THE
Red
ZONE

Amie Knight

DEDICATION

There was only one person I could dedicate this one to. See, *The Red Zone* isn't just a romance. It's the story of a man's homecoming and the unwavering love he has for his baby sister. So, it only seems fitting I dedicate *The Red Zone* to my baby brother. There's only one brown-eyed boy I love more than him, and he happens to be his son. And after all, he did help me name this book.

This one is for you, Will LaLiberte, since you insist on having a grown-up name even though, to me, you'll always just be Ty. I love you, Scootie Pootie.

PROLOGUE

Lukas

SOMETIMES WHEN I LAY IN BED AT NIGHT THAT FATEFUL DAY RACED through my mind over and over again. On repeat. And this night was no different. Sweat would bead on my forehead and my heart would race.

I may have been in my hometown of Summerville, Alabama, but my mind, it was in Florida. It was the best game of my career and the worst day of my life simultaneously. It haunted me. I thought I'd relive it as long as I walked this earth.

I was at the top of my game, the height of a career I'd been building on since peewee football when my mom had to help me into my pads.

My mom.

Just thinking about her sent a pang of sadness through me that was indescribable. Unimaginable. We'd been beyond close, best friends even.

That pang had never stopped and that day never failed to flit through my mind like an old movie reel, flashes of light, quietly speaking voices. It always started with me playing the best game I'd ever played.

I was on the field, sweat thick and slick under my helmet. The smell of fresh grass heavy in the air and on my dirty uniform. The clock was counting down and we were there, right in the red zone. I could smell victory. Because that day I'd played one hell of a game. We were in the fourth quarter and the pressure was on and damn if I wasn't excited because the fourth quarter was my fucking jam. I was what my team called a fourth quarter player and when I was in the red zone I was even better. They didn't call me Lukas "Last Minute Lucy" for nothing. I could pull a game out of my ass at the last minute like a magician could produce a rabbit from a hat.

I surveyed the field and checked the defensive formation, made the count, and the center snapped the ball back. I faked left, made like I was going to pass, but saw a hole in the other team's defense and ran like the wind. I was fast. Twenty yard line. Ten yard line. I felt a hand on my ankle as I landed in the end zone, but it didn't stop me. I lay there, my smile big behind my mouthguard.

We'd won, which was no surprise to me. There wasn't a doubt in my mind we were headed straight for the Super Bowl that year. We'd had a killer season, after all.

The after game festivities were as usual with interviews and fans and autographs. I distinctly remembered looking up in the stands that day after the game where my momma and Ella usually sat when we played at home. She'd told me the week before she wouldn't make it since Ella had a school dance that weekend.

The locker room was loud with the aftermath of a hell of a game. I barely heard my cell phone ringing from my locker after I showered. I didn't recognize the number, so I almost didn't even answer it, but some unknown force implored me to. I lifted it to my ear while drying my hair with a towel.

"Hello."

Jones, one of our linebackers, gave me a slap on the ass and I waved him off with my middle finger and a smile.

"Luk," a soft female voice said from the phone.

"Yeah?"

"It's Aunt Merline." Her voice was barely above a whisper and I could hear it trembling with emotion.

And this feeling came over me. It was like I knew. My stomach dropped. My face felt hot and my hand shook around the phone I held tightly to my ear.

I swallowed hard. "What's wrong?"

She was my mother's sister, but she never called me. Sure, I saw her when I went home for holidays and breaks, but that was the extent of our relationship.

She gasped and hiccupped out a sob that I felt in the deepest, darkest depths of my soul. "It's your momma, baby."

My head shook of its own accord. No. There couldn't be anything wrong with my momma. I'd just talked to her on the phone right before the game. She'd called and told me to break a leg as usual. She was a drama geek and I was a football player, so I informed her like I always did that you never said that to a quarterback. She'd laughed the way she always had. Carefree. Like she didn't have a care in the world when she shouldered more than most people could. But that was just my momma. Amazing.

It couldn't be. Aunt Merline was wrong. She had to be. Just no. She and Ella were all I had left. Them and football. That was my life.

"No." It was a whisper, a plea, a prayer. I'd already lost my father to a drunk driver when I was fourteen. How could my mother be gone now, too?

"It was a heart attack. Instantaneous. She didn't suffer. It was quick."

Why did people say that? That they didn't suffer. Was that supposed to make me feel better? Make me feel like a pivotal part of me wasn't missing? My eyes stung. My chest burned. I dropped the towel from my hand and placed my palm there right over my heart, where it hurt the worst.

I leaned into my locker, my head nearly inside. I didn't want to be here in this room. I needed to be alone. A lone tear slipped down my cheek and my jaw worked, but nothing came out. What could I say?

"You there?" Aunt Merline croaked out.

I took a deep breath that felt like I was inhaling water instead of air and swallowed again, because there was a question I desperately needed the answer to.

I pushed the words out that my body wanted to hold hostage even as my brain was screaming them. "How's Ells?"

A deep sigh came from the other end of the line. "I don't know if she gets it. I don't know if she understands, Luk." Silence was heavy over the phone until she finally said, "I think you better come home."

And that was that. It was the beginning of the end for me really. I'd leave behind my team and the Super Bowl ring in exchange for a mediocre team closer to my hometown and much farther away from my dreams.

I always knew what would happen when my momma passed. I'd get Ella. After all, she'd never be able to live on her own and I'd rather die than see her in one of those homes. She needed me and I needed her. And as I lay here at night, I couldn't help but think of how I was failing her. It'd only been two months since my mother died. Since I'd been traded to the Alabama Cougars. Since I'd been juggling more than I could handle. I felt like I was drowning every day. So I swam. And swam and swam. Against the tide, into waves that knocked me clear over and took me right back to shore, and still I tried again.

I did it for her, the little girl who had stolen my breath from the beginning of her life. I'd been fourteen when they'd told my mom she was having a girl. It had felt like fate to Momma and me. Daddy had left us the greatest gift before he'd passed.

My momma had sat me down with tears shining in her eyes and explained that our lives were going to change forever and not just because she was having another baby. No, this baby would have a genetic disorder called Down syndrome and she'd need extra attention and care and most importantly love. And God, did we love her. She was the shining light in all of my grim days since my mom had passed.

And I'd never give her up. I'd swim and drown. I'd jump and I'd fall. I'd try and I'd fail. But I'd just keep going. For her. Because Ella was my everything even when I felt like I had nothing.

Chapter
ONE

Scarlett

I PULLED DOWN THE FLAP-DOOHICKEY SUN BLOCKER THINGY AND LOOKED AT myself in the car mirror. Oh, sweet baby Jesus. My usual wavy, red tendrils were more like frizzy, red snakes at this point, but that was the price you had to pay for not remembering to set your alarm clock the morning before you had to be at work early. My vibrant green eyes shot daggers back at me from the mirror. And crap, but I had parent/teacher conferences today. My poor parents were just going to have to suffer right along with me. Did they think I liked looking like this? Just as I flipped the doohickey back up to the roof of the car, the car behind me honked and my foot came off the brake in shock before I stomped it back down. And that's when I felt it; the warm, wet feeling of my still hot coffee that was sitting in the console, in my pretty Ms. Knox tumbler Alex had given me for Christmas last year, soaking into the cream linen of my nice work pants. Oh. My. God. This could not be happening and why the hell did that car honk at me? I frantically searched for a napkin or anything to try to clean up the mess and came up empty.

Morning traffic was still at a dead stop in front of me, so I rolled down my car window and leaned my head out, fluffy red clown hair and all.

"What the hell is wrong with you?" I yelled at the man in a black Lexus SUV behind me. I already knew what was wrong with him. He was a pompous, entitled asshole and I could tell from his flashy car alone.

His window came down and his head popped out, expensive sunglasses covering his eyes. I couldn't get a good look at him, but I was sure he was good-looking like most men who acted like douches. "You need to be watching the road instead of giving yourself a look over in the mirror, sweetheart," he snapped.

I pulled my fluffy head back into the car in complete shock. Oh no, he didn't. I had half a mind to get out of the car and charge over to his window and scream in his face like a banshee. What the hell did it matter if I checked my face in the mirror when traffic was stopped? And where the hell did he get off calling me sweetheart? Freaking lunatic. God, I wanted to get out of my car and give him a piece of my mind. My face was hot with anger and I sure was fired up. My mother referred to these tendencies and outbursts as my redheadedness. Her mother had been born with this affliction as well. And when my redheadedness wanted to come out there was no stopping it. Well, there was. Today what stopped it was warm coffee crawling up my butt crack.

I pushed my head out of the window again with the strength of a gale force wind. "I'm not your sweetheart! You turd!" I yelled before I rolled the window back up of my small, blue Mazda 3 and ground my teeth. Traffic started moving in front of me, thank the sweet Lord, because I was only two seconds away from a full-on hissy fit. Yet another symptom of my redheadedness.

I cranked up the radio, blasting "Little Red Corvette" because in my mind there wasn't anything that a little Prince couldn't fix. Traffic had only made me slightly late for school. I was only a bit behind my usual schedule, so I was still in before the students and I dashed through the hallways of The Cottage School. I darted in and out of dark corners as I practically ran to my classroom like a secret agent. In my head *Mission Impossible* music played in the background as I darted and weaved, determined for no one to see my coffee pants.

I made it to my room with time to spare and ran to the supply closet in the corner behind my desk for a change of clothes. When you taught children with special needs, you had to be ready for anything.

Especially a clothing change. Alas, today I had no one to blame but myself.

I was leaned up and into the closet when I heard a tiny voice from behind me. "Did you poop in your pants, Ms. Lettie?"

I spun around, shocked and mortified, backing my coffee stained behind up and mostly into the small closet. With a red face, I answered, "No, Joshua. I spilled my coffee in the car this morning."

His face screwed up in confusion. "But how did you spill coffee on your butt?"

"An accident in the car," I said lightly, like it wasn't a big deal so he would stop talking about it. But I should have known better. I taught kids with autism. Down syndrome. And almost none of them had a filter. Especially sweet Josh. He was a child with high functioning autism and I could almost always count on him keeping it 100 percent real. Sometimes that was awesome. Sometimes it sucked. Like today.

"Like a poop accident?"

I let out a nervous giggle, my eyes darting around the room to make sure no one else heard him and thankfully, we were still blessedly alone. My ninth graders could be merciless when they went in on me. There were only six of them. They were only thirteen years old, but I was outnumbered and most days outsmarted by my kiddos.

"No, Joshua. I told you it wasn't a poop accident and I really wish you would stop saying poop. It's not a nice word."

I turned my back toward the bathroom that was luckily adjoined to my classroom, a luxury a lot of the special ed teachers didn't have at The Cottage House. Today I thanked God that this was the case as I backed toward the bathroom, my change of clothes clutched to my chest.

The Cottage House was a private school for children with special needs that ranged from ADD to autism. We had a wide range of children, which made my job all that more important and fun.

I was relieved to see Joshua had moved on and was unpacking his belongings into his desk as I closed the door to the bathroom.

"I've already seen the poop, Ms. Lettie. It's too late." I heard through the door.

I couldn't help but smile as I changed my clothes even though I was supremely embarrassed because this was it for me. These kids. They were my life. My everything. They made my days brighter. They were my reason. My momma had told me a long time ago to find a job that gave me a reason to get up every morning. And they were it. Poop talk and all.

I now wore a pair of yoga pants and a The Cottage School sweatshirt, but at least it didn't look like I'd soiled myself.

The classroom was filling up fast and the laughter and boisterous voices pervaded the space, making my smile wider.

"Hey, Ms. Lettie." I heard from behind me.

Ella, one of my kiddos with Down syndrome stood there, her soft caramel eyes shining up at me. Her sweet grin melted my heart. I knew we weren't supposed to play favorites, but I couldn't help it. Ella was absolutely one of my most favorite people in the entire world. And not just because I'd known her for what felt like forever. She was the beginning of it all for me. She'd been my very first reason.

"Hey, Ellie Bellie!"

She laughed like she always did when I called her that and immediately went in for a hug and I was right there with arms wide-open. If I'd learned anything in my years teaching special needs, it was that lots and lots of cuddles were required. It had taken time for me to get used to all the hugs, but now I was one of those people, a religious hugger, and I knew all the healing properties another person's arms around you held even if it did take me time to figure it all out.

I held Ella close, cherishing our relationship. It really was one of a kind and even though I was already short on time, I would conjure up some for this. It was a specialty of us teachers, pulling extra time out of thin air. I had student-teacher conferences today during my lunch and planning period, which meant I needed to get my day going right away. And I wasn't at all nervous about seeing Luk, Ella's brother, again. After all, I'd only been his tutor in high school. He probably didn't even remember me. I mean, I barely remembered him. I didn't think about him at all. Especially late at night when I was in bed. I particularly didn't think about how big and broad he was or how gorgeous his lips were. It had been ten years. That would be desperate and I definitely wasn't that.

Pulling out of our hug, I tapped her sweet button nose with my finger and hurried up to the front of the classroom. "Alrighty, friends. Let's put our things away so we can get started."

I turned toward the board to write today's schedule when I heard from behind me in a very poor attempt at a whisper, "Ms. Lettie had an accident in her pants on the way to school." Quiet giggles broke out across the classroom from behind me.

I snapped my head around, my face one of complete no nonsense, and everyone quieted as my eyes perused the classroom at the pace of a snail. I cleared my throat and turned back to the board slowly to continue writing and barely held in my laughter. These kids always made me laugh even if at often times it was at my expense.

Chapter
TWO

Scarlett
Age 14

I TAPPED MY FOOT, MY PENCIL AGAINST THE GLOSSY TOP OF THE LIBRARY table, and every freaking thing I could tap quietly because what I really wanted to do was bang my head on the dang table in front of me.

I was supposed to meet someone in the school library who needed help in French. Madame Quattlebaum had all but begged me and I think that was simply because high school teachers didn't need to beg. They had the upper hand.

And that was mostly why I was so pissed right now. Because I was wasting my damn time. And I didn't use the D word lightly. I took a deep breath, inhaling the sweet scent of old books and new alike, and told myself I loved this smell and I could wait another five minutes.

And for those five minutes I stared at the clock and felt my face grow hot. I could have been at home practicing my clarinet, or reading a good horror book, or listening to my new Prince album. In fact, I could think of a million things I'd rather be doing right now than waiting on the inconsiderate person who was wasting my perfectly good afternoon.

After another fifteen minutes, I pushed my chair back so hard, the loud scrape made me wince as I stood and started to collect my French textbook and worksheets. I felt eyes on me from the table nearby and turned that way to find what looked like three upperclassman boys looking at me and whispering. I was pretty sure at this point my face was exactly the color as my dark scarlet hair. It was no coincidence I was named Scarlett Knox. My momma had told me and everyone who wanted to listen on more than one occasion that she'd been all gung ho in naming me Taylor after her favorite uncle who'd passed during her pregnancy. But after twenty-four hours of intense labor she'd had to endure on Labor Day of all days, I'd finally arrived. She was so dramatic. They'd plopped my mucus and blood covered body on her chest and all she'd seen was my head full of flaming red hair. She'd described it so many times I could see it in my head. Which was just awful. Her holding her yucky baby with red hair and looking at my dad with gaga eyes and saying I had to be Scarlett. Scarlett Taylor Knox. Cliché as hell redhead. And then the woman had the audacity to never even call me by either of my given names, instead opting for the nickname of Lettie.

The boys at the table giggled again and I ran my tongue over my teeth, checking my braces for food. I shoved my stuff in my bookbag and slung it over my shoulder before pushing my black, thick-rimmed glasses up the bridge of my nose.

Lord, but I was a mess and I knew it, too. It wasn't that I didn't care, but I was only a freshman. I didn't really have any interest in boys yet, being the late bloomer that I was. And most of the boys in the small town of Summerville, Alabama, I knew too dang well to be interested in. For instance, like good ole Jeremy Lawton sitting at the table with the other boys who were giggling like fifth grade girls instead of the high school students they were. He'd picked his boogers and eaten them in the fifth grade. I pursed my lips. *You weren't laughing then, were you, Jeremy?*

Immature jackasses, the lot of them. I pivoted on the heel of my army green Converse, my eyes to the floor, ignoring the boys still whispering and laughing softly across the room and took one, two, three steps forward before I face-planted right into a broad chest that was covered by a startling white T-shirt that smelled like fabric softener and sunshine.

"Oomph," I grunted as large, warm, tan hands landed on my shoulders, straightening me so I could look up into the eyes of none other than the star quarterback of Summerville High. The one, the only, Lukas Callihan.

I wasn't short for a girl at five-foot-six and still he towered over me, at least six-foot-two, his frame at least three times wider than mine.

I stared up at him, speechless. Which wasn't abnormal for me. I was the quiet, shy type on a regular day and running face first into the school's most popular boy was definitely not a typical day for me. At all.

He looked down at me, forehead wrinkled before glancing past me and around the study space in the library. I continued standing in front of him, dumbfounded because that's what shy, possibly hormonal freshmen girls did.

His questioning eyes landed on the boys across the room. He smiled and raised a hand in greeting. "Hey, Marcus."

Marcus, a junior who flipped his eyelids inside out at me in the cafeteria when I'd been in the third grade, waved back.

"I'm supposed to meet my French tutor here." He looked down at a piece of paper in his hand and I noticed his nose was straight and narrow and he had some stubble on his chin. And then what he'd just said registered in my small, fourteen-year-old mind. I froze in place, my eyes wide, my face pale. Because no. There was no way in hell I was tutoring a senior in French. Especially not Luk Callihan. No way. No how.

I tried to moonwalk backward, slowly, quietly, hoping like usual no one noticed me. Prince was waiting at home. I could listen to "When Doves Cry" and have a good cry like I sometimes did for no other reason at all than I was a crazy teenager. Probably most kids my age weren't listening to Prince since his music was older than me, but I didn't care. I was in love with the man and his lyrics.

Luk looked at Marcus again. "Do you know a Scarlett Knox?"

Marcus snickered and his gaze flew to me. "She's right there, man."

Booger boy chuckled low and I wanted to take my shoe off and chuck it at him.

Brown eyes as dark as night landed on mine and that line between his brows was deeper than twenty seconds ago.

"You're Scarlett?" His voice was laced with disbelief and my hackles rose.

I straightened my shoulders and pushed out my still non-existent chest. I just wasn't there yet. I hadn't had my period. Or gotten boobs, or really any shape.

"Yep," I popped out, probably snappier than I should have. Yes, I was freshman, but I'd been in the advanced program in our school system since the fourth grade when I'd started taking French. I was on my fifth year and ole Mister Quarterback here was on his second mandatory year for graduation. He may have been a senior to my freshman, but I could run French circles around his very nice-looking behind. Not that I noticed his delectable derriere.

His lips turned down into a frown. "But you're like thirteen."

I cleared my throat. "Fourteen," I snarked, my teenage sensibilities thoroughly offended, my face flush as the douches across the room watched on. Jesus, I was embarrassed. And just like any time I was embarrassed, I became inevitably angry. It was my defense mechanism, this anger. It kept me from being sad or hurt.

I could feel my temper heat along with my face.

"What French are you taking?" he questioned, clearly not believing anything I was saying.

"French Two, Advanced," I answered, pulling my backpack higher up on my shoulders and trying to step around him.

His hand reached out, grabbing my arm as I tried to pass by.

"Hey, where are you going?"

I shrugged his warm hand off and ignored the way my belly

fluttered at his touch. No, there would be no belly fluttering. No swooning. No dang pitter-pattering of the heart. I was a logical girl. I didn't even really care about boys. Especially good-looking seventeen-year-old jocks who couldn't pass level two French. Absolutely not, I willed my stomach.

"You should have been here thirty minutes ago. Our tutoring session is over. You missed it," I deadpanned before heading to the door with the red exit sign above it.

"Aw, come on. Practice ran over," he called out, but I didn't bother to turn around as I answered him.

"Not my problem, Mister Quarterback."

I heard a guffaw from the douche brigade right before Luk called out, "Tomorrow, then?"

I turned around, which looking back I realized was the biggest mistake of my high school years. Because when I did, there he stood looking all masculine with his square jaw and slightly large but narrow nose. But that didn't stop his expressive face and eyes from looking desperate and pleading. So, I caved. I folded like a soft deck of cards because he was just too handsome and too sweet in that moment for me to do anything but freaking give in.

I shrugged my shoulders heavily for effect before I pushed the exit door open. "If you can make it on time."

I stepped out into the sunlight, paused on the steps, and took a deep breath, pressing my shaking hands to my stomach. There was no way in a million years that I was going to tutor the most popular, sought after boy in school. No matter how sweet and pathetic he looked at me with those brown puppy dogs that were meant to destroy young girls with one small glance. No way! I was Lettie Knox. Too skinny. Too tall. Too red. Too nerdy.

I'd have to beg Madame to find another tutor for Luk. There was no way this was going to work, especially since he hadn't even had the decency to show up on time. That part didn't surprise me. I found that most of the guys in school who were big shots didn't care much about anyone other than themselves. They were self-absorbed and cocky. That's what I told myself Luk was. One of those boys. Even though my eyes had told me different, but it wouldn't be the first time they'd deceived me. I didn't have time for boys, especially ones like Lukas Callihan. No, there was no way in hell I was showing up tomorrow.

It was tomorrow and I was back. I didn't want to be, but here I was, walking back into the library as slow as I could possibly manage because let's face it, Luk was probably freaking late anyway.

Imagine my surprise when I moseyed over to the table to find him already sitting there looking smug as hell.

"You're late," he said through a smirk.

I checked the cell phone in my hand. "Two minutes."

One of his thick eyebrows shot up and my stomach did that flippy thing again that made me want to hightail it right out of there. "But still late."

I rolled my eyes as I sat down. Great. We were off to a fantastic start. I'd spent the morning doing my own begging, but Madame Quattlebaum still insisted I help out. Because this was Alabama. Where football reigned supreme and we couldn't have our star player at Summerville High school not playing because of his grades. The fate of our beloved Cavaliers would fall solely on my shoulders and Madame had no problem breaking that down for me.

I looked at him again. Hard. It was okay. He wasn't all of that and a bag of chips. I always pictured the guy I'd date would be super intelligent, anyway. Maybe an engineer type. Not a jock. I could do this. I would be the best French tutor ever in the shortest amount of time.

"Well, let's get started. Do you have your French book?"

He leaned back in his chair and his big leg brushed mine and I felt goose bumps break out on my thigh. What in the hell was wrong with me and my stupid body? I jerked my knee away and cleared my throat.

We got started. I was efficient. Professional. I didn't giggle like some silly schoolgirl when he smiled. Which he did a lot. I was calling it a win.

While Luk worked on a worksheet, I grabbed a bag of Skittles from my bookbag and opened them. I sat them on the table and a few spilled out.

"Dibs," Luk said quietly before grabbing a few from the table and shoving them into his gorgeous mouth.

"You can't call dibs on something that's not yours."

I didn't let anyone have my Skittles. Not even my baby brother, Ollie, who had me wrapped around his pinky finger.

He didn't say anything as he grabbed more and ate them one by one, smiling at me the whole time. I bet he got everything he wanted. I bet his parents were rich and his life was easy and no one had ever said you can't have my tasty snack not one time in his entire privileged life.

I'd only agreed to a thirty-minute tutoring session with Luk, but we ran over another thirty and the whole time I had to remind myself not to breathe too deep. Because goodness, he smelled good. Like the sunshine and pine trees and mint. It was like being in my grandma's backyard right next to her herb garden. It was one of my most cherished childhood memories and I told myself it could be the only reason I liked his smell so much.

I made sure we didn't touch to keep those pesky goose bumps away that made girls full-on stupid. I made sure to not look at him too much. I made sure to hide the rest of my bag of Skittles.

The truth was tutoring Luk wasn't all that bad. He was smart and seemed like a genuinely nice guy. He had an easygoing personality and of course we all knew he wasn't hard on the eyes. He was focused at least. I found teaching him French actually enjoyable and I never ever noticed his plump lips and the way they shaped around some of my most favorite French words. Never.

And on that note, I closed my book. "Time's up," I squeaked out. We both stood up too quickly at the same time, and my forehead collided with some part of his large noggin.

"Ow." I rubbed the front of my head and looked at him to find him sheepishly smiling while holding the side of his head. "Sorry."

"Nah, it was my fault." He packed everything up in his bookbag and I did the same, making sure to keep my eyes to myself. It was hard. A boy had never caught my attention before and it seemed Luk had it in spades. It didn't help that he was so nice and not at all the douchebag I thought he was. I had a feeling this was going to be the longest semester of my life.

Pushing my frizzy hair behind my ears, I made my way to the library exit, deciding that the best course of action was to get the heck out of there.

"Hey, wait up."

I turned and there he was, every glorious inch of him. And he was smiling at me. And his teeth were perfect and his hair was sublime, hanging just a little over his eyes. It just wasn't fair.

I raised my eyebrows in response because that was all I had. That smile had rendered me speechless and that was saying something because I was what my mom liked to call the mouth of the south because while I was on the quiet side, when I really had something to say I let it fly.

He walked forward until he stood next to me. "Can I give you a ride home?"

He was still doing that sweet smiling thing that made my heart go pitter-patter and my hands sweat. How dare he ask it so casually? So nonchalant that for a second I almost believed it wasn't a big deal if I got in his old blue Ford truck that he parked in the senior lot every morning.

The car he drove older, more experienced girls his own age around in. Hypothetical girls, of course, because I didn't watch him. Ever.

My lips trembled as I tried to force a small smile and tucked my fingers under the bookbag straps at my shoulders. "No, thanks. I only live a couple of blocks away. I'm fine to walk." I shot him another quivery smile before pushing the double doors open, but I didn't get very far.

"Come on, Red. I don't mind. It's the least I could do. And it's getting dark out already."

Red. If my entire body could have eye rolled then it just did. Unfreakingbelievable. Was he kidding me? I scoffed before turning to give him a look. I realized real quick in that moment that Luk was far from perfect and I'd never been so relieved. Maybe this whole crazy crush thing would take a hike. "How very typical of you, Luk. I've never heard that one at all before." My voice was thick with sarcasm. "Red? Is that the best you got, Mister Quarterback?"

His smile disappeared even as a slow smirk appeared. With eyebrows raised he said, "Mister Quarterback? How original. And you're giving me shit?" He shook his head like he couldn't believe it.

After our tutoring session I'd come to the conclusion that Luk was far too smart to be so cliché. I'd been so very wrong. Like I hadn't heard Red before. It was time to go. And I had to get home before it really did get dark and my daddy lost his mind.

"Night, Luk." The humid Alabama heat smacked me in the face, practically taking my breath away.

"Hey, Red!" Luk called out from behind me.

I turned my body but kept on walking backward slowly. I really did have to get home. I smiled sardonically. "I bet you don't even know my real name."

He ran a hand through that thick mane of hair and pursed his lips. "Of course I do. Your name is Scarlett." His eyebrows danced and he grinned at me and God he was cute.

It was time to get the hell out of there.

I spun around and picked up speed, but there was no escaping Luk. He jogged to catch up to me and fell into step beside me. I tried my best to ignore him, but he wouldn't allow that either.

"Red suits you, you know."

This time I actually did roll my eyes.

His laugh was low. "It's not just about your hair." His eyes glanced over my frizz and I immediately felt self-conscious. But then his eyes met mine and he had that dang sweet grin on his face. "It's your attitude. It's just you. Red."

I wanted to roll my eyes again, but instead I asked, "How's that, Mister Quarterback?"

I didn't look at him this time, instead opting for watching my white tennis shoes kick up asphalt on the school parking lot.

He snickered before answering, but I didn't dare look up. I could tell he was still grinning from ear to ear, so I kept my eyes on my shoelaces to keep my heart from beating out of my chest. "You're a spitfire, feisty. Ya know. Red."

He said it so matter-of-fact. And I couldn't even argue with him. In fact, the boy had me pegged. But that didn't stop me from trying.

"You think after one afternoon tutoring session you know me?" I sassed. And I realized this was totally the pot calling the kettle black, but man, I was grasping at straws. I didn't want to like him. I didn't want to think he was nice and funny and sweet enough to offer me a ride home. It was all too much.

I could feel his eyes boring into the side of my face, but I made sure not to look at him. "Scarlett." He said my name so quietly I almost thought I didn't hear him. I thought maybe I was mistaken until he said it again, this time grabbing my arm to stop me from walking. "Scarlett," he said softly again and boy my name was loaded. It said all kinds of things. Like stop walking and look at me.

So against my better judgment I lifted my eyes to his and we were so close I could see each individual beautiful eyelash that surrounded his baby browns. I could smell that minty pine scent again and had the urge to close my eyes, but I didn't. I just stared up at him, begging him to say anything so I could leave.

"I know I don't know you, Scarlett." His hand landed on my

shoulder and my breath stopped. I was wearing a tank top and we were skin to skin. My stupid teenage heart almost stopped. And then he finished me off, practically killing me dead with his pure sweetness. "But I think you're cool and I want to be friends. Is that okay?"

Was that okay? Was that okay! Of course it was. How could anyone tell this boy no? He was perfect. And God, I was doomed. I was going to turn into one of those girls. The ones who lost their minds when a boy was near.

But I couldn't help myself. I just nodded and shrugged his hand off and started walking again.

I was relieved when we arrived at the back gate of the school so I could make my exit. I didn't like that he seemed to have me pegged already and we'd only hung out twice and the first time only for mere minutes.

"Well, I'm going to head out." I nodded toward the gate with my head before opening it up and stepping through.

Luk followed me out. "Since I can't interest you in a ride, I guess I'll just walk you home." And then he did it. He nudged my shoulder with his in that way friends did when they shared an inside joke or were picking on each other.

The butterflies were back in my belly and my face was warm and it had nothing to do with the humidity. That was it for me. That's all it had taken for my poor fourteen-year-old heart to be claimed. A boy asking to be my friend and a simple shoulder nudge.

Chapter
THREE

Lukas

"**Y**OU'RE PISSING MS. LETTIE OFF." ELLA WAS PERCHED ON THE couch watching an old rerun of *General Hospital*. The girl loved her soaps. She wasn't even looking at me, but I definitely knew she was talking to me. Because Ella didn't say anything unless she had something to say and it seemed like right now she was the one who was pissed, not Ms. Lettie.

"Quit swearing." I was cutting up a salad and watching the chicken bake in the oven of my momma's old kitchen. The house I had grown up in. The house I'd probably die in. God, she was worried about me pissing her teacher off and here I was worried that my life was a fucking mess. I couldn't even begin to think about Ella's beloved Ms. Lettie. She was the least of my worries.

"Piss isn't a swear word. There's a note in my bag." She finally looked at me. "You missed another meeting." Ella was a child of few words, but the ones she said always counted for a lot. But she was always listening and she always, always knew what was going on.

Fuck. But it was just a long list of shit I was fucking up every day. I didn't how my mom did it. Took care of two kids by herself most of her life and worked every day. I was past the point of struggling and I'd only been doing this for three months.

I put the knife down and walked out of the kitchen and into the living room until I stood directly in front of the TV. Ella looked up at me with her sweet, almond-shaped eyes and my heart broke. I was screwing this whole thing up and she didn't deserve it. She needed more than I could give her. My work schedule was grueling. I was forgetful. I was terrible at juggling family and football. She needed more. She needed her mother. I needed mine. And at that point I would have pretty much given anything in the world to bring my momma back. To make this better for all of us. Because the truth of it was, we sucked without her. She completed this family. Made it better. Made us whole.

"Where is your bag?"

She stared at me and then back at the screen like she was looking right through me. "Come on, Ells. Detective Chase is going to have to wait today. I need your bag and the letter."

Nothing. So I turned and shut the TV off. And her face. Man, it looked like she wanted to punch me in the nose, but instead she stood and went to her room, then came back quickly and shoved her school-bag right into my stomach before storming back the way she came.

I took a long, deep breath, trying to keep my shit together but feeling at my wits' end.

Dear Mr. Callihan,

This is the second time you have missed Ella's parent/teacher conference for this quarter. The first time you missed our meeting, I assumed it was an oversight on your part and now I can only assume you have a blatant disregard for my time. So that no more of my valuable time is wasted, I thought maybe we could schedule a phone conference since you are so obviously busy. Please contact me Tuesday thru Thursday evenings from 7:00 p.m. to 9:00 p.m. only.

Regards,
Ms. Lettie

Her phone number was followed by her very abrupt sign off. I stared at the letter in my hand. Wasted her time? She thought I did this on purpose? The sheer gall of the crazy woman. I didn't care if Ella liked her or not. She was insane. Certifiable. Teachers didn't send letters home like this, did they? Didn't she know that Ella's mother had passed and I'd had to take over? Did the woman not have a freaking heart? I was in the middle of my meltdown when my cell phone rang.

I was so engrossed in the letter, I picked the phone up without bothering to look who was calling.

"Hello," I said, still glancing over the letter like I'd misunderstood something. Because surely this letter wasn't real. Because fuck, this lady wasn't nice.

"Luk."

Fuck me running. It was Aunt Merline and I knew exactly why she was calling because she'd been calling every week since my mother had passed and every week we'd had the same damn conversation.

"Hey, Aunt Merline." I tried to sound upbeat, goddamn jovial. Anything to stave off the inevitable conversation I knew was coming.

"How's Ella?"

That's how she always started it.

"She's good. Just watching her soaps." I was the worst liar in the history of liars and even Aunt Merline could tell.

"No problems?" Her voice was laced with accusation. I'd made the mistake of confiding in her the first few weeks I'd moved home to take care of Ella. I should have known better. Now, she was using everything I'd told her about how hard of an adjustment it had been against me.

I couldn't hold in my sigh. "I don't have time for this, Merline. Did you have a reason for your call?"

"If you let me take care of Ella, you'd have all the time in the world. You could go back to playing for that fancy ass football team in Florida instead of that second rate team you've had to settle for here." She paused for added drama. "You could have your career back."

My fist clenched, inadvertently smashing the letter from Ms. Lettie. It always made me so angry when Aunt Merline talked about me abandoning Ella. Because that's exactly what it would be to her. I couldn't fathom it. No matter how bad I sucked at being a stand-in for my mother.

"It's not what Mom wanted, Merline." I had to bring out the big guns. She wasn't backing down. We all always knew how this scenario would play out. I thought I would be older and probably retired from football. I thought Ella would be older, too, but time and fate weren't on our side and I wasn't sure that God was anymore either. My faith in everything had taken a nosedive the last three months.

My mother had always made her wishes clear. In the event that anything happened to her or when it inevitably did because it was the way of things, parents died before their children, I would take Ella. I'd always known it. From the time I turned eighteen and my mother had a talk with me about it.

She'd been torn up about it and had even used the word burden. But I'd assured her Ella could never be a burden. I loved her. Of course I'd take care of her. And she wasn't a burden now. I just sucked at this. Bad. Way more than I could have ever anticipated. If anyone was a burden, it was me. I was the burden.

"Your mother had no idea she would be leaving this earth at the pinnacle of your career or when Ella needed her the most. It's not fair to either of you. Please, Lukas, let me help you."

I laid the letter from Ms. Stick-up-her-ass on the counter and used my fingers to massage my temples. "You can't help us, Merline. We just need to get the hang of things." No, the only person who could help us was gone.

Ella had come back in the room at some point while I was on the phone and I looked over at her watching her soaps and acting like she wasn't listening to this very conversation and I knew she was. She heard everything. She shouldn't have to listen to this shit on top of everything else. It killed me.

Merline was prattling on about how much help she could be if I would just let her take Ella and as I watched Ella, all I could think about was how she hadn't grieved properly. It was like she was totally in denial of Mom's passing. She didn't talk about it. Didn't cry about it and most definitely was in denial. I'd tried to take her to counseling, but children with Downs were as notoriously stubborn as they were sweet. She'd flat out refused to talk to anyone, instead opting to completely ignore the therapist their entire sessions.

And that was the kick in the ass for me. It wasn't that I was playing for a mediocre football team or that I'd had to uproot my life. I'd do it again in a skinny minute for Ella. It was that Ella was floundering and I had no fucking idea how to fix it. She was breaking my damn heart.

"Listen, Aunt Merline, I need to go." I didn't bother saying goodbye, knowing she'd call back tomorrow with even more reasons that I should let her have Ella. I knew she meant well. She loved Ella, but fuck, I loved her, too, and Mom wanted me to do this. She knew I could do this. I just had to figure out how.

Picking up the piece of paper, I walked to the living room and sat beside Ella on the couch. She didn't even glance my way. It gutted me, but I had to admit I'd sucked the first month after Mom's death. I'd been dealing with my own shit and hardly noticed how she was coping.

I placed my arm on the back of the couch behind Ella. "Bring it in, Ellie Bellie."

She turned her head slowly to mine. She was wearing her eyeglasses and the lenses were Coke bottle thick. She was the cutest thing I'd ever seen. I loved her more than football. More than Miami in the summer. More than anything in the world.

"I said bring it in."

"I heard you." She turned back to the TV. "I'm watching Detective Chase right now."

I let out a long sigh. Lukas Callihan, amazing quarterback, had fucking nothing on Detective Chase from *General Hospital* and Ella made sure I fucking knew that shit every chance she got. She'd been obsessed with him for years and even told me on more than one occa-sion that he was her boyfriend and she was going to marry him.

I sat up and grabbed the remote from the table and paused the TV. "Can Detective Chase wait just a minute? I need to talk to you."

She sighed dramatically like it was the end of the world and leaned back on the sofa, which allowed me to wrap my arm around her and bring her to my chest.

She nestled in, despite herself. We'd been doing this her whole life. I doubt she even realized she did it. It was just second nature.

"You ready to talk about Mom yet?" I asked into the top of her sweet apple smelling hair. She always smelled like fruit. She loved long baths with bath bombs and body sprays and lotions from Bath and Body Works.

I was met with complete silence. So, in Ella speak, I knew that meant hell to the no she didn't want to talk about it.

"Well, when you're ready, I'm ready." I uncrumpled the letter from Ms. Lettie in my hand and smoothed it out, showing Ella I was serious. I never could just tell her anything. I had to prove it. "I'm sorry I missed your conference again today." I sucked in a shaky breath. I wasn't used to apologizing to her. Up until three months ago, she'd looked up to me like I was a hero straight out of an action movie. Now, it was like we were miles apart. I wasn't even sure if she liked me any-more. "I know I've been fucking up, Ells. I'm going to work on it. I'm going to be better, okay?"

Still she said nothing, so I pointed to the part of the letter where her teacher had left her phone number. "I'm going to call Ms. Lettie to-morrow night and talk about how you're doing in school. And I prom-ise I won't miss anymore meetings."

She snuggled further down into me and I wrapped both of my arms around her, hugging her to me. "I'm sorry, Ella."

I'd cried two times in my entire life. The day Ella had been born and the day my mother had died. So, I was shocked when my eyes welled up. God, I needed help and not the kind where I just passed Ella off to someone. She needed stability and me. It was why I had moved home instead of sweeping Ella away to Florida with me. Children with Down syndrome thrived when they had a strict routine. I knew uprooting her from her home and school after losing her mother would be too much. I'd just have to uproot my own life and I did.

Her small arms came around mine. "Just be nice to Ms. Lettie. I love her. Don't make her mad anymore."

Using my hand to rub the back of her soft brown hair, I promised. "I won't. I'll be nice to your teacher and I won't miss anymore meetings and we are going to get through this because we are together and that's all that matters."

"Okay, Lulu."

I grinned at her nickname for me even though it made my heart wrench. My mother had called me that for as long as I could remember. She didn't care that as I got older it embarrassed me. She'd yell it out in the middle of a park and I'd want to crawl under the mulch to hide. Now, I just wanted to hear it one more time.

But I still had Ella and that was a hell of a lot. I looked down at her tiny frame against my large one. She was little and short like my mom while I was big and tall like my dad. In that moment with her arms wrapped around me, I was acutely aware of all I had lost and exactly how precious what I had left was. I needed to step up my game. And I wasn't talking about on the field.

Chapter
FOUR

Scarlett
Age 14

I WASN'T FREAKING OUT. NOT EVEN A LITTLE BIT. I MEAN, LOTS AND LOTS OF girls had probably sat across from Lukas at the dining room table in his house. Oh. My. God. No, I wasn't going to have a heart attack. We were just studying for French and I was totally playing it cool. Because we'd been doing this thing for just over a month and I was totally used to Lukas and his devastatingly good looks and sweet nature. I was so over him. My crush was yesterday's news. Today was a new day and that meant I didn't even hardly notice him adorably chewing the pink eraser on the top of his pencil while he read from his textbook.

"What do you think, Red?"

I blushed down to my toes because I hadn't heard a word he'd been saying. I'd been too busy giving myself the pep talk I always did when we were together, except this time I was at his house. I'd never been to a boy's home, and definitely not a boy like Lukas.

I looked down at my own book and let my scarlet hair cover my flaming face before answering. "I'm sorry. I wasn't listening. I was daydreaming."

Lord have mercy on my stupid mouth. Why did I say daydreaming like a damn fool?

He snickered. "Yeah, what are you daydreaming about? Or should I say who?"

That little comment had my head jerking up and my eyes flying to his in a panic. Did he know? But how could he? I'd been playing it totally cool until, ya know? Today. When he'd decided we should meet at his house after practice because he had a test the next day and wanted to study for it, I'd stupidly agreed, like I did for just about anything he wanted because I was officially one of those silly girls who adored a boy who hardly noticed me.

And now he was looking at me with a hitch to his lips that told me he knew exactly what I was thinking about. A certain knowing sparkle twinkled in his brown eyes. Oh, man. He was seriously about to call me out on my crush. And I couldn't bear it. I would die of embarrassment.

I knew what he saw when he looked back at me. Wide green eyes, pale, white face. Paler than usual, I mean. Because I wanted to melt into the floor. I'd do pretty much anything to get out of this very moment.

"You were daydreaming about a boy, right?" His eyebrows danced suggestively and I tried to swallow, but my throat felt too dry.

A nervous tickle started at the back of my throat that turned into a full-on coughing fit. The kind of coughing that had Luk jumping from his seat and pounding on my back even though I tried to wave him off.

"I'll get you some water." He went to the kitchen that was just off the dining room. I could see him getting some water from the tap through the bar that separated the dining room from the kitchen. After he filled the glass he made his way back to me.

"Sorry," I croaked, taking the glass of water and throwing some back.

"It's okay." He was grinning like a knowing fool while taking his seat again. "You okay?"

"Perfectly fine. My spit just went down the wrong pipe." For the love of God. What was wrong with me? Why did I have to turn into a mindless nitwit when he was around? I bet those sexy older girls he drove around in his truck didn't talk about their spit.

25

"Sure it did." His voice dripped of disbelief, but I chose to ignore it. I was of the mindset deny deny deny and avoid avoid avoid.

"Okay. Now, what did you ask me?" I wanted to get back to work and off the subject of my daydreams, but Lukas couldn't be swayed.

"Come on, Red. You can tell me. I thought we were friends." He poked out his bottom lip and his brown eyes instantly transformed into sweet puppy dog eyes. Heck, I almost wanted to reach across the table and give his head a good rub. He was still sweaty and dirty from practice, but that wouldn't deter me. I was willing to take one for the team.

And he had to go and call me Red again. It did make me feel like we were friends. Like we were something more than just study partners. It made me feel like what we had was special. After all, he had a nickname for me. One that wasn't just about my red hair. No, he'd made sure to tell me he thought it fit me, my personality. And all that did was serve to make me like him even more. Damn him.

I almost stuck my finger out and pushed that bottom lip back in. Instead, I turned the page in my book and pretended to play dumb.

"Let's start with the vocabulary section for this chapter."

"Let's start with the crush 411 instead."

"Let's not," I sang back, trying to sound bored when my heart felt like it was going to run right out of my chest. "And you sound like a girl. Pshhh. The crush 411." My eyes rolled.

"Jesus, Scar. I thought we were friends. You can tell me about you and Jamie. I saw you hanging with him at lunch the other day."

And I was choking again. Only this time Luk didn't hop up from his chair to help me. He only laughed his big guffaw deep laugh that boys in my grade didn't have yet. Thank God. Or I'd probably be flunking all my classes because that laugh did all kinds of things to me.

I sipped my water, stunned that he had somehow come to the conclusion I liked Jamie. Jamie was just a friend. And then I rolled my eyes because it turned out that even seventeen-year-old boys didn't have a damn clue. And I counted my lucky stars.

After I set my water on the table, I shook my head with a smile and pointed to the French book. "Can we stay on task, please?"

He pursed his lips. "We always stay on task." He was pouting and it was pretty darn cute. His puppy dog eyes were back. "So, you're not going to give me the dirt on you and Jamie?"

"I didn't think big, strong football players cared about 'the dirt,' Mister Quarterback." I smirked.

That lip hitched up on one side again and I licked my suddenly dry ones. "You couldn't be more wrong, Ms. Knox. We are the worst gossips. Locker room talk and all."

"I'd rather not be locker room fodder for the football team, Luk."

Shaking his head with a smile, he said, "Sometimes you talk like a school teacher. You know that?"

"Thank you." I pretended to write something in the notebook in front of me.

He chuckled low and I cursed the goose bumps that sprang up all over my arms.

"I guess I'll just have to ask Jamie."

My head flew up. "Do not even think about it." It wasn't my business to tell him that Jamie would have more interest in him than me. We were friends and that was it. I was horrified at the prospect of him asking Jamie about us, like I'd implied it instead of Luk just assuming something was going on.

So I turned the tables. "Why don't you tell me about all your girlfriends since we're friends and all now?" I grabbed my Skittles out of my bookbag because this was quickly turning into a Skittles emergency. I shook the packet and a few escaped onto the dining room table.

My plan to change the subject wasn't working. He just grinned that charming smile that made all the girls at school drool. "There's only one girl I date, Red. Her name's football."

I raised my eyebrows for effect. "And will you marry her, too?"

"That's the dream." And he meant it. "Dibs," he finished, grabbing my Skittles that had landed on the table. He had this far off look on his face that said it all. He wanted football more than he wanted anything in the world. And for some reason that brought me immense pleasure. It meant I wouldn't have to deal with the boy I was crushing hard on being with another girl. I could settle for friends, just so long as I didn't have to watch him swallow another girl's tongue in the hallway. I could deal with Luk dating football. That was totally doable.

"What are you smiling so big about over there?" His question interrupted my thoughts.

"Who, me?" I looked around the room like he could have possibly been talking to anyone else when we were the only ones in the house. "I'm not smiling."

His eyebrows popped up. "Yes, you are. And you're still smiling."

"I'm not."

"You totally are. Are you thinking about your boyfriend, Jamie?"

My face got hot. "Absolutely not."

"I hope not. You could hurt a guy's ego thinking about another dude and smiling like that while you hang out with him."

"Like your ego couldn't stand a little hurting?" I doodled on my paper so I didn't have to look at him and pursed my lips, but secretly I was thrilled at the prospect of him being just a smidge jealous. It was only right. Because I couldn't think about anything but him lately and I hated it. God, I wanted clueless, oblivious Lettie back. Not this flustered, hot for quarterback Scarlett. She could take a damn hike.

He threw the last of the Skittles into his mouth and I asked, "Why do you always do that?"

"Do what? Steal your candy?" His mouth was full of Skittles and I giggled because I somehow actually understood what he said.

"No. Call dibs."

He nodded. "Ah." His face grew serious and his forehead wrinkled right between his brows. "It was something me and my dad used to do."

"Used to?"

He ruffled the pages of his textbook, his eyes anywhere but on mine. "Yeah, he died a couple of years ago." A slow smile crossed his face like he was remembering. "My mom used to joke about never making enough food for me and Dad no matter how much she cooked. Her growing boys, she would say. We'd fight over the last of everything. The last bowl of chili, the last pork chop, the last brownie. We'd call dibs and grab it as quickly as we could." His smile was so melancholy my chest ached. "When I called dibs, I always ate it all, but Dad never did. When he called dibs he always shared it. He was a really good dad."

I let out a long sigh, knowing only one thing to say. "I'm so sorry, Luk. He sounds like he was a great dad."

I couldn't imagine at my age losing either of my parents. It made me incredibly sad for him.

His anguished eyes finally met mine over the table. "He was. He was amazing." He grinned big, his teeth on full display. "He would have liked you, Scarlett. A lot."

My breath caught because I didn't think anyone had ever paid me such a huge compliment. What was Lukas trying to do to me? Didn't he already know I was madly in love with him? This seemed like the final nail in the coffin.

I went back to doodling because I couldn't look at him. I just couldn't. He didn't say anything for what felt like a full five minutes but in actuality was probably only a few seconds, but it made me stop my doodling and lift my eyes. And he was looking at me. And he wasn't smiling goofily like I'd grown used to.

He was studying me. Like a puzzle he'd love to solve. His perfect pink lips serious, his eyes zeroed in on mine. His deliciously square jaw ticked and the silence between us was so thick you could have cut it with a knife.

I thought maybe I stopped breathing because all of a sudden I could hear his inhale, his exhale. Was that his heart beating or mine?

"We're home!" a woman's voice said from the front of the modest

29

home and it scared me so badly I jammed my knee into the bottom of the table.

"Shit," I whisper-yelled.

"Wow. Watch that mouth, Red." He winked at me and my banged up knee was long forgotten because holy shitake mushrooms that boy was hot.

I was staring at him in a teenage girl daze when a woman with dark hair and dark eyes like his came into the dining room. "Hey, Lulu. You have company, I see." She eyed me and I could immediately see the resemblance. She was a female version of Lukas. She was gorgeous.

I smiled with my mouth closed to hide my damn braces and pushed my frizzy hair behind my ears because this woman intimidated the heck out of me. She was too pretty to be someone's mother.

I didn't miss her nickname for him, though. I bit my lip and grinned at him at the Lulu bit.

"Give me a break, Mom. Stop calling me that. I'm not a baby."

She saddled up next to him, a toddler with dark hair on her hip. "I'm Diana," she said to me. "You must be Scarlett, Luk's tutor."

"That's me," I said quietly.

She turned to Luk. "Can you take Ella for a bit? I'm worn out and this cold is kicking my behind. I'd love to lie down if you guys are about done."

"Sure, we were just wrapping things up." He grabbed the little girl. I couldn't really see her face well, but he held her up in the air and stuck his nose under the hem of her shirt and pressed his lips to her belly and blew hard. She giggled loudly and I sat there like a fool, swooning my dang face off.

He pulled her down until her face was level with his and even though I could only see the back of her head, I could see Luk's plain as day. And it didn't take a rocket scientist to see that he was totally in love with this baby girl.

"Hey, Ellie Bellie." He kissed her on the mouth with a loud smack that made her giggle again.

"Lulu," she cooed so he smacked his lips to hers again.

I could feel my cheeks hurting I was smiling so hard when he finally turned the child and placed her in his lap facing me so I could see her.

"This is Ella," he said as he sat her down on his knee. I felt my smile fall as I took in her face. Something wasn't right. Ella didn't look like most of the children I had seen. I studied her features while she took in mine. All the while, Luk was strangely quiet.

And even though Ella wasn't a traditional looking child, I couldn't say that she wasn't stinking adorable. I just knew that something wasn't quite right and when my eyes finally lifted over Ella's head and found Luk's, my thoughts were confirmed. He looked at me like he'd die for this child and if I said or did anything crazy to upset her or him that he would throw me the hell out of his house so fast my head would spin.

"Ella, this is Scarlett." He was speaking to the baby, but he was definitely talking to me. His eyes never left mine. His face was serious, grave even. His shoulders were high and tight and that gorgeous jaw of his was ticking again. He was waiting on me and I knew that whatever I did or said next would determine the rest of our friendship and how it was going to play out.

I surprised him and myself. I'd never seen a child like Ella before and I wasn't exactly sure what to do, so I just went with my gut. I stuck my finger out near her hand.

"Hey, Ella," I said softly and gave her a smile. She wrapped her tiny fist around my finger and promptly brought it to her mouth and gave the tip a good gnaw. "Does that taste good?" I cooed and giggled and she smiled back at me from behind my finger and her fist and a ton of slobber.

I looked up, my eyes hitting Luk's above her head. His eyes were heated on mine. Almost like he wanted to eat me right there at the dining room table. I had no idea what that look meant then. I was too young, too inexperienced, too childish.

31

But finally he smiled and his shoulders dropped and I could see that whatever I'd done, I'd passed some test. Because he was easygoing, goofy smiling Luk again.

"She has Down syndrome," he said softly.

I shrugged. "And I'm a ginger."

Pursing his lips, he shook his head. "No, Scarlett. Ella has Down syndrome. She's *really* different."

I nodded even though I'd never heard of it, but I studied her face. Her teeny tiny nose. Her big, slanted eyes. Her perfect little mouth. "She's really cute."

Luk smiled like I'd given him the universe. "Cuter than me?" he questioned.

"Definitely."

"Well, damn. You're stomping all over my heart today, Red."

"I didn't think you had a heart, *Lulu*."

"Ah. You're not playing fair now. That nickname is top secret." His cheeks were pink and for once I'd managed to turn the tables. For once he was at my mercy, all embarrassed and flustered. And it was adorable.

"I can't imagine why," I said through laughter before pulling my finger from Ella's mouth and holding both of my hands out palms up. "Can I hold her?"

Luk passed small Ella over to me with only a slight look of apprehension and the smallest bit of hesitation, but she didn't mind a bit. She stood on my thighs while my hands cradled her up under her arms.

"All right, Ella. I'm Scarlett." I stared down at Luk's eyes peering up at me from Ella's face. And my heart melted just a little bit more. She smiled at me, her grin wide for such a small mouth, her little square teeth perfect. My eyes darted to Luk's quickly before returning to hers. "But ole Lulu over there likes to call me Red."

Luk scooted his chair around the table and forward until his knees pressed to mine and his body towered over me. I wanted to move mine back, but I was caged in by his long legs, broad shoulders, and long arms. He reached around Ella and grabbed her tiny hands, leaning closer to speak into her ear.

"Can you say Red, Ellie Bellie?" When she didn't say anything, he repeated, "Red."

She turned her head and sweet eyes met Luk's over her shoulder. And I just stared on, totally enraptured, completely, utterly losing my heart to none other than Mister Quarterback.

Ella uttered a sound I couldn't be completely sure was Red or not, but Luk moved his hands back and placed them over mine under Ella's arms and lifted her high over our heads.

"That's right! Touchdown!" he yelled, while Ella threw her head back and laughed high above our heads.

Lukas

I MADE MY WAY TO THE LOCKER ROOM FEELING LIKE I HAD BEEN HIT BY A Mack truck and that wasn't too far from the truth. Because I'd been sacked no less than twenty times in the last two hours by dudes who were almost twice my size and I wasn't a small guy by any means.

But I was starting to get used to it. It seemed that the team hadn't quite warmed up to me yet.

I felt a hard shoulder push mine and then all of a sudden Jackson Wells, the team's tight end and also the biggest pain in my ass, brushed past me and entered the locker room in front of me like I wasn't even there.

"Lukas, Last Minute Lucy my ass, man," he muttered, throwing me a quick look over his shoulder like I was shit on his shoe. "I'm still waiting on that last minute. Any minute, really." His low, sardonic chuckle hit my ears like acid. "When are you going to throw the fucking ball, Callihan?" The motherfucker was laughing at me.

I gnashed my teeth together and pretended to not hear him. I didn't need these guys. This was just a job I was here to do. If anything, they should be kissing my fucking cleats. I was their best shot at any kind of hope for a playoff game. I'd definitely taken a step down or maybe five, but you didn't see me giving them shit nonstop.

These assholes. I knew what they were doing when we were running plays. For the last two months they'd been kicking my ass. Hazing me. The offense wasn't blocking me and the defense damn sure wasn't taking it easy on me. And I had the bruises to show for it. I thought for sure that shit would be over now, but no, it was still happening and it didn't seem like it was going to be changing anytime soon.

I'd do what I did every evening after practice and ignore them. I'd grab my shit from my locker and get the hell out of there, opting to shower at home where I didn't have to listen to second rate players heckle me.

"Or hand the ball off or something," Wells continued as I undressed as quickly as I could so I could pack my shit up.

I just had to get out.

"Hah. He's not vertical long enough to throw or pass shit," Trevon Childs, wide receiver, piped in, laughing. "Someone needs to teach him to stand up first."

The gnash of my teeth turned into a full-on grind. I'd teach him something. Like how to keep his fucking mouth shut.

Fuck.

Motherfucking fuck. Teach. I totally forgot about contacting Ella's teacher. After our talk last night, we'd had dinner and I'd fallen asleep with her on the couch. I'd woken up alone this morning when the timer on my phone had gone off. She'd obviously gotten up and gone to bed on her own. I'd meant to contact Ms. Lettie last night during the special hours that she deemed appropriate in her letter but between football and Ella, I was fucking worn out and I'd just passed out.

It was okay. I'd call her tonight.

I grabbed my phone out of my bag and closed my locker. It was 4:00 p.m. Ella should have just gotten off the bus from school, so I shot her a text to make sure she got home okay. Allison, the sixteen-year-old who lived next door, chilled with Ella until I got home. She usually sent the thumbs-up back to let me know she was okay and home, so I stood there patiently waiting and freaking out at the same damn time.

I didn't get home long after her, and Allison was a great help, but I liked to know that she made it off the bus and into the house okay.

"Fucking Christ," I said under my breath while I wiped my forehead with my shirt. My entire body screamed in pain, but I somehow managed to stop the groan that was sitting right on my lips.

"Waiting on a call?" the big linebacker from beside me asked someone in a low, growly voice I'd only heard on a few occasions. Mason didn't talk much at all from what I had seen over the last two months. And he definitely didn't talk to me. He wasn't an outright asshole like some of the guys, but he sure didn't mind clobbering me on the field.

I kept checking my phone while I put my shit back in my locker and grabbed my bag.

"Lucy, I asked if you were waiting on a call."

I slowly looked away from the phone and up at him. Yes, I said up because Mason Stark was huge at freaking six-foot-five. "Are you talking to me?"

His blue eyes twinkled back at me. "I'm looking at you, Lucy. Ain't I?"

Feeling like I still wanted to be an asshole since the man hadn't talked to me since I'd been here, I turned around and checked behind me before looking back at him. "I'm sorry. You sure you're talking to me?"

"Quit being a dick." He took off his pads and nodded at my phone again. "Who you waiting on to call?"

I rolled my eyes at him. "You wanna gossip like fucking girlfriends now? When you haven't had the decency to even speak to me in two months?"

He turned and positioned his body right in front of mine. "The street works both ways, brother. You came here with a chip on your shoulder the size of fucking Africa and you want to act like we're the problem?" He stepped away and pulled a clean shirt over his head.

I got the thumbs-up from Ella on my phone and relief coursed through me. She was home. She was safe and now I needed to get there and make dinner, but first I'd deal with this.

"Yeah, you guys really rolled the fucking welcome mat out for me."

He shrugged with a smirk. "Like I said, Lucy. It's a two-way street." He nodded toward my phone. "Your girl finally get back to you?"

I rolled my eyes. "It's not my girl. I was making sure my sister got home okay."

"Damn, and here we all thought you needed to move back home because you knocked some chick up."

Was that what these assholes thought? That I'd moved home because I'd gotten a

hometown girl pregnant? I didn't think about girls. Before all this shit had happened, I lived and breathed football. Girls were an afterthought.

"Well, did she?" Mason spoke again.

"What?"

"Did your sister make it home okay?"

What the fuck was up with this guy? All of a sudden we were buddies now? "Yeah," I said, making my way to the exit.

He followed behind. "Good. Then we can go get a beer. My treat."

What. The. Fuck?

"Can't. I don't drink." I'd never had a sip of alcohol. My father was killed by a drunk driver. Alcohol had taken something precious from me. I'd never let it do that to me again.

I dashed through the parking lot to my car, Mason heavy on my heels. I didn't know what the hell his problem was, but it felt like some kind of set-up. The team didn't matter. Ella did. She was who I had to focus on.

I opened my car door, ignoring whatever it was Mason Stark was getting up to. The only thing I needed was my family, what little was left of it anyway.

Chapter
SIX

Scarlett

"FOR GOD'S SAKE, OLLIE. IF YOU STEP ON MY FOOT ONE MORE damn time." I was pretty sure my big toe on my right foot was bleeding and my big toe on my left foot was broken.

Ollie looked down at my feet and then back up at me with a smile. "I can't believe you thought this was a good idea. And I'm not talking about inviting me. I'm talking about actual ballroom dancing. What the hell possessed you to do this?"

"I don't know. I thought it would be something fun." I was lying like hell. I'd let the old lady next door sell me classes as some kind of fundraiser so her dance class could go on a cruise or some craziness. That's right, Sylvia Valasquez was dancing up a storm with the ninety-year-old love of her life in the Bahamas and I was going to be toeless by the end of the night.

"You could at least try, Ollie. It's a simple waltz, not brain surgery."

His brown eyebrows shot to his hairline. "Lettie, this ain't *Dancing with the Stars* and I'm no Maksim Chmerkovskiy."

I rolled my eyes and pierced him with a glare. "Oh, I'm all too aware of the fact you aren't Maksim Chmerkovskiy." No, Maksim would be rocking my world right now, not destroying my feet.

"Rude," Ollie grunted before landing his heel to my toe again. But the timing was a little convenient.

"Ouch! You did that on purpose!" I stopped dancing and Ollie let my arms fall and placed his hands on his hips.

"Prove it," he demanded.

My own hands went to my hips. I couldn't believe this. I'd asked my stupid brother for one damn favor. I should have known. Oliver Winston Knox may have been only a year younger than me, but he was ages more immature. It was a good thing he was ridiculously adorable and could get away with anything.

His hazel eyes were a stunner and they worked the whole cuteness thing to the limit. It didn't hurt that they were framed in the thickest, darkest eyelashes ever. Even his hair was thick and wavy and framed his face perfectly. Ollie was the dark to my light. Everywhere I was milky white he was beautifully bronzed. And while I was an obnoxious shade of red, he was all dark-haired gorgeousness. He took after my father. And I took after my grandmother. I'd drawn one hell of a short straw.

Through gritted teeth I said, "Stop embarrassing me, Oliver."

He pursed his lips. "What the hell did you expect? I play football. I'm not a damn dancer."

I screwed up my face. "Don't they make you take ballet or something? Isn't it supposed to help with sports?"

He just stared at me in a way that screamed what the hell are you talking about and where the hell do you get your information from.

I felt a nudge to my back.

"Dance!" my dance teacher, Christian, yelled about two inches from my ear. He followed it up with two hand claps in quick succession and then proceeded to yell "Dance" in Ollie's ear as well, his accent thick with French that sounded quite a bit contrived if you asked me. But that didn't stop us from jumping into each other's arms like two terrified children. It was the mustache. It looked like a double-edged sword. It was dark and pointy at both ends and he twirled and rolled it like an evil cartoon villain as he taught class. I knew this already and it had only been twenty minutes.

"Dance!" he yelled again and we sprang into action to the worst interpretation of a waltz I'd ever witnessed in my life.

"This is your fault," Ollie whispered where only I could hear.

"Yeah, yeah," I mumbled before landing on his toe with the arch of my foot. *Take that, butthead.*

He glared at me. "You should be telling your loving and kind brother how nice it is of him to make time in his grueling football schedule to take dance classes with his sister."

Grueling football schedule my ass. My brother played college ball, but he also had plenty of time to date by the looks of his Instagram account.

Christian came breezing by with a long-legged blonde in tow. "Dip!" he yelled, causing me to jump and for Ollie to practically throw me back.

"Christ," I whispered, dipped back almost to the floor, a wide-eyed Ollie cracking a smile.

"This dude is wild."

I nodded.

He pulled me up and kept on moving because honestly we were both scared the maniacal mustache twirling Christian would come back and yell at us in his fake French accent. He only stepped on my feet twelve more times in the next five minutes. I'd be icing those puppies tonight.

When Christian did a final pass with the blonde still in tow, Ollie eyed her and I pursed my lips and glared because I knew exactly what was coming.

"Damn, I'd butter the hell out of her biscuit." His eyes were glued to her legs.

My face scrunched up in disgust. "Ew. No one wants to hear about your butter."

He turned and dipped me again and leaned his face into mine and waggled his eyebrows. "Lots of girls like my butter, Lettie." He pulled me up to my feet and swayed me from side to side.

I made a horrible gagging sound that made everyone in the room turn around and look at us. "Sorry," I mouthed to an older lady who looked at me like she wanted to punch me in the face.

A fist landed on my back, causing me to cough. "Scarlett, my lovely, are you okay?"

Christian pounded on my back again and then twisted his diabolical mustache.

Holding a hand up, I said, "I'm fine. I swear." If he hit me again, I was in serious danger of losing a kidney or a lung.

"Dance!" he yelled and we fell back in step, Oliver laughing quietly.

"That was not even a little bit funny."

"Come on. It was a little funny. Besides, you asked for this. You could have brought any other guy in the world and you asked me."

He was right. Damn him. But I didn't have any other guys I could ask. I'd never even had a serious boyfriend. Most of the teachers at The Cottage House were women and I'd been a really late bloomer. Like junior year of college late and I wasn't even sure if I'd ever fully bloomed. I mean, I had my boobs and curves now, but I was still a really awkward ginger.

But I couldn't tell Ollie that. He'd pick on me forever and ever. And ever.

"Not all of us are out there whoring it up, Ollie."

He smiled, his teeth big and white, and I couldn't help but smile, too. That smile could end wars and it had. Like the time he'd skipped school and my mom found out or the time she'd found a dime bag of pot in one of his old dirty socks on the floor. She'd be all crazy, waiting on him to come home, and he'd walk in the door and see her face and he'd pull out the big guns. That damn smile. And she'd melt like ice cream sat out on the counter too long. My mother wasn't the only woman in the greater Summerville area who was a sucker for Ollie's smiles. Rumor had it he was a complete manwhore.

"You better not be whoring it up, Scarlett." The line between his forehead was deep and his eyes flickered with thought. "Are you see-ing someone? Who is it? Do I know him?"

I should also mention that Ollie was also completely over the top protective of his big sister. It didn't matter that I was a year older and ten years wiser, the boy watched out for me. He had my back.

Damn him. Now I was feeling all sweet toward him again even though my feet ached. I didn't need a boyfriend anyway. I had Ollie and my daddy. And no man would ever love me and treasure me as much as they did. Our parents had retired to Florida recently but that didn't stop me from being a daddy's girl.

"There's no one, Olls. Calm the heck down."

He raised an eyebrow. "Are you sure? Because if there was I would need to vet him and make sure he was good enough for my big sister."

Now I couldn't help but crack a smile. "Of course there's no one, Ollie. There never has been and there never will be. I'll be an old cat lady, but without the cats because I'm allergic." Jesus. That was so, so sad.

He stopped dancing but didn't let go of me. "What are you talking about, Lettie Knox?"

Rolling my eyes, I answered, "You know what I'm talking about." I threw him a look that said it all. That I had never had a boyfriend and that I had never ever been in love. And that I probably never ever would.

His face came closer to mine. "I hope you're talking about what an amazing catch you are and that any man who ever had the complete honor of dating you damn sure wouldn't deserve you."

Sweet, sweet, naïve Ollie. He didn't get that men didn't want a sassy redhead who spent more of her days taking care of her gobs and gobs of kids than worrying over a man who I knew wouldn't call anyway.

"Okay, class. That's enough for the day. You all were simply amazing."

I guessed Christian hadn't seen Ollie stomping all over my feet.

I took off my heels and changed into a pair of sensible, nude flats.

"Pizza?" Oliver questioned, his hands tucked into a pair of black sweatpants pockets. I looked behind him at the blonde ogling the way his biceps bulged in his white T-shirt.

"Sure. I told Hazel to meet us here so she could do dinner with us."

He swallowed hard enough I saw his Adam's apple bob up and down. "Hazel's coming?" he squeaked out.

I narrowed my eyes, studying him. He'd been doing this lately whenever I mentioned Hazel. I couldn't figure out what was going on with him and her, but I was positive it was nothing good.

"Yep," I popped. "She wanted to do dinner, so I told her to meet us here since the pizza place is close by."

He grinned crazily. "Great. Super. I can't wait to see her."

He was so full of shit. Oliver was my brother. A brother I happened to be very close to. I may not have known the details, but I knew when he was lying his face off. Like he was this very minute.

Behind Ollie, I saw Hazel walk in the door to the dance studio sporting her usual baggy hoodie and jeans.

"Good, because here she comes."

Ollie jumped like someone had pinched his ass and turned, spotting Hazel. "Hey, Hazel," he said with a slight quiver to his voice I'd never heard before in my life.

"Hey, Ollie." Her eyes danced behind her big, black, thick-rimmed glasses and I giggled. I had no idea what was happening, but whatever it was it had Ollie doing a pee pee dance and had Hazel feeling pretty confident. I decided I liked it.

"How was class?" Hazel asked, pulling the scrunchie off her wrist to tie her thick, long, brown hair into a knot at the top of her head. I was surprised it was down when she walked in because she almost always tied it up at the top of her head, giving the excuse that it was too much hair but never ever cutting it.

Ollie looked around the room like he didn't hear her, so I answered.

"It was good. Ollie destroyed my toes with those big ole clog hoppers of his and talked about buttering people's biscuits. Ya know? Just the usual."

Ollie's eyes flashed to mine accusatorily before looking at Hazel with red cheeks.

She shot him a big smile. "Yum. I like butter."

"I bet you do," he mumbled, scratching the back of his head.

"What did you say?" I asked, thinking I'd heard him wrong.

But Hazel interrupted. "We should head out." She looked around the room that was still full of people. "Looks like they're getting ready to shut this place down."

I studied the face of the girl who had been my best friend since I was six years old and in kindergarten. The same girl who had thrown down on the playground the day two little brats were trying to bully me off the swing. She'd left school that day with a black eye and my deepest affection. I loved Hazel Jones almost as much as I loved Ollie. And they had never ever acted this way. I was thrown and didn't know what to say, so I swung my eyes to Ollie, waiting on some clue, but nothing. He was too busy looking at his sneakers, his hands tucked deep into his pockets.

"Okay. Well, let's head out." I grabbed my stuff and started to walk out of the building, still eyeing my brother and best friend.

The cool air smacked me in the face. I'd grown up in the south, but I'd never get used to the temperature changes. It had been a warm seventy-five degrees earlier in the day and I was guessing it was closer to fifty now. I was wearing a short-sleeved A-line dress, so I rubbed my palms along my upper arms, trying to warm them as we walked the block to Luigi's, the only pizza place in Summerville.

"Wait," Ollie said from beside me. "My car is right here and I have a jacket inside. Let me grab it."

He walked around his parallel parked car and I grilled Hazel quietly. "What the hell is going on?"

She shrugged her shoulders. "What are you talking about? Nothing is going on. Nothing at all."

I was shocked. Hazel kept nothing from me. We told each other everything.

"Here," Ollie said, throwing his jacket over my shoulders and then pulling it back. "Sike."

"Stop playing." I grabbed the jacket from his hand and draped it back over my shoulders, feeling blessedly warm.

We took off for Luigi's, Ollie and Hazel flanking me.

"Speaking of playing. When are you coming over to play again, Ollie?"

My head spun to Hazel so fast, I thought it was going to fall right off my shoulders. What?

Hazel looked at me innocently. "Video games, of course." Her gaze swung to Ollie's. "To play video games again. When are you up for it?"

Her eyes were smoldering at Ollie and I looked between the two of them as we walked, confused as hell.

"You know what?" Ollie looked down at a nonexistent watch on his wrist. "I don't have time for pizza, after all. I forgot I told a friend I'd help him move a TV."

Hazel and I stared at him like he'd lost his mind.

I pointed to his wrist. "Ollie, you're not even wearing a watch."

He smiled. "Yeah, well, I should go. I'll see y'all later."

He leaned in to kiss me on the cheek and I tried to hand him his jacket.

"No, you keep it. I'll get it from you later."

I looked at him like he'd lost his damn mind and I wasn't sure that he hadn't. "Yeah, later. If you're not too busy moving TVs and all."

"Funny girl," he said to me and waved at Hazel, not even sparing her a glance as he started jogging down the block back toward his car.

"Bye, Oliverrrrrr!" Hazel yelled down the road, and Ollie did that thing where he didn't turn around and just threw his hand up over his head.

"What in the absolute hell was that about?"

She pushed her hand through my arm and pulled me toward our favorite pizza place. "What are you talking about?" She picked up speed and it felt like we were practically running up the street, but she wasn't getting out of this that easily.

"Stop playing dumb, Hazel. Spill! What did you do to my sweet baby brother?"

Her eyes were wide. "Me? What makes you think I did something? And that boy is not sweet."

"Because I saw you eyeing him like a piece of filet mignon."

She gave me a totally fake laugh. "You're being ridiculous."

"Hazel Jones, you better not traumatize my Ollie."

Her eyes rolled. "Please, girl. That boy can hold his own."

She opened the door to Luigi's, but I paused at the threshold and pointed at her. "I fucking mean it. That's my brother and I will cut you."

She laughed and this time it was real. "I hear you, crazy lady. Put down your scissors."

"Ha. Ha. Ha. You're hilarious."

"Can we at least get some food before you cut me? Yeah?"

"Fine." I gave her a final look of warning before we entered the pizza place. I'd never cut her. Not even for Ollie, but she didn't need to know that.

As we were taking our seats my phone pinged with a text. I clicked, not recognizing the number.

I'd love to schedule a time to connect with you about Ella. My apologies for not respecting your time.

That was all it said. But I knew exactly who it was and all of a sudden the phone in my hand felt like I was holding dynamite instead. Lukas was messaging me. Did he know it was me? He wasn't all like hey, Scarlett, let's meet up for drinks and rehash old memories and talk about why I haven't spoken to you in ten long years.

I had to admit, part of me loved giving Luk a hard time, but I thought he had intentionally missed our meetings because he was avoiding me, but maybe I was wrong. Maybe he didn't know I was Ella's teacher. Maybe this wasn't him avoiding me. Maybe he just had no clue who Ms. Lettie was. Oh my Lord. That had to be it. He had no clue who I freaking was. I grinned.

"Who was that and why are you smiling like that cat who ate the canary?"

Hazel's questions snapped me out of my thoughts. "What? Who? Nothing." God, I was worse at this than she was.

She reached around in the booth, snatching the phone out of my hand in the process. It was so fast I'd barely blinked and she was scrolling my phone, reading the text already up on the screen. What the hell? It was like she was a ninja instead of a freaking video game store manager.

Her forehead scrunched up and she turned the screen of the phone toward me so she could show me a text I'd already seen. "What the hell about this made you smile?"

"I wasn't smiling."

Pursing her lips, she threw me a sardonic look. "You were totally smiling and you're smiling now, you weirdo."

I smacked my teeth. "You don't know what you're talking about."

She turned the phone back toward herself and read the text again, her eyes squinted, her attention laser focused on it. And I couldn't have that. I couldn't have her figuring everything out.

"How about you give me the phone back now?" I grabbed for it only to be dodged.

"Ella. Hmm." She tapped her finger to her chin dramatically and held the phone high above my head. For such a small girl, she had arms like an orangutan.

And then I saw it. Realization painted her features. It was like I could see the little light bulb over her head turn on. And it was bright. Too damn bright.

"Oh my God. Is this from Lukas?"

I didn't say anything, so her eyes widened. "The Lukas! Like star quarterback Lukas Callihan you mooned over our entire freshman year of high school."

"It wasn't our entire freshman year."

She was totally embellishing. It was only the last half of freshman year. And this was getting so embarrassing.

"Give me the damn phone, Hazel!" I lunged for it again and this time I actually got it. Shoving it into my bag, I ground out, "It's not a big deal."

Her eyebrows flew up. "It seemed to be a big deal a minute ago when you were trying to keep the phone from me." She stared at me. "Wow, I heard he was home. And about his mom. How is Ella taking it?"

Shrugging, I said, "I don't know. She doesn't really talk about it."

She wore a complete shit-eating grin. "I can't believe your dream man is home. And you're teaching his baby sister. It's like fate!"

"Let's order the food." I was ignoring this. I wasn't going back there. With him or her.

She opened her menu and looked at it even though we'd been coming here at least once a week for years. We never looked at the menu and we always got the same thing. "Fine. I won't mention that Lukas Callihan messaged you. Or how formal it was. I won't mention that it seemed like he didn't even know who you are."

"Drop it, crazy lady."

She laid down her menu and threw her hands up in front of her. "It's already dropped."

After we ordered food, Hazel picked up her phone to respond to a text, so I did the same. I may have grinned a little as I typed it out because I'd liked to give Lukas shit years ago, but it seemed that now I loved it.

Chapter
SEVEN

Lukas

WAS SHE FUCKING FOR REAL? WHO IN THE HELL DID SHE THINK she was? Not even my mother had talked to me like this. I read over the text again and again because I still couldn't believe it. This woman had more balls than the whole damn NFL. That was a lot of damn balls.

> **You have a very hard time following directions, Mr. Callihan. I specifically gave you exact instructions on when it was appropriate to contact me. Was this a mistake or another bout of completely disregard for my time? Again.**
>
> **P.S. Ella hates peanut butter and jelly.**

Ella didn't really hate peanut butter and jelly. Did she? I made it for her almost every morning for lunch. God, it had been a long time since I'd even considered what she liked and didn't. She'd liked them at one point. Right? God, now this woman was making me question everything. This woman who I didn't give two shits about. What did I care what she thought about me and how I took care of Ella?

I was childish as hell, so I programmed in her number and added her as a contact that would show as She-Devil From Hell whenever she messaged from now on. I wouldn't be caught off guard again.

I realized I'd been meaning to contact her for days but kept getting thrown off. Between Ella and football, I was a fucking mess. I was barely getting enough sleep and this woman was going to complain about me not contacting her at the exact hours she'd requested. The whole thing seemed absurd and definitely a power trip. Besides, how the hell did she know what Ella liked to eat? She was just her teacher.

It was only 5:00 a.m., but I had no fucks. I wasn't putting up with this shit anymore. I hit reply faster than I ever had in my life and started mashing the buttons on my phone harder than probably necessary.

"Ella, you up?" I yelled as I sat up in bed, still typing my text to the teacher from hell.

My feet landed on the cold hardwood as I finished and pressed send. I felt good about my text until I actually hit send and then I realized it might have all been a huge mistake.

Me: Teach, what exactly crawled up your ass and died?

That may have been a touch dramatic, but I was sick of taking her shit. It wasn't easy juggling a demanding career and raising a child. I had no idea how single mothers did it.

My first order of business was taking a piss, so I walked to the adjoining bathroom off the master. It had been weird taking my mom's room in the house and for the first few months home I didn't, but I needed my old room for my gym equipment and when I'd finally decided to take it out of storage, I definitely felt like I couldn't use my mother's old room for a gym, so here I was, using it to sleep in. It was still weird as hell, but I was making do for Ella.

The tiles were cold against my feet. I turned the light on and looked at my almost twenty-eight-year-old self in the mirror, practically feeling like I was one hundred.

"Ella!" I yelled again. "Get up!"

Walking to the toilet, I noticed someone had once again removed the toilet roll from the dispenser and not replaced it. That someone had to have been Ella and it wasn't the first time she'd done it. I wasn't sure why she came into this bathroom, removed the almost empty roll, and never replaced it, but stranger things had happened and at this moment in time I had bigger fish to fry.

I did my business and noticed my phone buzzed from the bathroom counter while I did.

Oh, I couldn't wait to hear what this teacher said to me. I was part nervous and part elated as I picked up the phone after I washed my hands.

She-Devil From Hell: Excuse me? You must have meant to send this to one of the other countless women who are no doubt in your phone.

I couldn't help it. When I left the bathroom, I was grinning from ear to ear like a complete loon and maybe I was. This was the most fun I'd had since I'd moved home. This here was right what the doctor ordered. Why did she sound like a scorned woman? Like she was my girlfriend? Oh, this chick was completely crazy and I dug it. Hard.

Before I typed out my response, I poked my head into Ella's room and she was still under the covers, her head under her pillow. I sat down on the side of her bed. "Don't make me do it, Ellie Bellie."

"No, Lulu. Go away," she groaned from beneath the pillow.

"You wanna do this the hard way or the easy way?"

She rolled over onto her stomach and held the pillow close over her head. Sweet stubborn Ella. She was impossible to get out of bed every morning. Mom had been resorting to this since she'd been a small child.

"I said go away!"

I laughed quietly. She only got more adorable when she was angry. And she was pretty much angry every day before 9:00 a.m. She loved her sleep.

I set my phone down on the nightstand. The crazy teacher could wait. I pulled back Ella's covers and gave her side a poke.

"No, Lulu."

I stared down at her. "Then you need to get up. I can't have your teacher pissed at me. She's already giving me a hard time."

She turned her head toward me and gave me the stink-eye. "What did you do to Ms. Lettie? You're mean to her."

I was offended. "Me? Are you kidding? She's the spawn of Satan." I gave her side another poke. "You're gonna make me do it, aren't ya?" This time my poke was more of a tickle.

She laughed and moaned at the same time like I was both hilarious and the worst brother in the world.

"Fine. Fine. I'm getting up."

"Good," I said, standing and grabbing my phone, then heading toward the kitchen to start a big breakfast for Ella and me. Ella always did Zumba in the mornings before school and watched her soaps after. She never deviated from the plan, so it was no surprise to me when she came into the living room and turned on her Zumba DVD while I started cooking up eggs.

"Want eggs this morning?"

This time I didn't get an answer or even an acknowledgement. If she didn't feel like talking to me, she just didn't. It had always been like this. But since the peanut butter and jelly comment, I was questioning everything. "Do you even like eggs?"

No answer.

Still, I made the eggs and some bacon and by the time I was done, my phone was burning a hole in my pocket. I sat down, Ella across from me, our breakfast plated on the table, and I picked up the phone, smiling as I started to type out a text.

"You're a jerk."

My smile fell and my head flew up. "What? Why?"

"Because you called her Satan."

I grinned and set the phone on the table. "I didn't actually call her Satan. I said she was the spawn of Satan."

Ella poked her eggs angrily with her fork.

"Chill out, Ellie Bellie."

"I like her." She stuffed some egg into her mouth.

I nodded, taking a bite of bacon. "I know you do."

"Then be nice."

She wanted me to be nice. I guess she didn't realize how awful Ms. Lettie she-devil was being to me.

There was only a piece of bacon left on the plate between us. I looked up at Ella, her eyes on the bacon as well. I stabbed it with my fork quickly. "Dibs."

"Fine," she grumbled at me, shoving the last bit of egg into her mouth.

I didn't know what she was grumbling about. I always shared with her. I tore the bacon down the middle and placed half on her plate and shot her a grin. Dibs just wasn't as fun without Mom and Dad. In fact, it sucked.

We finished breakfast in relative silence just how Ella liked it most days. I loved Ella more than anyone in the entire world, but now that I couldn't even confide in Aunt Merline without her trying to convince me to give her Ella, I had no one. No one to sit and chat with about my day. And I was having shitty days. No adult conversation at all, really. I had no one, except her. And I just kept telling myself over and over again that she was enough.

I cleaned off the table and started to pack us both lunches when a thought occurred to me. "Hey, Ella. You still like peanut butter and jelly, right?" I called from the kitchen. She was in her room, but I knew for a fact that the girl could hear like a champ. She was a top-notch listener.

"No," she called back and I stood there, feeling dumb as shit.

Thinking I heard her wrong, I said, "Excuse me?"

"I said no."

Her teacher had been right. I stopped packing lunches and walked back to her room, knocking before I pushed the door open a crack. "Can I come in?"

She didn't answer me, so I went on in and watched her load up her bookbag and put her glasses on her face. She couldn't see well at all without them, but she did a hell of a lot of other things well. My mom made sure Ella was as high-functioning as she could be. She put her in schools and classes and never treated her like a kid with special needs. And thank God for that, because I was already struggling.

"If you don't like peanut butter and jelly then what did Mom pack for your lunch every day?"

"She didn't pack my lunch."

"What?"

Using her pointer finger, she poked her own chest. "I pack my lunch."

I wanted to scream what again, but instead I closed my eyes, placed my hands on my hips, tilted my head back to the ceiling, and prayed. I didn't use to be a praying man, but it seemed like I was now. I prayed for the patience of a father that I absolutely wasn't. I prayed for the patience of a mother because that was what I was going to have to be now. And I prayed for Ella because Lord knew she needed both of those and all she had was me.

And then I prayed for me because just when I thought I couldn't get any worse at this parenting thing, a tiny girl would trick me into packing her lunch every day even though she didn't like it all.

And then I laughed. It may have been the first time in two months. It started out with just a small shake of my chest and then a tiny tickle in my throat and before I knew it my hands that had been on my hips were covering my wet eyes and I was letting loose huge, grand guffaws that were less close to genuine laughter and leaning more toward complete hysteria.

I pulled my hands away and used the backs of them to give a good wipe under my eyes before looking over at Ella. Her bookbag was on and she was ready to take the bus to school, but I didn't miss the small smile that was playing at her lips. I hadn't seen too many of those either lately and my heart ached at that small smile. It was better than nothing. And that was what I'd be left with without Ella.

We both missed Mom so much. It was like we were in survival mode.

Still smiling, I asked, "So what have you been eating if you don't like peanut butter and jelly and you usually pack your own lunches?"

She shrugged, her small grin growing. "Ms. Lettie's lunch. It's good. She brings a hot lunch every day."

And then I laughed again. Because not only had this devious angel been tricking me, she'd been tricking her dear, sweet Ms. Lettie, too. And for some reason that made me ecstatic. I'd felt slighted by this teacher that Ella had grown to love so much. Like maybe Ella preferred her to me, but now I knew. Good ole Ms. Lettie and I were on an even playing field and even though the spawn of Satan didn't know it yet, I always played to win.

"Well, the gig's up, kiddo. Looks like you're back to making your own lunch. Better get it done before Allison comes and gets you for the bus."

"Fine." Her words were grumpy, but her face was anything but. It seemed like Ella thought this situation was as funny as I did. God, she'd really pulled the wool over both mine and her teacher's eyes. I had to give it to her.

While she set about making herself a ham and cheese sandwich that I took note of for future reference, I shot off a text to my favorite teacher.

Aww, Teach. You feeling jealous about all the women in my phone? ;)

I shouldn't have felt so damn good about firing off that text, but honestly this was the only adult interaction I'd had in months that wasn't me getting my ass handed to me on a football field. I was enjoying getting this woman fired up.

And as I packed my bag for practice and got into my SUV, I wondered what she looked like. If she was older or younger. And then I kicked myself in the ass for even thinking about it. It was none of my damn business and my hands were already full.

I turned into the stadium, laughing at myself. Because this woman was probably a hundred years old and had been teaching students with special needs for forever and here I was thinking about if she could possibly be my age and hot. God, I wanted her to be hot.

I wondered too damn much about this Ms. Lettie. All the way to practice and the whole time my team failed to block me and sacked the shit out of me. I knew this couldn't continue past the off season or we'd be fucked. No connection. No love for each other, but for some reason I couldn't be bothered to care at the moment. I had my own shit to deal with.

So when Mason tried to talk to me again, I threw in my headphones and ignored his ass. I checked my cell to see if I'd received a reply text from Ms. Lettie and I hadn't.

As I changed, I tried to think back to if I remembered a Lettie from ten years ago in town. Back then, Summerville had been a small place, but over the past ten years it had experienced a huge boom of growth.

Summerville used to have only one Walmart and, well, nothing else. Now, it was a booming suburb of Birmingham. In ten years it had changed completely and there were more people here that I didn't know than I did.

It was on the ride home that I heard the ping for a text, but I didn't text and drive, even though it nearly killed me to wait until I got home to check it. So when I pulled into our old garage that I needed to clean out ASAP because it still had a ton of Dad's old shit in it and I could barely fit my vehicle, I reached into the console and grabbed my phone.

I read the text and I read it again. And then again, my heart pounding in my chest like I'd run around the block five thousand times, my hands gripping the phone for dear life because I had to be wrong. I couldn't be right. And I went back. Back to late afternoons in a quiet library after school, an adorable redhead leaned over my textbook, the sweet smell of Skittles on her breath as she enunciated a complicated French word. I went back to late evenings at my house, baby Ella bouncing in that same redhead's lap, their faces close, my heart so full compared to how it felt now. It just couldn't be, but could it? And then I read it again, just to be sure.

She-Devil From Hell: You're mistaken. I couldn't care less about the copious amounts of women in your phone, Mister Quarterback. All I care about is Ella and her well-being and education.

There was only one person who ever in my whole life had called me Mister Quarterback and I hadn't seen her or spoken to her in over ten years. And all of a sudden, that seemed way too damn long.

Chapter
EIGHT

Scarlett
Age 14

ELLA WAS SITTING IN MY LAP AND HOLDING ON TO MY HAIR FOR DEAR life.

"One two, buckle my shoe," I sang and she laughed. I was trying my hardest to get her to say one, two. She'd done it a few days ago and I'd felt like queen of the world. Teaching Ella things was becoming my new addiction. The last couple of months of tutoring Luk had turned into me teaching her, too. It was pretty awesome. And I felt accomplished, like I was really making a difference. And not for Luk. For baby Ella.

And while I taught Ella, Luk just stared at me with some kind of look in his eyes I couldn't quite understand. But he'd been giving it to me a lot lately. Like now. He was looking at me like he was angry or very, very serious or maybe like he wanted to crawl inside of me. I couldn't quite figure it out. My fourteen-year-old mind couldn't quite wrap my brain around these looks he gave me when I held his baby sister like I did.

"What are you looking at, Mister Quarterback?" I found the only way to deal with my awkwardness about his looks was to be a smartass, and he found the only way to deal with my smartassness was to be a smartass back.

Except today.

"My Red."

And that threw me for a loop. My stomach dipped. His Red. Now, why did he have to go and do that? Why did he have to make this whole crush thing so much harder on me than it needed to be by teasing me? I ignored him.

"Three, four shut the door."

But Ella wasn't having it. She pulled my frizzy hair into her fist and stuck it in her mouth.

"Yuckies, Ellie Bellie." I pulled my hair out of her mouth.

She giggled.

"I think that's my cue to get home." It seemed like I spent more days over at Luk's house than not now. We really were friends. He was doing great in French and hardly needed my help at all anymore. We just hung out for the fun of it. Me just a little ole freshman best friends with the star quarterback of Summerville High. It seemed unimaginable and yet there I was sitting on his sofa playing with his baby sister, whom he loved more than life.

But I was trying my darndest not to get attached. Luk was leaving for college soon. We didn't talk about it. But we didn't have to. I'd heard the rumors. Most of the rumors at school were about the football players and let's face it, Luk was the star football player. He had a big future ahead of himself. I'd heard it said plenty of times that he would be playing pro ball one day. But most of the rumors nowadays centered around his immediate future. He had a full ride to a college in South Carolina. And he'd be leaving in just a few short weeks.

He took Ella from my arms before I could hug her bye.

"Wait," I said, leaning over and giving her a squeeze while he held her in his arms. "Bye, baby girl."

Luk crowded in, making sure to wrap an arm around me, too, and I hoped he didn't feel the goose bumps on my arm the moment his warm hand made contact with my cool shoulder.

"Bye-bye," she cooed back to me and I kissed her chubby cheek.

We broke apart and I finally let out the breath I'd been holding. I couldn't deal with Luk calling me his Red and breathing in his intoxicating high school boy scent. It was too much on a regular day when he didn't try to make me swoon.

"Mom, I'm walking Scarlett home!" Luk yelled.

"Okay, go on. I'll keep an eye on Ella. Bye, Scarlett!" she called back.

Luk always walked me home. Over the last few months I realized he was a real gentleman through and through. I'd miss him when he left.

The walk to my place was an unusually silent one. There wasn't much that Luk couldn't find to talk about. I may have been quiet and awkward, but he seemed to make up for it in spades. He never let me feel uncomfortable around him. He would carry the conversation if he had to and sometimes he did. And it wasn't because I felt awkward or out of place with him. It was because I loved hearing him talk. The things he said. How he said them. Even at my young age I knew Lukas Callihan was something special. Every hour felt fleeting, every moment so precious.

When we got home, it was already dark out. I stepped up onto my porch feeling differently—strung tight like a rubber band about to snap. He'd been too quiet, too reserved tonight. It made that moment right then feel momentous, important. When I looked back at Luk standing down on the sidewalk in front of my porch it felt like there was an electricity in the air I'd never experienced before. My skin felt tight. My body felt restless and the little hairs on every surface of my skin stood up.

A lightning bug flew past his head and I smiled uncomfortably. Anything to make this feeling stop. Or to keep it forever. I couldn't decide which was worse. Never having this feeling again or feeling it every day for the rest of my life. It was too much, this buzzing under my skin as I looked down at him, this desperate pressure on my chest to say something big.

Running a hand through his gorgeous curls, he choked out desperately, "Scarlett." His face looked pained and I panicked.

I took one step down the porch, my foot hitting the wood a thud that seemed ominous. "What's wrong?"

He looked past me, staring at my front door in thought, his eyes too serious. He drew that plump bottom lip I dreamed about at night into his mouth in thought before releasing it.

He squeezed his eyes shut and tilted his head back to the sky and let out a deep sigh. "Fuck," he said to that sky like it had done something horrible to him.

Worried, I came down the last three steps quickly and stood in front of him, my heart beating out of my chest. He was wearing a blue and white plaid flannel over a bright white T-shirt and I pulled at the lapels of that shirt, begging him to look at me.

"What's going on, Mister Quarterback?" I didn't normally touch him like this, so unabashedly. But he didn't normally look this upset either.

Taking a long breath in, his head lowered slowly until his emotional eyes crashed into mine.

I clung to those eyes while my hands clung to his shirt as he raised his hand to my face and placed his palm lovingly to my cheek.

Oh, God. What was happening? My eyes slipped closed as he stepped in and the scent that was purely Lukas washed over me. His palm was warm against my face and I leaned into it, thinking maybe he'd never touch me like this, beyond thankful for this singular moment.

A cool forehead pressed against mine and our breaths mingled. But I kept my eyes closed, thinking I was probably dreaming because this couldn't be real. Lukas only liked Scarlett Knox on a platonic level, never as more. He'd never hinted. Never touched me. And definitely never cradled my face tenderly or laid his forehead to mine.

Except he was. Right now. God, how I hoped I would never wake up in that moment. My hands fisted the front of his shirt. I never wanted to let go. Not today. Not tomorrow. Not ever.

"I wanna call dibs. So bad," he whispered almost against my lips and my knees trembled.

He wanted to call dibs, but there were no Skittles to be seen. No candy, no food, no remote control that he'd taken from me too many times to count over the last few months. My voice quivered. "On what?"

But I knew. I knew what he was saying and it was too good to be true. And too late. Way. Too. Late.

"You." His voice sounded as tortured as my heart felt. His thumb rubbed my chin. His eyes held me captive. "I wanna call dibs on you, Red."

His other hand came up until it cradled the other side of my face and all of a sudden I was enveloped in him. Just him and the most romantic moment of my life. His hands on my cheeks, his body close to mine, my hands clinging to him for dear life. Because this was it. It was the moment every girl who'd ever liked a boy ever wished for.

His nose brushed the side of mine, the stubble on his face scratching me, making me shiver even though I was pretty sure I was the hottest I'd ever been.

He didn't ask to take my first kiss. I didn't expect he would and I would've said a thousand yeses anyway. So, when he leaned in and pressed his warm lips to mine, I exhaled slowly. And he breathed in, sucking that very oxygen into his lungs like it was everything to him.

He didn't take it further. He just held my face like I was something special and kissed my lips chastely, his soft lips pressed to the heat of mine. It was how a girl's first kiss should be. Romantic. Devastating. Sweet.

He pulled back and my lips followed his, but he used his thumb to stop them, pressing right there at the pillow of my bottom lip.

I opened my eyes and sad, brown ones were waiting on me.

"I'm leaving in a few weeks, Scarlett. As soon as school's over. I have football camp in South Carolina at the beginning of summer."

I nodded, my heart breaking even though I already knew. "I know."

His thumb roamed my lips while his words destroyed me. "I'm leaving and you still have three years of school left." He gave me a sad smile and I wanted to use my fingers to wipe it away, but instead I just enjoyed the feel of his thumb on mine. "But I couldn't leave without at least doing that once. I had to. Forgive me?" His voice was so quiet it could have been a whisper, but I heard it loud and clear. He was leaving. I was staying. This was over. Whatever this was now. Because in the last ten seconds it had seemed to change drastically and I was way too young and immature to understand more than that I wanted to kiss him again. More. Harder. I wanted his hands on my skin and not over my clothes. I wanted more than a simple kiss. I wanted to taste the inside of his mouth. I wondered what his tongue would feel like against mine like I'd seen in too many movies.

I stupidly wanted to beg him to stay. To tell him I could visit him. That I'd be here when he came home to see his family, that I'd wait, but the resolve on his face kept me in check.

I stepped back and his hands fell. I had to preserve what was left of the rest of my young heart. It may have been in tatters, but it was still there, beating wildly, firmly in the clutches of my very first ever crush.

"It's okay," I said, lying. I could pretend. I was good at that. I'd been pretending the last few months, so I'd had lots of practice. I was getting dang good at it.

I kept backing up until I backed right back up the porch steps I'd just come down moments before. Before everything had changed in the span of seconds. Before he'd kissed me. Before he'd ruined everything and made my dreams come true all at once. Part of me wished I could press rewind. Part of me wished I'd never come down those steps, that he'd never devastated my mouth with his sweet kiss. The other part of me never wanted to forget it. The other part of me wished I could press pause instead.

"Red," he ground out, his hands back in his hair, pulling at his pretty curls, his face tortured. "I'm sorry, I—"

I held my hand up. "No, it's okay, Luk. I get it." I nodded, trying to convince myself along with him. "I really do." I threw him a paltry smile. It was freaking pathetic and I instantly regretted it. "I should go."

I took one last look at his gorgeous face, trying to memorize it because I knew this was it and I kept backing up until I felt the door at my back. I pushed my hand behind me until I found the doorknob and turned it and slipped inside, closing it behind me swiftly. The living room was dark and I was so, so thankful. I was pretty sure my mother and my brother were at some sporting event he was doing, so at least no one would witness how pathetic I was. I slid down the door until I landed on my behind. With my knees to my chest, I cradled my head in my hands and finally let the tears fall.

Even through my sobs and hiccups I could hear what sounded like a kick to my front porch and the word, "Fuck," loudly from Lukas's mouth.

I held my cries in as best as I could until I heard the crunch of the driveway pavement beneath his sneakers walking away.

The first few days after it had happened, I dreamed of it. I held the memory of his hands on my cheeks and his lips warming mine close to my heart, cherishing them, knowing I'd never have them again. Until I didn't anymore. Until those memories hurt me more than they comforted me. Until I felt like they broke me somehow. Until I realized the kiss had somehow ruined the little time I'd had left with Luk. Why had he kissed me? Had he somehow figured out how much I adored him and felt sorry for me? Why hadn't he just left and let me keep my heart intact?

I avoided him the last few weeks of the school year. I didn't go by his home and pay my favorite baby girl any visits. I didn't look at him as I passed him in the hallway. I avoided the library where I knew he'd study. He wanted a clean break and that was what I gave him. He didn't avoid me, but he didn't come for me either. He didn't say goodbye before he left for school and he damn sure didn't contact me in the years after.

It was silly, almost immature how I still thought of him ten years later as the one who'd gotten away. As the one who'd broken my teenage heart and stolen my first kiss.

Chapter
NINE

Scarlett

I WAS LATE FOR SCHOOL AGAIN. I'D PROBABLY BE MORE WORRIED ABOUT IT IF it wasn't a regular occurrence and if my boss didn't give a rat's ass. He knew I was a good teacher and believe it or not, those weren't too easy to come by. Especially in the special education variety. Besides, it wasn't like I intended to be late. I was a Southern girl. We were habitually late creatures. It was just in our DNA. There was no getting around it.

Imagine my surprise when I saw the black Lexus behind me again. Traffic was light, so I didn't get the chance to check my teeth in the mirror or anything just to piss him off. I could see the silhouette of his ridiculously expensive glasses and I rolled my eyes as I pulled into the school parking lot.

What I was surprised to see was that he was pulling in right behind me. Holy shit. Was he following me in so he could tell me what a crazy person I was for yelling at him in traffic? Better yet, was he following me because he was a parent and I had yelled at him?

As I pulled past the line of parents and headed back to the teachers' lot, I let out a sigh of relief. He'd turned into the carpool line. He may have been a parent at the school, but there were a lot of kids here.

I did check myself in the mirror in the lot and add a little red lipstick to my lips. I got out of the car feeling like a million bucks. I may have been a little late, but I looked good today. I had on a red pencil skirt and white silk blouse that I had tucked in. I wore my black pumps with the red bottoms sans stockings. My hair was down and tamed around my face in soft curls and I'd even thrown on my pearl earrings and necklace. It was a rare day that this teacher got her act together in the morning, but today had been a good day thus far. Ollie had woken me up when he'd left early in the morning for football practice before school, but I was thankful for it when I looked down at my freshly pressed outfit.

But maybe I was having a good day because I'd been enjoying a string of texts between me and a certain quarterback. Messing with Lukas and teasing was becoming something of an obsession and I'd become ridiculously attached to my phone over the last few days.

I grabbed my laptop bag with my school supplies and headed in, my heels clacking down the hallway, my hips swaying like I knew I was having a good day. Because I was, even if I was doing it a little later than I should be.

Even Vice Principal Vega seemed to notice. "Hey there, Scarlett. You're looking nice today."

Oh, I knew what he meant by nice because his eyes were feasting on the length of my legs as he said it. But there was no way I was going there. He was my superior. It didn't matter that Victor Vega had a head full of beautiful, thick, black hair and a killer smile. He was a tall glass of Spanish water that I wouldn't mind sipping at all. If he wasn't my boss. Besides, I knew the likes of him would destroy me. I knew his type. His type had damn near ruined me in high school. I'd have to stay far, far away from what some of the older girls called "The Puerto Rican Papi."

"Thanks, Principal Vega." I didn't look back as I passed him by, but secretly I enjoyed his attention. This girl didn't get hit on by too many guys. Especially ones who looked as good as him.

I entered my classroom with my chest puffed out. It was just one of those days. One of those *awesome* days.

A few students were milling about already and I greeted them as I made my way to my desk at the back of the room. I even stopped and did a little twirl in front of Joshua's desk. *See, no poop today, buddy!*

Only to my surprise and ultimately my demise, I spotted a very big man behind my desk and sitting in my chair mid-twirl. And for once my black pumps didn't make me look great because I was so stunned at the sight before me I went down like a large sack of potatoes, rolled ankle and all.

I lay there for approximately five seconds, looking up at the ceiling and praying for something to happen. Anything really so I didn't have to face the man behind my desk. I was unprepared. I had just fallen. I'd done a twirl, for Christ's sake. Kill. Me. Now.

I slammed my eyes closed and prayed a little and then I used my right hand to pinch my right side just to make sure this wasn't a bad dream.

"You okay, Ms. Lettie?" a little boy named Gavin asked from my left side.

I kept my eyes closed. "Yes, buddy. I'm fine. Because this is a dream. A very bad dream."

Because the man I thought I saw mid-twirl before I went down could not be here. This whole thing could not be happening.

"I don't think so," came his little voice again, in a mild stutter with a bit of a lisp. It was adorable and all, but God, I just wanted to sink into the ugly, dirty carpet around my head.

A shadow fell over me that I could see even behind my eyelids. And I knew it was too big to be one of the kids. *Wake up. Wake up right now*, I pleaded with myself.

"Need some help there?" That voice. Oh, dear Lord, that voice. I knew it. I remembered it like it was yesterday. It may have held the same inflection and bit of teasing. It may have still been laced with a thick Southern accent I'd recognize anywhere, but it was deeper, more gravelly and so much sexier. Damn it. Damn it. Damn it.

I squeezed my eyes closed harder. "Nope, I'm good," I squeaked out.

I felt him squat down near my head, but I dared not open my eyes because I was still in denial and my theory was proven when his voice sounded a lot closer. "I'm all for women falling at my feet, but this seems a little extreme, Red."

My eyes popped open of their own accord and sure enough his face was right over mine, looking down. And God, he looked good. Better than he should have. It just wasn't right. He was all tan, manly, and scruffy, and I was pretty sure that pine woodsy scent I'd loved in high school was multiplied times ten. I wanted to hold my breath, but I felt like what I had to say was more important.

"It's just as cliché now as it was then." I glared up at him. Well, I tried to glare. I probably looked more like Popeye since I was wincing a bit from the fall.

One of his thick, perfectly groomed eyebrows hitched up. "What's that?"

I pursed my lips. "Red."

He grinned, his perfect white teeth almost rendering me blind before pressing a big hand to his chest. "You're wounding me here, Scarlett. And I thought we were friends."

I felt my eyes get big. He had to be kidding me. He'd kissed me and then didn't contact me for over ten years. That didn't constitute as friends in my book. At all. In fact, when I thought about that day my chest pinched in a way I didn't like a darn bit.

"I bet you say that to all the girls."

His smile was back and despite how I wanted to throat punch him for surprising me, I felt my own lips begin to tip up.

"Only the ones I like."

"Oh, I bet there are plenty of those," I said under my breath, beginning to sit up.

He stood up and put his hand out. "What was that?"

"Oh, nothing." I grinned so hard my teeth hurt. It was fake. It was the smile of a girl in full-on panic mode. I didn't want to take his outstretched hand, but I didn't want him to know that, so I tentatively reached out, but he grabbed my hand roughly, full-on, and pulled me from the floor.

"Sorry about that, Mr. Callihan," I said, releasing his hand quickly and straightening my skirt and blouse, looking anywhere but directly at him. "I was just giving a twir—"

"Oh, I saw you showing off your ass-sets. I'm thoroughly impressed, by the way." Damn him. The inflection on the ass part of that word wasn't lost on me, but I wouldn't feed into it. I wasn't taking the bait this time. Besides, I couldn't very well tell him the poop/coffee story. That would be almost as embarrassing as falling on my ass in front of the boy I crushed on forever ago. Almost.

And then it occurred to me. The Aviators sat right there in the pocket of his white T-shirt. Holy shitake mushrooms. He was the black Lexus driving douchebag who yelled at me. Of course he was. Because my life was like a damn episode of *I Love Lucy*. Wasn't that just freaking rich?

Good Lord. Lukas was responsible for the coffee incident of 2019. Now he'd most definitely go down in history. As if he hadn't already.

"So, how are you?"

My eyes flew to his. What the hell was he doing? He was wanting to chat like we were old friends. I studied his genuine eyes. Because he thought we were. He thought we were old friends and that we were going to catch up. Hell, he even looked excited to see me. Holy shit. He could not do this. I wasn't fourteen and stupid and we were not picking up where we left off because in reality there was nothing to pick up. Still looking at his eyes, I noticed they were harder than they were ten years ago. But that hardness made sense. He'd lost his mother, after all. I thought of the day in his house when he'd told me about his dad. And now all he had left was sweet Ella.

I walked past him to my desk and stood behind it, putting some much needed distance between us. I felt for him. I really did. I knew how awesome his momma was. How much he loved her. I wanted to hug him and tell him how sorry I was. But I wanted to save myself more. It may have been selfish, but I was Ella's teacher now and we hadn't spoken in many years. Our relationship was purely a professional one and would continue to be.

But that didn't stop me from taking everything in. I didn't miss the way his eyes followed me. I didn't miss how good he looked in those damn jeans. I wondered how he got them on because they were tight in all of the good places. The places I tried desperately not to look at. I picked up a pile of papers. I had no idea what they were or what they said, but I needed to look anywhere but at the fine man standing in front of my desk with his hands on his hips. That smile still firmly in place. How did he get bigger? Broader? More devastatingly handsome.

"What can I do for you, Mr. Callihan?" I said to the pile of papers, ruffling them around like I was studying them instead of freaking the hell out.

"God, Red."

I looked up. I couldn't help it. The tiniest bit of pleading in his voice made me.

"Come on. Cut me a break and tell me how you're doing." He tucked his thumbs into the pockets of his jeans. I decided that was about all that could fit in them, they were so snug. And then I noticed the class behind him quiet, all studying us. They were all seated. All being too well-behaved.

They knew the rules and hardly ever broke them. My kiddos were the best, but I could tell they were on pins and needles just like Luk, waiting on my answer.

My eyes found Ella's sitting in her desk patiently even as her eyes volleyed back and forth between Luk and me.

My gaze traveled back to Luk's and I gave him a small smile. I told myself it was for Ella. "I'm good. How are you?"

"I'm better. I'm excited to see you." His stare trekked down the length of my body and back up before landing on my eyes again. "God, you look gorgeous, Red. You're beautiful."

And just like when I was fourteen when my spit went down the wrong pipe and I felt like I was choking. Why did this man do this to me? I started to choke and Luk rushed around the desk and pounded me on the back twice.

"Same ole, Red. I didn't mean to make you choke."

Kill me now.

I took two steps away and held a hand up while I caught my breath before asking, "Is there a reason you came by? Is it about Ella?"

He shook his head, his face serious, almost solemn. "No, I just had to see for myself. I had to see if it was you. Ella calls you Ms. Lettie, so I had no idea."

My cheeks burned. "Yeah, all the kids call me that. It's easier than Scarlett for some of them to say and my momma always called me that anyway."

"It's sweet." He said it like he thought I was adorable.

I nodded and moved around the stapler on my desk. "Well, I have a class to teach." I was sure that would get his ass moving and out of my classroom.

"Sure thing. Maybe we can get together some night and catch up."

What the hell did we have to catch up on? Maybe we could catch up on how I thought we were friends and he'd kissed me. Or maybe we could catch up on how he didn't talk to me for ten years after that. Yeah, I knew I was harping on it, but damn, I wasn't going to let bygones be bygones. He wasn't going to get my friendship so easily again. He'd let me down once. Fool me once, shame on you. Fool me twice, shame on me.

"Have a good day, Mr. Callihan."

"Damn, it's like that, huh?"

I totally played dumb. "I'm sorry."

He nodded and walked backward a few feet, his thumbs still adorably tucked into his pockets, his eyes dancing with mirth, even though his mouth wasn't smiling. "You know what gave you away?"

I didn't answer. I wasn't feeding into this. I wasn't doing whatever it was he thought we were doing.

"It was the Mister Quarterback. I hadn't heard that one in a long time." He let out a low chuckle that sent goose bumps up and down my arms.

Do not engage. Do not engage, Scarlett. He wants you to giggle or smile or choke on your spit again. Don't do it.

He turned on a heel and walked over to Ella's desk. His gait slow and self-assured, and I wanted to kill him because I was anything but sure. I was a wreck. One freaking meeting and I was ruined. I'd fallen on my ass. I'd choked. Fuck. My. Life.

Bending down low to reach Ella, he said, "I love you, Ellie Bellie. See you after school." He pressed a kiss to her temple and made his way to the exit.

Ella studied my face before turning to shout at her brother, "You said you weren't going to piss her off, Lulu."

He threw a smile over his shoulder to her and his stare flashed to me before returning to hers. "She doesn't look pissed to me. And watch your mouth.

"See you soon, Scarlett Knox."

His eyes were full of promise. This was bad, bad, bad. His cocky ass left the classroom completely unscathed, unlike me. My hip was already twinging from the fall, right along with my pride.

Chapter
TEN

Lukas

I'D BEEN LATE FOR FOOTBALL PRACTICE AGAIN THIS MORNING, BUT I couldn't be bothered to give a fuck. Not one single one. I'd been fined a hell of a lot of money and Coach had been pissed, but it had totally been worth it. Suspecting that saucy old Ms. Lettie was Scarlett was one thing, but sitting there in that seat and watching her walk in all fucking grown up and beautiful had just about killed me.

Scarlett Knox, the only girl in high school who'd made me want to do something other than play football. The only girl who'd made me want to skip football practice in exchange for tutoring lessons. My tender-hearted, good-natured, sweet friend, Red. She'd been adorable then, mature more than her years and kind beyond measure. I'd instantly liked her. I hadn't been surprised when months later, I'd had feelings for her that were much more than friendship. I'd thought about her through the years, always wondering how she was, what she was doing, what lucky asshole she'd ended up with.

I couldn't believe she was still in town. Teaching Ella of all people. And looking damn fine. I hadn't had much good news lately, but Scarlett Taylor Knox still in Summerville, Alabama, was definitely good news.

Jesus, thinking about high school made me feel all kinds of things and they weren't all just about Scarlett. I'd lost my dad then, but I'd still had my mom. At least I'd had her. I was happier then. More carefree. And Scarlett, she'd been a friend I could confide in. Our tutoring sessions had turned to friendship faster than I'd thought possible, but she was just a special person. One of those instantly trustworthy people, and when I'd introduced her to Ella, she'd proved that. She hadn't let me down when she'd looked at Ella like any other toddler and I knew what it was like when people didn't. By the time Ella was two, I'd gotten enough stares to know that not all people were accepting and nice when it came to kids with special needs or really anyone who was different. It didn't matter to them how much we loved Ella. How kind she was. How she sucked her thumb and called me Lulu and I felt like I was on top of the fucking world. No, certain people didn't care how beautiful and wonderful my sweet girl was.

But Scarlett had. Right away. I could picture it now. Baby Ella sitting on Scarlett's skinny legs, her red hair wild around her head, her glasses down on her nose where they too often slid and drove her crazy. She'd push them up and give Ella a big smile full of braces and crooked teeth and still I'd thought she was the greatest thing since sliced bread.

She'd been adorably nerdy on the outside then, but on the inside was a damn beautiful bombshell. And now that she was an adult, it seemed like the bombshell had emerged and I was in a shitload of trouble because I couldn't stop thinking about her. I wanted to text her, call her. I wanted her to give me a hard time like Ms. Lettie had. Those sharp worded texts were what was getting me through my long, sucky days.

She hadn't seemed pleased to see me in her classroom. I thought she would have been happier. We'd gotten along really well when we'd been kids. I wondered if she was still upset about how I'd left things, but I'd known in my heart it had been the right decision. For her. I'd put her first. I knew she would have never seen it that way, but I'd made that decision solely for her. Maybe I shouldn't try to contact her anymore. Maybe it wasn't fair to her.

"What you daydreaming about over there, Lucy?"

Fuck. Mason wasn't going to give up apparently. He was still trying to strike up a conversation with me every chance he got. He was still kicking my ass on the field, right along with the rest of the team, though, so I just ignored him.

I shrugged and ignored the ache in my rib as I grabbed my phone from my locker.

"Don't tell me I knocked your ass mute, Callihan?"

I blew out a long breath and checked the phone to make sure I got the thumbs-up that Ella was home. When I saw it, I finally answered Mason. "Nah, man. I can take a hell of a lot harder hits than any of you can give me."

And wasn't that the truth. I'd been taking them left and right lately and not just on the football field.

He raised his eyebrows at me, before he lowered them, his eyes narrowing like he was trying to figure me out. "No one knows what you can take, Lukas. You don't let anyone around here know anything about you. And you sure as hell don't give a shit about us."

Lukas. It was the first time he'd used my real name. It made me feel things I didn't want to feel. It made me want and need friends that I didn't have time to enjoy. I snatched my bag from my locker, pissed off. Didn't he fucking realize I had more on my plate than I could deal with? I didn't have time to worry about hurt feelings and getting to know the guys. I was here to do my job. A job I now needed to support Ella.

I couldn't acknowledge this right now. I was still reeling from realizing Scarlett was still in town and all grown to boot. I started walking at warp speed to my Lexus. I thought I'd almost made it when I felt a big hand on my shoulder, squeezing.

"Hold up, man." Mason's deep voice stopped me in my tracks.

Closing my eyes a moment, I hoped for the patience not to lose my shit on him before I turned around.

He didn't pull any punches. He just started right in. "Didn't you ask to be traded to this team?"

I gripped my bag tightly in my hand as I answered. "Yeah." He wasn't getting more than that. It wasn't any of his damn business.

He stared at me long and hard for a minute before he shook his head slowly, his jaw ticking. Dude looked like he was going to beat my ass in this parking lot and he very well could have. He was bigger and stronger.

Nostrils flaring, he said, "Then why the fuck won't you even try? Why come back home to play for a team that needs you and not give it your all?"

I dropped my bag and stepped forward until my chest brushed against his. I was so angry my whole body was burnt up with it. Was he fucking kidding me? I tried my hardest every fucking practice. I was giving everything my all. I was gived all the hell out. "I give it my all every fucking practice," I spat two inches from his face.

He shook his head back and forth slowly before landing his pointer finger right to my chest. "Not just on the field, Lucy. You're fucking up. Your attitude stinks. You're letting the team down."

"It's not my fault the team sucks!" I shouted.

And he was on me, his forearm to my throat tight, my back to the driver's door of my SUV. He had cornered me and he had the leverage and he was cutting off my air supply.

With his forehead practically pressed to mine, he growled, "You're a part of that sucky team, Lukas Callihan, and you better get fucking used to it. You decide if it sucks. You decide if it gets better. Because you're a part of us now, whether you like it or not. Fucking act like it."

With a sudden burst of angry energy, I shoved him off me and sucked in air through my lungs, trying to catch my breath. This crazy motherfucker was trying to kill me.

I leaned over, closing my eyes, breathing deep until I finally caught my breath. When I looked back up, Mason was leaning down into my side mirror, pushing around his blond hair. He'd obviously messed it up in our almost scuffle.

I stared at him because what the fuck was going on?

Still smoothing his hair, he asked, "Where should we go to dinner?"

Again, what the ever-loving fuck was happening? "Excuse me?" I rubbed at my neck where he'd held me down.

"I said, where are we going to dinner?" He patted his stomach. "I'm starved."

I picked my bag up off the ground, shaking my head because I was confused as hell. "You're insane."

He finally stopped checking himself over in the mirror and stood to his full height. He gave me a huge, toothy grin that I'm sure had all the ladies swooning, but all it did was piss me off.

"So are we going to dinner or what?"

I pushed past him and opened my door and threw my bag inside. "You tried to choke me to death," I accused.

He lifted one blond brow. "You're being dramatic. I'd never kill you. I can't win games if my quarterback is dead." At this he looked thoughtful. "I didn't take you for the dramatic type."

I hopped in my car and closed the door. I cranked it up and rolled down the window. "I can't go to dinner, you crazy motherfucker. I have to get home to make dinner for my sister."

He took a couple of steps backward like he was heading toward his own vehicle. I let out a sigh of relief that this shit was finally over for today. I was tired and sore and over everything.

"What are y'all having?" he yelled from next to a giant, white truck.

I had no clue what the hell the crazy man was talking about. "What?"

"What are y'all having for dinner?"

I was tempted to pretend I didn't hear him and drive the hell off, but now that I knew what kind of crazy he was hiding I decided against that shit. "Whatever is in the fridge!" I yelled back.

He nodded before opening the door to the white truck and climbing inside. And when I said climb I meant climb because homeboy was big, but that damn truck was huge. Before he shut the door he called back, "Sounds good to me. I'll follow you home."

The man had insulted me. And almost choked me, but I just rolled my eyes while I put my window up and pulled out of the parking lot. Mason Stark seemed like he was looney as a bedbug, but no one else was beating down my door to have dinner with me and Ella. I'd just have to take what I could get. And right now all I had was a deranged linebacker.

Chapter
ELEVEN

Scarlett

Lukas: I was wondering if you wanted to come over sometime.

Oh, dear Lord, but I couldn't deal with him right now. Why was he texting me? I couldn't handle it. Not on top of everything else. It was the third Friday of the month and on the third Friday of the month me and my part-time teacher's assistant, Jessi, took the kids on an outing. CBI trips were what the grown folks called Community Based Instruction. It was supposed to help my kiddos navigate real world situations in the community. We taught them to shop for groceries, to go bowling and rent their own shoes. Hell, one time I thought it was a brilliant idea to do a camping trip, but that's a horror story for another day.

So, while Luk clearly had enough time in his day to shoot off a text, I was in the throes of a chaotic Walmart shopping trip, complete with one child taking off on a handicap cart. Those things were faster than I ever thought they could go. And another kid had disappeared. He'd been hiding amongst the paper towels. Who knew there was so much room down there? Kids did, that's who.

We were frantically making our way to the cash register and I was only sweating a bit when I got the text I'd been expecting for days. Everyone was paying for their items and I was in Walmart hell. That hell consisted of an impatient cashier who rolled her eyes as I helped each child. When I finally got everyone settled, my quiet guy Nathan asked to go to the bathroom. I couldn't let him go into the men's room alone. Nathan was a child with autism who had just recently become verbal. The mere fact he'd asked me to go to the restroom and not wandered off to find one like he had in the past was miles from where we were at the beginning of the school year.

Another text popped up.

Lukas: To discuss Ella, of course.

I rolled my eyes because he'd already missed two meetings to discuss Ella. I left Jess in charge of the rest of the kiddos checking out while I took Nathan to the restroom, full of questions. Did he really want to discuss Ella? Did he want to catch up on old times? I only had an obligation to meet with him about Ella. I didn't think rehashing the past was anything we needed to be doing.

We stepped into the ladies' room with me deep in thought, so I almost missed the older lady right on the inside. She stopped us with a hand to Nathan's shoulder. I wanted to thump her knuckles. My boy didn't enjoy being touched by strangers.

"Oh, sweet boy," she cooed. "You're far too mature and handsome to be using this bathroom."

I had a million words on the tip of my tongue and none of them were kind or nice or words I would use in front of my kids, but lucky for me I didn't have to.

Nathan shrugged her hand off and looked her dead in the face. "Yes, I am. I am very handsome." His pointer finger came out and pointed at her face. "You are old. With saggy skin and hair on your lip. You are not handsome."

I slapped my hand over my mouth to cover my smile as the lady gave me a scowl and pushed past us to exit the bathroom. As soon as she was gone, I pulled Nathan in for a big hug.

Even though what he said hadn't been what someone would call polite, it wasn't a lie and furthermore he'd spoken to someone he didn't know. I was beyond proud.

"Good job using your words, buddy!"

He didn't hug me back, but I was used to this with my kids. I didn't take it personally. I stood at the front of the bathroom while he went and did his business. It gave me a chance to respond to Luk's text even if I didn't want to.

Me: If you'd like to discuss Ella, I'd be happy to schedule an appointment with you at the school, Mr. Callihan.

There, I kept it strictly professional when in reality I wanted to keep it strictly dickly. I was doing well. I would've given myself a pat on the back if Nathan hadn't been watching me while he was washing his hands.

We made our way back to the register just in time for the last kiddo to be rung up. Sweet Ella was up and I grabbed my hair products out of the bottom of the buggy and set them on the conveyer belt.

She turned to me, hand out. I was no fool when it came to her, so I handed her a twenty so she could pay for me. I watched, making sure she handed the money over. She didn't say thank you, but the more you pressed her, the more stubborn she became, so I said nothing when the cashier handed her the change back. I'd talk to her about it later.

She handed me back the dollar bills before throwing my loose change in the bottom of her pink purse. *Girl, take all my pennies!* I'd have put up a fight if I had any left in me, but at that point, I was ready to wave the white flag. They'd won. I'd been defeated.

My phone pinged and I looked at the screen as we made our way out of the store.

Lukas: What if I wanted to discuss you?

Another text popped through quickly after.

Lukas: You're cute, trying to keep things professional between us, Red. But I really, really like it when you call me Mr. Callihan.

Well, if I wasn't frazzled before I was now. What did that mean? Like, was he being serious?

Another text.

Lukas: Like I really like it. ;)

I looked around, thinking the man was spying on me. And the winky face. What the heck did that mean? Was he flirting with me? Or was he kidding around and wanted to hang out as friends? And why hadn't I had a serious boyfriend so I would know what the hell was going on? My face got hot in anger and excitement and I decided to chuck my phone in my bag and forget about it until I got the kids back to the school and to their parents. And that's when I realized Luk would be picking Ella up. I was only slightly panicking as I drove the kids back to the school. Lucky for me, all of the Walmart shenanigans had worn their behinds out.

When we arrived at the school, most of the other children had already been dismissed, so I wasn't surprised at all when I saw Luk standing out front in the carpool circle. I parked the van and helped unload the children and didn't give him the time of day. Well, my eyes didn't. My mind was fully on him, which was why when I stepped out of the van, I missed the last step and almost went down like a ton of bricks. Luckily I caught myself with the door handle.

I shook my head at myself. Because I was a damn mess around Luk. Part of me loved the giddy feeling he gave me even after all these years. The other part loathed the clumsy prepubescent inner me. She was a damn fool and I was over her fumbling ass.

I tried to walk past him like I didn't see him, but you know he wasn't down for that. Not even a little bit.

"Not even a hello, Red?" he questioned and all the kids paused. A few parents milling around waiting on their kids noticed, too, and I clenched my teeth so I didn't snap at him.

I didn't like being embarrassed at my place of work. I took my job seriously. These kids meant the absolute world to me. I didn't need their parents talking about me and Luk. I didn't need the inevitable rumors that would come from one nonchalant comment. I was not dumb. I'd seen many a teacher taken down by one silly rumor.

So, I corrected him sharply. "Ms. Knox," I snapped.

He hummed low so only I could hear as I walked by him. "I really like that, too."

I swung my gaze to him and narrowed my eyes before heading into the school with most of the parents tagging along behind me. His ridiculous flirtations were unnerving and not proper at all.

I quickly handed off the children and backpacks while Jess assisted. Eventually the only people left were me, Jess, and my old friends, the Callihans.

It was perfect timing to get things off my chest. I smiled softly at Jess. "Do you think you could take Ella outside for a bit? Mr. Callihan wanted to discuss some things with me."

She nodded. "Ella, wanna hit up the teachers' lounge and see if they have any good snacks?"

I'd never known Ella to turn down food, so when she took off with Jess, I wasn't the least bit surprised.

As soon as I knew they were out of earshot, I turned to Luk, who'd made himself comfortable in my seat again. "What are you doing, Luk?"

He grinned his boyish grin and my heart did a stupid thump thump. "Having a seat. Practice today kicked my ass."

I shook my head. "No, what are you doing with the texts?"

He stood up slowly and gave a long, languid stretch that caused his black T-shirt to ride up so I caught a glimpse of his gorgeous hard stomach. My mouth went dry.

He dropped his arms and shrugged. "What's the big deal? I thought we were friends."

I nodded. "We were friends. Ten years ago. Now, I'm Ella's teacher and you are her guardian. Unless you have something to talk to me concerning Ella, it's completely out of line for you to text me or call me."

There, I said it. I laid it all out there.

He quirked a thick eyebrow at me. "So, we're not friends anymore?"

Pursing my lips, I answered, "Luk, we haven't spoken in ten years."

He nodded and his eyes lit with understanding, but it was completely wrong.

"You're mad."

I took a step back. "What?"

"You're mad about how things ended between us. I don't blame you."

I wasn't mad. Was I? That was ten years ago. Sure, I'd been mad then, but I definitely wasn't mad now. I was smarter and less naïve and completely ready to deny. "This has nothing to do with ten years ago, Luk. And everything to do with the fact I'm Ella's teacher."

He nodded again. "Fine. I get it."

I almost felt bad. But then I remembered how much this job meant to me. And my heart. I remembered how I was saving it for someone who deserved it. Someone who would earn it. But still I couldn't help myself. I was always a sucker for those baby browns. "But if you need anything at all, Luk, I'm here. I adore Ella and I'm always here to help."

He gave me a pathetic smile as he backed out of the room. "I appreciate that, Red, eh, Ms. Knox," he corrected himself as he diverted his eyes.

The fourteen-year-old me wanted to chase him out of that room and beg him to be friends with me again. Anything. Because those months had been the best. Luk had been the best. Until he hadn't.

Chapter
TWELVE

Lukas

MASON HAD JUST LEFT. IT TURNED OUT HE MUST HAVE HAD AS MANY friends as me because he came over to have dinner with me and Ella for the past four nights. She'd instantly taken to him much to my chagrin. I got it. He was a giant, easy on the eyes football player. But the girl was practically eating out of his hands. She even talked to him when she wouldn't talk to me. And Mason ate that shit up and made sure to give me a cocky grin. It pissed me off to admit it, but he was a good guy. I'd immediately known when he'd taken one look at Ella and given her the biggest hug and told her how beautiful she was. She'd blushed and he'd sat down on the couch and asked her to watch TV with him while I prepared dinner. And it was a wrap. That's how Ella and Mason's friendship was born. Over old episodes of *General Hospital* and subpar meals cooked by me. After dinner she always asked him to come back and he hadn't let her down yet. Damn him. He was so fucking likable even after he'd almost killed me in the parking lot. I had no idea how he pulled it off.

He'd left tonight and Ella had disappeared and I decided that something wasn't right. Something was wrong. Something was very, very wrong. Ella had been strangely quiet and hidden in the bathroom most of the evening. I'd knocked twice to only be told very forcefully that she'd be out soon. Well, soon was like an hour ago and I was starting to get worried.

Instead of being the overbearing parent figure I knew she didn't want, I paced outside the bathroom door like a lunatic.

When she finally deemed it time to grace me with her presence, I was terrified that something was wrong. Two hours in a bath seemed like a ridiculous amount of time even for Ella, who loved her baths and bath bombs and lotions.

I scratched at the back of my head, playing it cool like I hadn't been a nervous wreck for the last hour. "What's up, Ells? How was your bath?"

Her shoulders shrugged beneath her silk pink robe. "It was fine."

I followed her to her room. "What took so long? Was something wrong?"

"Nothing's wrong. I need my privacy."

That was code for get the hell out of her room, so I left quickly before she decided to start changing in front of me, which she would. Ella didn't have a problem with being shy like the rest of the world. She merely issued her 'I need privacy' warning for others, not herself. She could be naked as a jaybird in a room full of a hundred people and not give it a second thought.

I walked into the hallway and past the bathroom before backing up and deciding to go in and check to make sure everything was indeed okay. She had been in there for what seemed like forever.

Immediately upon entering, I realized what a horrible, horrible mistake I'd made. I saw the razor. I saw the hair. And still I felt like maybe I wasn't seeing it right. So. Much. Hair.

No, she wouldn't have done that, would she? She was still so young. She wouldn't have shaved down there. She must have done her legs, but her legs weren't that hairy. I'd seen them just this morning and there was no way in hell they'd been that hairy. I would have noticed, but all the hair that was stuck to the side of the tub and on the floor told a different story. And it wasn't a story that she'd given herself a haircut. Not the hair on her head at least.

I was horrified, disgusted, and most of all I didn't know what the hell to do. This was one of the many reasons that Ella needed a mother. She was a teenage girl and I was a big, doofy, jock football player brother. Not a damn woman.

I walked out of the bathroom, my hands over my eyes like I could somehow block out what I'd just seen, but even with my palms placed firmly over my eyes, I could still see it. The dark, curly hairs everywhere.

Fuck. This was awful. What did I do? What did I say? Jesus, was she a mess down there? Who the fuck told her this was a good idea? My questions were endless and I had not one answer.

After pacing the floor for what felt like the millionth time tonight, I decided I could be an adult about this. Not the teenage boy I wanted to be. I could calmly walk into Ella's room and ask her about it. We could talk rationally because I had to make sure I never walked into another clusterfuck like that again. I felt like I was scarred for life.

I was pulling my hair out of my head with one hand as I knocked on the door with the other. "Can I come in? You decent?"

"Yeah," Ella answered and I was thankful for that. Because when she felt like it sometimes she would just straight up ignore my ass.

I slipped into the room and noticed she had on a long pink night-gown. For fuck's sake, she was dressed like a damn seven-year-old and I was pretty sure she'd just shaved her pubes. How the hell was this my life?

I closed my eyes and took a few deep breaths before I could speak on this.

"You meditation?"

My eyes flew open. "What?"

"You meditation? That's what Ms. Lettie does when we misbe-have. She does meditation."

I felt myself fight off a smile even though I was in a straight up state of panic. "Meditating," I corrected her. "And yes. I was meditating."

"Why?"

Holy shit. Would she think I was mad at her about the hair thing?

I mean, I wasn't exactly pleased about it, but I wasn't mad. I just didn't know what to do or why or how I should talk about it with her.

"You know what? I'll come back later." And I fled the room and closed the door behind me like the complete pussy I was.

I had no idea what to do and before I could even register what I was doing, I was texting Scarlett and begging her to come save me.

Me: I have an emergency with Ella. Can you please come to the house now?

I shouldn't have messaged her. It was clear from our last encounter that she wasn't interested in anything with me, even a friendship. She wanted to keep things platonic between us and while I thought that sucked because I could really use a friend and maybe something more, I was trying my damnedest to respect her wishes. Scarlett must have still been the nicest person on the damn planet because it may have been nine at night, but she responded right away.

Red: Of course. On my way.

I spent the next fifteen minutes hoping and praying that Ella didn't come out of her room and that she did her usual lotions and deep hair conditioning. I couldn't face her yet. This whole thing was beyond embarrassing and awkward more than I could ever imagine.

I never in all my life thought I would have to deal with something like this and then I wondered if she had done this before. Maybe my mother had already talked to her about it?

But then, wouldn't she have told her to clean the damn hair up? Oh, God. The hair. Every time I thought about it, I gagged a little and then felt terrible about gagging.

When the doorbell rang, I dashed to it, relief coursing through me. Scarlett would know what to do. She probably dealt with embarrassing shit like this all the time being a special education teacher.

I wrenched the door open quickly. "Hey, Scarlett, come on in." I moved the hell out of the way because I needed her to get her ass in here so she could make this better and save the damn day.

"Is your emergency that all of your clothing was burned in a fire?"

My eyebrows pinched together. "What?" I shook my head confused. "No."

She did a slow perusal of my bare chest all the way down to my basketball shorts. "Then where the hell are your clothes?"

I looked down at myself, thinking I looked completely presentable, nothing you wouldn't see a million guys wearing at the pool during the summer. "What are you talking about?"

She walked in, rolling her eyes. "Then what's wrong?" She looked around the room. "Where's Ella? What's the emergency?"

She was being too loud. I couldn't let Ella know I'd called her freaking out. "Shhh," I said, pulling her toward my bedroom down the hallway and closing the door behind us.

Scarlett looked around my messy bedroom and crossed her arms over her chest like she was uncomfortable. It was then I realized I'd just dragged a woman to my bedroom, who barely knew me anymore.

"Why are we shhing, Luk, and where's Ella?" She kept her voice down.

"We are whispering because I have an emergency and I don't want Ella to hear," I whispered back.

Once again, she looked around the bedroom before glaring at me. "This is not the kind of emergency I can help you with, Lukas," she said, her teeth clenched together.

Oh, shit. She thought I was having an emergency. Like in the bedroom. Like a sexy time emergency. I mean, I did, but she'd been clear about not wanting any part of that. "Nooo," I whisper yelled. "I'm having a pube emergency."

Her head jerked back and her eyes doubled in size. "What? Did you just say pube emergency?"

I nodded frantically like what I was saying was making complete sense because I was a fucking wreck over the pube crime scene in the bathroom.

Her nose wrinkled. "I don't know if I can help you with your pubes, Luk. There are professionals for that." Her face looked how mine must have looked when I walked into that bathroom minutes ago.

I ran both hands through my hair. "Fuck. I can't explain it. Just follow me."

I opened the door and pressed my finger over her lips to indicate she should keep quiet. The home I grew up in was a small one and Ella was a tiny damn spy. We creeped down the hallway and to the bathroom door, hoping like hell I'd somehow been mistaken. Because I damn sure didn't want to see that mess again. But when I turned on the light, there it was. Hair. Every fucking where.

I closed my eyes so I didn't have to see it. But then I felt Scarlett's hand hit my arm and then grip my bicep hard like she was scared she was going to get swallowed up by the hair monster.

"What in the hell happened in here?"

She was looking up at me with wide eyes and I didn't know what to say back. It was too embarrassing. It was too much, this whole situation.

"Did you do this?"

I flinched. "Me? Of course not!"

"Then who?"

She was being too loud, so I placed my palm over her lips and tried to explain again, this time with actual adult words. And I wouldn't get embarrassed. I wouldn't turn red, or stutter like a kid, I told myself.

"Ella did it."

My hand was still covering her mouth, but her eyebrows rose all the way to her hairline. She was obviously needing more information, so I continued.

"She went to take her usual bath. It took forever. She came out and went to her room like nothing happened and that"—I pointed inside the bathroom—"is what was left behind."

If I thought her sparkling emerald eyes couldn't get bigger, I was wrong.

I leaned closer to her face. "I'm going to let go of your mouth now, but you have to keep your voice down."

She nodded and I removed my hand slowly, but it was a huge mistake because her serious face instantly transformed into one of hilarity. She doubled over, her hands to her stomach, her laughter silent at first and then becoming booming and loud. I couldn't believe she was laughing. And so loudly. I was going to kill her.

Ella was going to hear, so I did the unthinkable and shoved Scarlett into the bathroom and went in after her and closed the door.

As soon as I realized what I had done, I felt my face contort into one of complete horror. Scarlett only laughed harder at the look on my face.

"Oh my God, look what you did. Now we're stuck in here with it," I accused her.

She didn't seem to care because she was too busy wiping the tears of laughter from her face as she giggled hysterically at my expense.

When she seemed to finally collect herself enough to stop cackling like a hyena, I asked, "Are you done?" I was moody as hell. My baby sister was shaving her private parts and Scarlett thought the whole damn thing was hilarious.

She busted into laughter again and held up a hand. "Not yet."

I leaned against the door, as far from the hair as possible, and rolled my eyes. She had to be kidding me. Didn't she deal with shit like this every day? I thought she would be more mature about it.

She quieted again and looked around the bathroom, even stepping forward and taking in the ring of hair around the tub before looking back at me. "You called me over here because Ella decided to do a little woman scaping?"

Is that what people were calling it now? And I didn't like her tone. How it insinuated that I was overreacting, because I totally wasn't. She was too young. This was too soon. How did she even know to do that?

I darted my eyes around quickly and then looked back at Scarlett. And why the hell didn't she clean up her mess?

Even though I was mad as shit and embarrassed more than I was that, I couldn't help but think how cute Scarlett was. Her cheeks flushed, her eyes sparkling up at me in humor. It reminded me of the months we spent together before I went away to college. When she was just a kid and I'd wanted more with her but known better. She'd given me shit then. I'd always liked that about Red. She'd never cared about my social status at school. Or that I'd been the star of the football team. If anything, she'd given me a hard time about it. She'd never been impressed with anything about me but just me. And Ella. Always Ella. There weren't any girls I'd ever brought home to my baby sister, but I'd trusted Scarlett with her and I hadn't been wrong.

Even now, as she looked around the bathroom, she seemed way more chill about this than me.

"I brought you over here because I have no clue what to do."

She nodded thoughtfully. "Is this the first time Ella has done this?"

"How am I supposed to know? Can we leave the room now? Can you be quiet? I can't be in here anymore." I swung the door open and headed to the kitchen, Scarlett behind me.

"Well, did you talk to her?" she asked once we entered the kitchen. Her voice sounded accusatory to my ears, but maybe it was just me feeling embarrassed that I hadn't.

I grabbed a cold water out of the fridge and opened it. "I tried."

She stared at me.

Why was she looking at me like that?

I held up the bottle of water. "Want a water?"

She continued to stare.

"Fine, I didn't talk to her. I thought about it, though. That counts for something, right?"

Rolling her eyes, she said, "Luk, what happened tonight is just one of the many girl things that is going to happen. Has she had her period yet?"

Period? She caught me mid-mouth full of water and I sent a spray of water across the kitchen that could have rivaled the sprinkler out back. "Period? Is she old enough for that?"

For fuck's sake. Was she? Did she have her period? I prayed that she did because how was I supposed to help her take care of that? Because I had no clue what to do. God, I was in no way prepared to take care of a teenage girl, especially one with special needs. I was completely and utterly fucked.

This time it was Scarlett who told me to be quiet. "Shhh, you crazy man. You're going to give the girl a complex."

I was going to give the girl a complex? I was being completely traumatized and she was worried about Ella. I paced the kitchen and guzzled my water. How was I going to navigate this whole thing? What was I going to do? I couldn't talk to her about these things. No one had prepared me for this moment. It was like I'd been thrown on the football field and never told the rules. That's how I felt. Like a fish out of water.

"Luk. Stop pacing."

I wondered if my mom had talked to Ella about any of this. God, I was praying she had. Ella maybe didn't retain the entire conversation but maybe she wouldn't be shocked to death when she got her period.

"Luk!" Scarlett's voice was loud. "Stop and look at me."

I turned and she stepped forward until we were toe-to-toe. Up this close, I finally got a look at her and man, she looked good. She was a sight for sore eyes and let me tell you, after witnessing the pubic hair massacre of the century, my eyes were beyond sore.

Scarlett's long red hair was in a knot at the top of her head and a few tendrils spilled down the sides and whispered along her ears and cheeks. For a minute there I was wishing I were those hairs. I wanted to touch her. She was wearing a white T-shirt and black stretchy pants, probably just her hanging around the house clothes, and she'd never looked more beautiful. Not a stitch of makeup, not a bit of fanfare, just emerald green eyes and juicy pink lips. She was stunning. And her mouth was moving, so I should have been paying attention.

"You can do this. You're a big boy. And Ella is loving and wonderful and open and she will be totally cool with all of this."

I shook my head. "I'm not cool with this. I have no idea what I'm doing. I don't even understand what in the hell happened here tonight." I looked back at the bathroom of horror.

Scarlett placed her hands on each of my shoulders. "But you love Ella. And really that's all that matters. The rest of this stuff will work itself out. Love goes a long way, Mister Quarterback." She was smiling sweetly up at me and she almost had me convinced. Almost.

"I think you should talk to her. Find out what she knows. And then report back to me like an undercover operative."

"No." Her head shook back and forth slowly, but she was still smiling, so I figured I hadn't lost her yet.

I put on the big puppy dog eyes that I knew she used to go gaga for in high school even though she'd never admit it. "Or you could talk to her for me."

Her arms fell and she glared, but that didn't deter me.

"Just this once. I promise I won't call you again with anything like this."

She still scowled and crossed her arms over her chest. I was losing her.

I held my hands up. "I promise and I'll get you some Skittles."

She let out a big sigh. "Christ, Luk. I'm not a kid anymore, but fine. I'll talk to her. Just for tonight. You're on your own after this because I know you can do it." She poked me in the chest. "And the red bag. That's the only kind I like."

And she'd lost me. "What?"

"It's the red bag of Skittles or none, Mister Quarterback."

"Gotcha."

She turned around the kitchen, her eyes perusing the space. "Got some kitchen gloves?"

"Probably, if I look around."

"You round those up while I go talk to Ella," she said as she left the room.

I breathed a deep sigh of relief and thanked God Scarlett had come over. I'd never tell her, but she was a lifesaver. I promised myself I wouldn't call her again. I wouldn't bother her. I'd learn to do this on my own. Even the uncomfortable stuff. I could do this.

Scarlett

I CLOSED THE DOOR BEHIND ME AS I CAME OUT OF ELLA'S ROOM. I WAS grinning like a maniac in an effort to not laugh out loud because Luk was going to lose his freaking mind.

He looked up from his phone, his face concerned, as soon as I entered the room.

I nodded toward the cell. "Everything okay?" I knew the answer to that question. Everything was not okay. Not even a little. He wasn't wearing a shirt. He'd answered the damn door with no shirt on and muscles everywhere. He may as well have been holding those babies up and saying, "Hey, welcome to the gun show." But that wasn't even the worst part of it all. No, the worst part was, he was wearing thin, low slung basketball shorts that exposed the V. And God, the V looked good enough to eat and I wasn't exaggerating. But still, not the *very worst* part. No, that was the fact I was 99.9 percent sure he wasn't wearing underwear and every time he walked I could see *it* swinging around underneath the fine, thin fabric of those things he was calling shorts. It was embarrassing the hell out of me. It was turning me on. It was freaking making me as red as my hair and I was doing everything in my power to not look below his neck. It wasn't easy. Not when he looked as good as he did. Which was a thousand times better than he did in high school and he'd looked damn good then.

He nodded and let out a long breath. "Yeah, just my aunt messaging me."

"You don't look too happy about it." I grabbed the blue rubber gloves from the counter and stared at the floor.

"Are you all right? You look a little flushed."

"Who, me? I'm fine," I said, swinging the gloves around like a maniac because I didn't know what the hell else to do. "Your aunt?" I changed the subject back. Things were getting more awkward by the moment.

Jaw clenching, he laid his phone down and ran his hands through his hair. I smiled, remembering how he did that even as a kid. "My aunt Merline is driving me nuts. She wants Ella." His face looked like he was in physical pain, but I knew it was more internal.

"Why?"

"Because she thinks I suck at taking care of her."

I bit my bottom lip to try and stop the question from passing them, but I couldn't help myself. "And do you?"

He looked at me long and hard and then looked at the bathroom behind me before raising his eyebrows.

I laughed. "Aw, come on, Luk. Tonight wasn't all that bad. Nothing that a little kitchen gloves, some bathroom cleaner, and Prince won't fix."

He let loose a low chuckle that immediately caused my nipples to harden beneath my shirt and I remembered he wasn't wearing a shirt and probably no underwear either, and I couldn't have that, so I grabbed my purse and rummaged around in the huge thing before I finally found my phone.

I put on "I Would Die For You" and slipped on the gloves. "Kitchen cleaner?"

His eyebrows shot to his hairline. "You gonna clean up that mess?" His eyes were wide.

"Yep. I'm gonna help you out this one time, Mr. Quarterback. Next time you're all on your own."

He handed me the cleaner wearily and followed me to the bathroom, Prince serenading us in the background.

"So what did she say? Why'd she do it? Has she done it before?"

I giggled, recollecting the conversation I'd had with Ella minutes before. He was going to die. Hell, he'd looked like he was going to die when I'd gotten here. This was going to be fun.

I grinned from ear to ear.

"Why the hell do you look so happy?"

"Me?" I asked, pointing a blue gloved finger at my chest. I was trying to keep cool.

"Yes. You, Red. You look like you want to laugh."

"Maybe I do. Broom," I demanded while I turned the bathtub water on so I could wash the hair down the drain. I'd need to sweep up the rest.

Luk looked around the room, frowning. "You don't have to do this."

I started rinsing the bathtub, the water drowning out Prince singing from my phone in the other room. "It's no big deal, honestly. Just go grab the broom."

The bathroom may have warmed from the steam of the hot water coming from the faucet, but when he left, I felt relieved. It seemed like that guy sucked the oxygen out of every room he was in with his big presence. It had always been like that. He'd always been too much for me. And that had always been the problem. Only, foolishly, I hadn't seen that then.

Luk did the sweeping and wiped down the bathroom while I swayed my hips to the little of Prince I could hear over us working.

"So, what did Ella say?"

Grinning, I said, "She mentioned Allison, her neighbor, has a boyfriend?"

"And?"

"Turns out Allison just started shaving. She watched a YouTube video."

Everything was on YouTube now and when I said everything I meant ev-er-y-thing.

"And?" He looked impatient and like he wanted me to spill everything right here and right now, which made it all the harder for me to contain myself.

I giggled, trying to contain most of my laughter. He was getting so worked up. It was adorable. "Well, Allison told her about shaving her girl parts and so Ella decided to try it."

He immediately broke out in a sweat at the mere mention of shaving girl parts and Ella in the same sentence. "Okay, okay," he said, nodding, and I could tell he was trying to rein his crazy in.

"But don't worry. She's already started her period and your mom taught her everything and has her all sorted. The worst you'll have to do is make sure she has pads and tampons." I honestly thought he'd be relieved at this bit of information. He wouldn't have to teach her how to use pads or tampons or talk about periods with her.

But I'd been wrong wrong wrong. Like so dead wrong and I realized that quickly when he blinked several times like he was seeing something that I wasn't. Then he weaved back and forth in a motion that told me this giant guy was about to go down and not in the good way. Like not in the way every girl dreams of, but more in the way that he'd probably get a concussion on the tile in the bathroom.

"Whoa there, big guy. Why don't you have a seat right here?"

I used my small gloved hands to push him down onto the toilet seat while he leaned over and put his head in his hands and rubbed the heels of them into his eyes hard like he was trying to snap himself out of it.

Shit, he was freaking out.

I took off the gloves and threw them to the side and ran my hands through his silky brown locks. I immediately knew it was a mistake. They were soft and my hands loved them. My hands wanted to stay there forever. His breathing was deep, so I continued to massage his head and shh him in an attempt to calm his breathing.

"Maybe Aunt Merline is right. Maybe I can't do this." He was talking to himself, but I heard him all the same. His words had been a shot right to the center of my chest. Because I knew without a shadow of a doubt that no one loved Ella Callihan like he did. No one. Not even me. And I loved her a hell of a lot.

But I just kept shhing and rubbing his head because I knew that sometimes the best thing you could do for someone was to let them have a moment to just lose it. To just have the meltdown of the century. And I had a feeling that this one had to do with a lot more than Ella and her razor.

After a good solid minute, he finally calmed enough to raise his head and look up at me. Sweet, worried, brown eyes practically melted me. "There you are," I whispered, pulling my hands from his hair and laying them in his lap.

"You doing okay?"

He shook his head slowly. "No, Red. I'm fucking this all up. I'm failing on every front. Football, life, Ella. Just everything."

God, he was breaking my heart wide-open. The poor man needed a friend and I wanted to be there for him. I really, really did, but I also remembered high school when I'd been there for him and he'd left me high and dry, his kiss still on my lips.

But still I couldn't help it. Just like then, his soul called to mine and all I could do was answer.

"You know, Luk. So many of my parents feel the same way. Like they are failing when really all they are doing is the best they can."

His forehead wrinkled like he was thinking.

I brought one hand up to his hair and ran it through the side and he leaned into it, clearly needing the closeness. "Are you doing the best you can?"

I already knew the answer to that. I just wanted to make sure he knew. Because Lukas had never done anything by half measures.

"I am," he croaked out. "But it's not good enough." He sat back, pulling away from my hands in his hair, and I stood up and moved back to the wall behind me and leaned against it.

"Why isn't it good enough? Because it isn't what your mom would do? Or because it isn't what your dad would do?"

He looked at the ceiling and let out a long breath. "I don't know, Scar. I don't think I can do this."

"Let me ask you something, Luk."

His head came forward and he looked me square in the eye.

"Is there anyone in the world who loves Ella as much as you do?"

He didn't immediately answer, so I kept going. "Does your aunt Merline know that Ella does Zumba every morning? Is she going to DVR all of her soaps? Does she have a big, strong chest that Ella likes to lie on at night when y'all talk? Does anyone who is left in this entire world know and love Ella as much as you do?"

His face crumbled like he was in inexplicable pain. I couldn't understand it. Why the thought of him loving Ella so much seemed to make him so sad, but I still went to him. And I wrapped my arms around his neck and pressed his face into my stomach even though it wasn't appropriate at all, but because he needed it.

It was his muffled voice into my stomach that delivered the saddest blow. "It's sad. Isn't it? That I'm all she has left. Just me, fucking up everything."

I shook my head and slowly lowered my knees to the floor, checking to make sure I wasn't kneeling in hair, until we were eye to eye. I took in his anguished face, the hard lines that hadn't been there ten years ago, the crinkles around his eyes from smiling. The sweetness I always saw in the depths of his baby browns and I thought that his baby sister had hit the jackpot with this one. Because as far as I could figure, there probably wasn't anything in the world better than being unconditionally loved by Lukas Callihan.

Taking his cheeks in my hands, so he would keep his eyes on mine, I whispered one of the truest statements I'd ever uttered. "I don't think it's sad at all, Luk. I think it's beautiful how much you love her. How you worry. How you care. How you love her enough for both of your parents and then some. And trust me, she knows it and loves you back just as much. Don't doubt yourself, Mister Quarterback. You got this."

"Fuck, Red." His voice was all choked up and his forehead hit my shoulder softly, so I wrapped my arms around his neck and held him. It was a solid ten seconds, because I counted, until his arms came around me. And we hugged because sometimes the best medicine was just a hug and a pep talk from an old friend.

"You good now?" I asked, grinning.

"I'm good."

I felt his nod against my shoulder.

"Well, good because we still have to clean up this hairtastrophe."

He rumbled a low laugh. "You're clever, Red."

I backed out of our hug and eyed him. "You're just now realizing this? If you recall, you would have flunked French without me."

He eyed me from my red hair down to my knees and back up. "Oh, I recall a lot of things."

Abort, my brain screamed, so I stood up fast and pretended like he hadn't come on to me. Because I was pretty sure he had. I threw on the pair of blue gloves and got to rinsing out the bathtub.

He got up off the toilet seat, grabbed the broom, and got back to work, and I kept an eye on him to make sure he wasn't going to fall on his face on the floor because I kind of liked his face.

I was swaying my hips and singing a little Prince while I rinsed the sink when I felt eyes on me. I turned and he was leaning against the doorjamb, broom still in hand.

"Enjoying the view?" Sarcasm was my scapegoat when I was embarrassed.

"Definitely," he answered without skipping a beat.

"Mmmhmm," I mumbled, feeling even more uncomfortable.

"What made you go into special ed?"

I turned toward him again, thinking I'd misunderstood him. "What?"

"What made you want to teach children with special needs?"

And that was a pretty personal question for me, but I couldn't not tell him. He and Ella were such a huge part of it, he deserved to know.

I shrugged like those few months hadn't changed the course of my life forever. "You and Ella."

The shock on his face made my own warm and I turned away. "What?"

He'd heard me just fine. He just couldn't believe it or maybe he didn't want to. Maybe he didn't want to think I'd remembered him and Ella and thought of them while he'd gone off to school to play ball and hadn't given me a second thought.

I turned off the water and wiped down the edges, giving him my back. "Ella. Playing with her, seeing how you loved her and how much a child thrived when given the right tools, there was only one choice for me. I always knew I was going to be a teacher, but Ella and you, you guys made me realize I was needed in special ed. And I don't have any regrets. It is one of the best decisions I've ever made." And that was the truth through and through. Were there hard days? Sure. Were there days where I felt like I'd lost my mind? Absolutely. Were there days where I cried my eyes out for those children? Definitely. But the good always outweighed the bad. I loved my job. I loved my life. And I had Lukas and Ella to thank for that.

He was quiet for too long after that, so after I'd exhausted cleaning every inch of that tub for as long as I could, I finally turned around to find him staring at me still.

I quirked a sassy red eyebrow because I was awkward as hell and I didn't know what else to do. I remembered that look. It was the one he used to give me in high school when I'd play with Ella. Now, I recognized it for what it was. It was something beyond worship and a little more than lust.

"You're something else, Red," he said seriously.

I laughed oddly, my chest vibrating with an awareness of what was to come even though I wasn't ready. I could still feel it, though. That inevitable pull between Luk and me. It had always been there, the undercurrent of us being something more. And now was no exception. It was there whether I liked it or not. Just like always.

"I hope that something is good," I joked, but he didn't waver in his seriousness.

"You have no idea."

Warmth spread through my body like a wildfire in a dry forest. He thought I was something good. And he was making no bones about it.

"I want us to be friends again."

He said it so easily, so casually, but the statement was loaded with seriousness.

I pressed my lips together, thinking while he watched on. It seemed like he really could use a friend. We could be just friends, right? Even though I was madly attracted to him? Even though after ten years he was still the boy turned man of my dreams?

But after tonight, how could I say no? How could anyone say no to this sweet man?

I stared at him pointedly. "Just friends?"

How the hell was I supposed to be just friends with the sexiest man on the planet?

He nodded, his eyes staying on mine. "Just friends. But friends hang out and do things together."

I nodded back. He wanted to be friends? So be it. In fact, I was in need of a male friend for tomorrow night and I couldn't chance it with Ollie's clog hoppers again.

Chapter
FOURTEEN

Lukas

I WAS A GRUMPY, GRUMBLING ASS MESS AND I HAD NO ONE TO THANK BUT Scarlett. The one damn person I wanted to see. I scanned the street parking in downtown and prayed I found a spot so I wouldn't be late.

I didn't know what I was going to be late for, but what I did know was I was going to get to see the woman I was thinking about nonstop. What I also knew was I wasn't allowed to pick her up so we could ride together. And finally, I knew there was a lack of fucking available parking in downtown Summerville and I was going to lose my ever-loving mind if I didn't find a space soon.

I finally found one about a block from the address Scarlett had given me the night before. I should have been apprehensive, but I was mostly just excited. I'd decided earlier in the day that there wasn't much I wouldn't do for my Red. Because I knew without a shadow of a doubt that there wasn't much she wouldn't do for me and Ells.

As I walked up the lit sidewalk of my hometown, warmth filled me up. I had missed this place with its small town feel. Warm streetlamps lined the walkways while people milled about, going from shop to shop and restaurants. It wasn't like this in Florida. This sense of home. It was different. It had felt fast-paced with my budding stardom pushing me forward constantly. Here, it just felt easy. Comfortable. And practices were getting better. I was still getting my ass handed to me, but it felt like the hits weren't coming as hard, in life and in football.

And as I walked up to a building with a huge storefront of lit windows with a beautiful girl standing out front, I was feeling like life wasn't just getting better. It was getting damn good. Even If I was firmly in the friend zone at the moment.

I walked closer to the girl with the red hair, who was inching her way more and more into my heart every day. She stood there in a long green dress that matched her eyes perfectly. That dress may have covered her, but it hugged all of her gorgeous curves like a glove and made her porcelain skin look like a silk backdrop. It took everything in my willpower to not stand there and stare with my mouth hanging open. So, I forced my eyes up and to her painted coral lips and peach cheeks, and my breath caught in my throat. Her thick, red hair hung loose around her shoulders and my cock instantly hardened behind my jeans. She was easily the most gorgeous woman I'd ever seen. It seemed unfair that she'd also be the best woman I'd ever known besides my mother. She was perfect in every way and I wanted nothing more than to walk her back to my car and take her back to my place, my bed where I could do everything I'd been thinking about doing to her for years.

I was standing there gawking like a lovesick fool when her voice snapped me out of it.

"You look nice." Her voice was small, her hands wound around each other in front of me. Looking adorably nervous, she reminded me of the anxious, sassy kid I'd met in the library all those years ago. Jesus, how the hell was I supposed to be friends with her? This would never work.

I ran a hand through my hair and looked down at my black T-shirt, dark jeans, and the only pair of black dress shoes I owned. I didn't really look nice at all. I looked casual and she looked fucking gorgeous.

"You look amazing." My eyes traveled the length of her again and landed on her high-heeled gold sandals. Her peach painted toes peeking out. Even they were adorable. I wanted to eat the woman whole. Right there on the street in front of the entire town.

"Thanks," she said quietly, still twisting her hands around each other nervously. I couldn't stand it another minute, her nervousness, not touching her.

I stepped forward and pulled her hands apart with my own until I held her soft ones in the palms of my rough ones. "You should have let me pick you up," I teased.

She'd been insistent I'd meet her here. I'd wanted to pick her up and bring her because it was the right thing to do and because I wanted to see her and be with her as long as I could.

She pulled her hands from mine. "This isn't a date, Luk."

I grinned. "You've made that abundantly clear, Red. But don't friends pick each other up from time to time?" I knew I was pushing my luck, but God, I loved pushing her. Her back talk and sass drove me crazy in the best possible way.

"They do. But most of my friends don't look like you." She eyed me up and down.

I didn't think my grin could get bigger. Wrong. "And what do I look like?"

Her cheeks were pink when she answered, "You know what you look like, Mister Quarterback."

Mister Quarterback. Fuck, but I loved when she teased me back. I stepped closer and the scent of fruit invaded my senses. I had the immediate urge to lick her from the tips of her toes, right to her mouthy lips that I adored. "But I really don't." I poked out my bottom lip.

She stepped forward and started walking toward the door to the building we were standing in front of. I fell in step beside her and nudged her with my shoulder like old times. It felt good. Right. "Come on, Red. Don't leave me hanging."

She turned to me, lips pursed, clearly annoyed, and I chuckled.

"Fine," she said, swinging the door open. "You look like sex on a stick. Happy now?"

I laughed big and loud because she seemed pissed off about me looking like sex on a stick.

We walked in and she whispered, "And how the hell did you ever get into that T-shirt? Is it painted on?"

She was all red-faced and huffy, and I couldn't help but laugh harder. We walked to the middle of a big room. I had no clue where we were or what we were here for, but I knew she liked my T-shirt a lot. Or maybe not the shirt but what was under it, so I stretched my arms over my head, gave a few flexes of the pecs and biceps, and threw her a wink and grin.

"You're shameless."

I took a small bow. "Thank you. And if you like, I can show you later how I got into this shirt. Or I can show you how I get out of it." I waggled my brows.

"Friends," she said forcefully, but I saw the slight tilt of her mouth. She was smiling. She couldn't help herself. Because I was sex on a stick and funny.

I was still patting myself on the back for winning her over and being awesome when others entered the big empty room and a man called out in an accent I couldn't place, "Okay, everyone. Let's get started!"

Scarlett turned to me with an evil grin on her face and put her hands up. I looked around as the music began to play. Music for a waltz I recognized. I spun in slow circles and watched the other couples start to dance before my eyes eventually landed on mischievous green ones.

"It's okay, Luk. I'll teach you."

Her words said she would teach me, but her voice said she was laughing at me and that she was being sassy as fuck. Her hands were in position and her body was full of challenge.

I stepped forward, man hands easily finding their spots. One at her waist, the other cupping her hand.

I took the lead like I'd done dozens of times, only this time I wasn't a foot shorter than the woman dancing with me and she wasn't my mother.

I quickened the pace and traveled the floor easily. It had been years, but it all came back to me.

As we moved around the dance floor, Scarlett's jaw fell open and her eyes looked like they were going to bug out of her head.

I just smiled and spun her around as a man with a pointy mustache walked by and clapped. "Scarlett, your partner tonight is divine, my darling."

She gave him a polite closed mouth smile as he wandered around the room before turning back to me and glaring daggers. "You have got to be joking," she whispered.

"I never joke about dancing, Red. It's serious business, you know?" I dipped her low.

She rolled her eyes at me and I brought her back up. "Why didn't you tell me?"

I chuckled. "Why didn't I tell you? You didn't even tell me what we were doing!"

"Damn you, Lukas. Why do you have to be so good? At everything," she said as I danced her around the floor.

My good mood instantly soured. There was a shit-ton I sucked at. Hell, at this point I was practically drowning in all the things I wasn't good at. "There's plenty I'm not good at," I ground out.

She shook her head, a tiny crease in the middle of her forehead. "No, Luk. You're gorgeous. And a good brother, and a really good friend for showing up when I didn't even tell you what we were doing." A small smile crept over her face. "And you can paint yourself into a shirt like a boss."

My mouth curved up. "Keep going, baby. You're doing amazing things for my ego. Tell me more about my painting skills."

She looked down between us. "Well, you didn't do too bad a job on those jeans, either."

I laughed and twirled her out and back in and her fruity scent hit me hard, making me stupid with want. When I pulled her back in, I asked, "What are you doing after this?"

109

"Taking my new dance partner for pizza."

I was starving, but it wasn't for pizza. That wasn't what I had in mind at all, but I'd take it. Spending time with her would have to be good enough for now. And it was. We danced the class away and then walked a block to a pizza place she loved.

I watched her eat pizza and drink Diet Dr. Pepper while she prattled on about seeing Prince in concert her senior year of high school and how amazing it was. I was sad I'd missed it. I was sad I'd missed anything with her at all.

I walked her to her car at the end of the night and shut her in. She smiled and waved at me through the window as I backed away and headed to my car nearby.

I jumped in quickly and cranked the car up so I could follow her home and make sure she made it there safely.

We pulled into her apartment complex and she parked in a space close to the building. I pulled in beside her and watched her get out of the car. She walked over to my driver's door, shaking her head and smiling.

"What are you doing, Luk?"

"Making sure you got home okay."

She nodded slowly, thoughtfully, looking down into my window at me, her eyes dreamy. "Where'd you learn to dance like that, anyway, Mister Quarterback?"

I smiled because I couldn't help it. I'd hated those lessons, but my mother had insisted I should know how to dance. Whenever I'd complain she'd just shake her head and say, "You don't wanna disappoint your wife on her wedding day, now, do you?"

I hadn't thought about it in years. And I'd never been grateful for those lessons until tonight. I'd say my momma was right and it wasn't the first time over the years I'd realized it.

"My momma was a dancer. She gave me lessons. She insisted. She was old-school like that."

"Your momma was everything, Lukas. Raising children on her own, working a full-time job, and making sure you were amazing."

My breath caught. My heart skipped a beat. "You think I'm amazing?"

She took a step back from the car and laughed. "Quit fishing, Lukas. You know how perfect you are."

I was far from perfect, but the fact she thought I was meant a hell of a lot. I stared up at her, my eyes full of questions. Mostly about why we had to just be friends.

She lost her smile and her face became serious. "You know friends don't follow each other home to make sure they made it okay."

My hands tight on the wheel, I shrugged. "Ya know, Red, the friend zone has never really been my thing."

Her eyes daring, she asked, "So, what *is* your thing, Lukas?"

I put the car in reverse and took a slow gander at her face. I stared at her thick, red hair that I wanted wrapped around my fist, down to her full lips I wanted around my cock. "Mmm, I'm thinking The Red Zone might be more my speed."

Pink hit her cheeks as she bit her bottom lip to hide her smile. "Good night, Mister Quarterback," she said, turning and heading for her apartment.

"Good night, Ms. Knox," I called back.

Chapter
FIFTEEN

Lukas

I COULDN'T BELIEVE I WAS DOING THIS. I WAS LEAVING ELLA WITH ALLISON. To go hang out in a bar and I didn't even drink. What the fuck was I thinking? I'll tell you what I was thinking. I was thinking about the last time Allison and Ella had been left alone for more than five seconds. I was thinking about all the things Ella could learn tonight. I was thinking of the Alabama Hair Party in my damn bathroom. That's what I was thinking about.

Allison and I'd had a long talk about what not to and what to discuss with my impressionable sister, but I had a really bad feeling that our talk had gone in one teenage ear and out the other.

I really just wanted to go home. I was already regretting my decision to go out, but Mason must have known I'd try to bail because he had me leave my car at the stadium, which meant I was riding shotgun in his giant white truck that looked like it was older than I was.

"Where are we going again?"

I was really damn tired and grumpy and just wanted to go home and check on Ells. Where I could think about Scarlett and her two left feet, sweet smile, and sexy as sin ass. Jesus, I was fucked. One go around the dance floor and I wanted to dance with her forever. She was still the fun, silly, Skittles-eating girl I'd adored. Only now, she was a woman and that was a deadly combination for me. I wanted her. Bad. I was almost 100 percent sure she was ghosting my ass. I hadn't talked to her in days. I'd tried texting. I wasn't feeling brave enough for a phone call yet, but I could see it on the horizon. She was the only good thing about my life at the moment besides Ella. I needed to talk to her.

"Damn, don't act so damn excited to hang out with a friend." He was giving me the side-eye and I was pretending I wasn't seeing his judgy ass gaze.

"Is that what we are now? Friends?"

Turning the radio down, he said, "Well, shit, Lucy. I don't wanna kiss you or anything, but I definitely think we're friends. Am I wrong?"

I thought how not long ago he'd tried to choke me against the side of my vehicle and now we were friends. And how now he paid me and my sister visits for dinner. Crazy fucker.

I shook my head and mumbled, "I don't understand you, Mason."

He huffed a sarcastic laugh. "And I'm supposed to understand you? Hell, half of the team assumed you came home because you knocked up a chick or something. But you're home to take care of your sister. Yet you tell no one. In fact, you act like you don't give a fuck about the team."

God, he wasn't starting on that shit again. And I was stuck in the damn truck with him.

Fuck. He was right about the team. I didn't give a shit. I had too many other things on my mind. It used to be I lived my life to play football and now I played football so I could live my life. Season would be starting soon and we definitely weren't playing like the well-oiled machine my team in Florida had. But how was I supposed to act like we were a team when everyone hated my guts? I ran my hands through my hair. "Everyone on the team hates me."

He glanced at me from the driver's seat, his eyes serious. "Nah, man. They don't hate you. They hate how you're acting."

I looked up at him. "How's that?"

"Like a complete dick."

I nodded. He wasn't wrong. But I was also having the hardest time of my life and it didn't have a damn thing to do with football. The truth of it was I hadn't had time to mourn my mother. Christ, Ella hadn't properly mourned her either.

I didn't say anything else. What was there left to say? I could have come clean about it all and told him everything. How I'd lost my dad who'd taught me to play ball. Who'd come to every game. Who told me I was going to be one of the greats. And then how I'd lost my mom, too. The woman who'd kept my dad's football dream alive by paying for camps with money we didn't have and carting my ass to and from practices in the middle of working long shifts on her feet all day. Everyone who'd believed in me was gone. That's what I wanted to say, scream. But I couldn't do that. Because I was a grown fucking man with a kid now. I couldn't afford to be sad. I had to keep my shit together.

I stared out the window in thought as he drove past the little shops and restaurants in downtown Summerville. It was a cute little town and part of me was happy to be back. The other part of me was sad that I didn't have more family here to enjoy the time with. I wasn't particularly fun to hang out with anyway. Although you'd never know it the way Mason hounded me. I didn't even have a clue why this man wanted to be my friend. I'd been a shitty teammate, definitely not worthy of friendship. I was starting to feel like I wasn't worth much lately.

We pulled up outside of a long brick building loaded with shops and restaurants. Mason parallel parked his monster of a truck right in front of The Mills. It was a place that had been in Summerville longer than I had. It was part coffee shop, part bar. The upstairs was usually crawling with college kids studying with headphones on and MacBooks and lattes on the tables in front of them while the bottom was more of the adult variety.

I waited on the sidewalk as Mason came around the truck saying, "We're meeting my neighbor and his sister. He plays ball for State." He shrugged. "He's not bad."

As we walked in, he finished. "Man, you should see his sister. She's a damn knockout redhead."

And just as he said redhead, I saw her there, sitting with what I could only assume was Oliver, her brother. I never had the pleasure of meeting him when we were younger, but she'd mentioned him plenty in conversation.

The look of surprise on her face didn't shock me. I was probably wearing a similar look. I shook my head with a smile because Summerville was a small town, but it wasn't this small anymore. It felt like fate, me seeing her there. And that scared the hell out of me because my good ole Red didn't seem to want to have a thing to do with me. And all I could think about when I wasn't taking care of Ella was her.

I'd been trying to keep my distance. I'd been trying to play it cool. Fate had other plans, though, and I had to say they weren't bad plans at all. At least for me.

We walked up to the table, my eyes glued to Scarlett's, and she looked like she'd seen a ghost. I took a bit of a guilty pleasure at the sheer panic on her face.

"Hey, y'all!" Mason's booming voice snapped me out of our stare-down and I looked over at him, waiting for the introductions, and he didn't let me down.

"Scarlett and Oliver, this is my buddy, Luk." He gave me a shit-eating grin. "You can call him Lucy. He's new to the team."

Scarlett's mouth hitched a little like she wanted to smile despite herself. "Hey there, Lucy." Her emeralds shined up at me knowingly. Ah. She wasn't going to acknowledge we knew each other, then.

Oh, so we were doing this. We were pretending we didn't know each other. Fun.

Oliver stood up and thrust out his hand. "Hey, man, I'm Oliver, but you can call me Ollie. Most of my friends do."

Looking Oliver over, I immediately noticed he didn't look at all like pale, creamy-skinned, redheaded Scarlett. He was dark-haired and tan and completely opposite.

"Nice to meet you, Ollie." I shook his hand. "Contrary to popular belief"—I eyed Mason—"I just go by Luk."

Ollie gave a low laugh as we all took our seats. Immediately, drinks were ordered. I opted for water while everyone else had beer.

"Have a beer, Lucy," Mason boomed.

My eyes met Scarlett's over the table. I didn't miss the softening in them. The understanding. It was clear to me in that moment she was one of the only people in the world that was left who really knew me. The whole me. The boy who'd lost his father me. The kid with a dream me. The man who'd lost his mother and was now raising his sister me.

"I don't drink." My gaze didn't leave hers. Those pretty greens were giving me strength.

"Why?"

Jesus. What the hell was this? Twenty fucking questions? I let out a deep sigh and my eyes finally left Scarlett's but only to take in the shift of her hand sliding across the table. She didn't quite make it to my hand before Mason interjected again.

"You a recovering drunk or something?"

The fucking nerve, so I let him have it. I turned and looked at him. "No, my dad was killed by a drunk driver."

His face fell and the guilt hit me hard. He didn't deserve for me to tell him like that, but I'd felt interrogated and defensive. "Damn. I'm sorry, man."

I shot him a sad smile. "It's cool. It was a long time ago. I was a kid." I always said that when people said they were sorry. But the truth was, losing someone never got easier. It only got harder. Because one day, years after they'd passed, you'd wake up and realize you forgot the sound of their voice, the pitch of their laugh, their smell. And that was the fucking sad part.

Football was the topic of conversation. An easy one for me even if I didn't feel like socializing, but I couldn't seem to keep my eyes off the fidgeting Scarlett. She seemed uncomfortable with me here and the thought made me a little giddy. Because I'd been uncomfortable for days thinking about her. Wanting to talk to her.

"So, Scarlett. What do you do for a living?"

I caught her mid-drink and a little beer might have come out of her nose. I grinned.

Wiping her face with a napkin and coughing, she tried to answer. "I'm a teacher."

I nodded. "How lovely."

She nodded back frantically while wiping her face with the white paper. "Mmmhmm."

Mason jumped in. "Yeah, you teach special needs, right?"

Her wide eyes flew to me as she picked up her beer glass and took a healthy sip after giving us a quick, "Yep."

I probably smiled a bit bigger than I should have and she glared at me from behind the napkin pressed to her lips and a silent chuckle vibrated in my chest. Five minutes in her presence and she had me grinning and laughing like a crazy person. No, like a happy person. Damn her. It had always been this way. Easy. Why was she fighting it now?

Mason looked at me from behind his beer. "Cool. Maybe she knows Ells. Where do you teach, Scarlett?"

Scarlett shot up out of her chair. "Excuse me. I have an emergency phone call." She darted for the front door, her hands frantically working her phone before stepping outside and pressing it to her ear.

Ollie looked out the clear front door and laughed. "She's a nut." He shook his head.

Mason leaned over the table closer to Ollie conspiratorially. "So, your sister. Is she single?"

I'd been watching Scarlett out the window as she waved her hands around frantically and talked quickly, but the minute Mason asked Oliver that question all my focus changed immediately.

Ollie laughed. "Yeah, man. As far as I know she's as single as it gets. Damn near lives like a nun. She's married to her job."

Mason leaned back in his chair, looking pleased with himself.

I wasn't pleased at all. In fact, I felt like I was going to be sick. The thought of Mason with Scarlett. It didn't fit. Not at all. They'd never work out. Besides, he was much older than her.

I couldn't stop the words from coming out of my mouth. "Aren't you a little old for her?"

Half of Mason's mouth kicked up in a grin. "Wow. You make me sound like an old man, Lucy. I'm only thirty-six."

I shrugged, feeling petty as fuck. "That's pretty old in football terms."

Now he leaned closer to me, his blue eyes dancing. "I'm not too old to kick your ass on the field."

He wasn't lying. He'd been beating the shit out of me. But right then I decided I'd die before I let him have Scarlett. True, it had been years since I'd kissed her goodbye, but she'd still felt like mine the moment I'd seen her come twirling into that classroom. He couldn't have her.

Mason leaned out of my space before I could tell him he couldn't have her. He took a long pull of his beer before looking out the window. "How old is sweet Scarlett, Ollie?"

Sweet Scarlett. I'd kill him with my bare hands. He did not get to call her sweet.

"Twenty-four," Ollie answered, his eyes volleying back and forth between us knowingly.

"Too fucking young," I said again, but our argument was cut short as Scarlett entered the room again and sat down.

Her smile was back. "Hey, what did I miss?"

Ollie smiled at us. "Oh, plenty," he said, while I answered, "Nothing much."

She looked between Ollie and me confused, but Ollie changed the subject.

"Who was that?"

"Oh, just Hazel. She wanted to talk about something quickly. I invited her to hang with us."

Oliver lost his smile and he swallowed hard and I grinned. Looked like whoever this Hazel was, she made good ole Ollie nervous. Looked like the evening was going to get a whole lot interesting and all of sudden I wasn't that gloom and doom about going out with Mason tonight. It was turning out to be an interesting night, after all.

"When will Hazel be here?" Oliver was looking at Scarlett, so Mason leaned closer to me so only I could hear.

"Damn. I wonder if all that gorgeous red hair is everywhere." He waggled his eyebrows. "If you know what I mean."

I knew what the fuck he meant and I was fuming. I could practically feel the hot air coming out of my ears. He would never find out if she was red everywhere if I had anything to say about it. And I did. I fucking did.

But Mason wasn't wasting any fucking time. "So, Scarlett, Ollie here was just telling us you're single?"

"He did?" Big eyes looked back and forth between Mason and I. "Well, yeah. I guess I am."

She lifted her beer glass to her lips but realized it was empty.

"Is that so?" Mason's voice was full of flirtation and I wanted to kill him. Dead. Really dead.

She gave him a tight, close-lipped smile before looking over at Ollie. "Let's do shots."

His smile fell. "What?"

"Shots," she said a little louder.

When Ollie only looked at her with a bit of confusion, she got up out of her chair. "Fine, I'll get them."

She walked to the bar and leaned over it, and I admired the way her denim shorts clung to her ass. Turned out so did Mason.

"Jesus. You see that ass, man? Fuck, she's hot," he said so only I could hear, but Ollie wasn't paying us much attention anyhow. He was checking out a brown-haired girl wearing a hoodie who'd just come in and had stopped at the bar to talk to Scarlett.

Scarlett made her way back over with another tall beer but without shots. She shrugged as she sat down. "Turns out, they don't sell hard liquor. Beer will have to do."

She took a healthy sip and I couldn't help but smile. She was ridiculous and adorable and fuck if I didn't want to kiss the beer right off her lips.

Hoodie girl came over and sat right in between Scarlett and Ollie. She nudged Ollie with her shoulder. "Hey there, Oliver." She was cute and I was praying that Mason switched his fixation to her, but I could tell right away that Hazel only had eyes for Ollie.

"Gonna introduce me to your friends?" she asked him, the flirtation blatant in her eyes.

He cleared his throat and swallowed hard, and I even saw a bit of sweat form on his forehead. He either had it bad or Hazel scared the shit out of him. Either way, it was good entertainment.

Ollie motioned to Mason. "That's Mason, our neighbor." His head nodded toward me. "And that's his friend, Luk. He plays ball with Mason."

Hazel's eyes landed on me and even though her lips weren't smiling, her eyes sure were and there wasn't a doubt in my mind that she knew exactly who I was. Her next words sealed the deal.

"Well, hey there, Mister Quarterback."

I grinned so wide, I felt my cheeks hurt. I pushed my hand out across the table and gave Scarlett a quick glance that sent her scurrying for her beer glass and throwing the liquid back while I shook a very knowing Hazel's hand. From where I was sitting, it seemed like Scarlett had called in a little help to get her through the night.

Hazel leaned over the table and reached for Mason's outstretched hand next. "How you doing there, Mason?"

He grinned at her. "I'm doing pretty well. I was just getting ready to ask Ms. Scarlett here on a date sometime."

My head snapped to him. Over my fucking dead body. It just came flying out of my mouth. "I think she likes younger men, dude." I was being an ass, but he was trying to steal my girl.

Jesus, I was out of my fucking mind. My girl. I couldn't even get her to return my texts and I was over here being a territorial asshole, but I couldn't help it.

Mason studied me with inquisitive eyes. He wasn't a damn fool by any means and he'd been seeing through my bullshit since I started with the team. I imagined he could see through it now.

Like a smartass, he said, "I imagine the next thing you'll tell me is that she has a thing for quarterbacks instead of linebackers."

My quick gaze landed on Scarlett chugging her beer while her eyes darted back and forth between Mason and me. "Damn straight," I said to Mason, but making sure to look at Scarlett.

"I'll be back. I'm gonna hit the head," Ollie interjected.

"Do you need me to go with you?" Scarlett asked, batting her lashes, and I held in a laugh.

Looking at her like she was a lunatic, Ollie answered, "No, I've been peeing all by myself for quite a few years now. I think I can handle it."

He started walking off and Scarlett eyed me before calling out to him, "Are you sure?"

Ollie shook his head and kept on walking, so a panicked Scarlett just kept right on drinking.

Hazel was watching Ollie walk toward the bathroom when Mason interrupted. "So, Hazel, what do you do for a living?"

Her head turned to his, smile in place. She was cute, in an innocent kind of way. "I manage the video game store a couple of blocks from here."

"Cool. Are you a gamer?" Mason questioned, intrigued with the tiny enigma that was Hazel.

"Sure am," Hazel answered distractedly, looking around the bar. I had a guess who she was trying to find.

Mason didn't seem to notice. "Sweet. Maybe me, you, and Scarlett could get together and do a little gaming." He shot me a cocky grin that made me want to kick his ass.

"Would y'all excuse me? I think I left something in my car." And Hazel was gone in a flash.

"I think Ollie said that Scarlett is busy with work. I doubt she has time to play games with you, Mason. Fuck off." I glared at him. The fucker. He was grinning. He knew what he was doing.

"Lukas!" Scarlett yelled, clearly scandalized by me telling Mason to fuck off. "Here," she said, reaching into her purse and producing a red bag of Skittles. "Have some candy and calm the fuck down." She drunkenly threw the Skittles down in front of me. "Taste the rainbow and take a damn chill pill." She finished the last of her beer and put the mug back on the table as gracefully as possible. Which wasn't that graceful at all.

I pushed the bag of Skittles back toward her. "I don't need to taste the rainbow, Red. I already know my favorite flavor."

Rolling her eyes, she asked, "And what's that?"

My face dead serious, I answered, "Red."

She pushed her lips out and gave me a whatever look. "That's not a flavor, Luk."

My eyes roved the expanse of her face. "Why don't we test that theory?"

Her cheeks turned a pretty shade of red. "Bathroom," she squawked before standing up and dashing to the bathroom as quickly as possible for a girl who wasn't too steady on her feet at the moment.

I shot Mason a look.

He just shook his head. "Your game sucks, dude."

I just kept looking at him.

He rolled his eyes and brought his beer to his mouth before saying, "Well, go on. Before she catches an Uber and leaves your dumb ass here."

I raced to the bathroom like a bat out of hell and parked my ass in the hallway and waited.

Chapter
SIXTEEN

Scarlett

OKAY, THIS WAS FINE. I WAS OKAY. EVERYONE WAS OKAY. THIS WAS NOT a time to panic. I mean, I was a little drunk. But I'd have to blame sexy ass Lukas and Mason for that. Admittedly, I'd been avoiding Lukas for a few days since our ballroom lessons. As he'd driven away that night, I'd realized Lukas and I could never be friends. It was a lie on his part and even more a lie on mine. It was never going to work. And now with him and Mason here I was stressed to the max. Ollie had told me that he thought our neighbor Mason might be interested, but I thought he'd been blowing smoke up my ass. I figured I was having drinks with friends. I now knew that wasn't the case. Goodness gracious, but those two both putting the moves on me were just a little too much for a girl like me. And where the hell had Hazel and Ollie run off to? I'd specially called her so I wouldn't be alone in this situation. How dare she leave me in my time of need? And I was drunk. She'd broken the hell out of girl code. I hoped whatever she was doing was worth it. And then I thought about what she and Ollie might be doing and I felt sick to my stomach.

I'd escaped to go to the bathroom, so I made myself pee while I took deep breaths and then after I washed my hands, I gave myself a pep talk.

"He is just Lukas Callihan. He is not God. You can resist him. You are his sister's teacher. He will probably leave and break your heart all over again. You can abstain. And you will."

Feeling strong and tipsy, I yelled, "Hell, yeah!" as I left the bathroom and plowed right into a hard wall of muscle. "Oomph."

I almost fell back on my ass hard, but two strong hands wrapped around my upper arms and held me steady. I blinked and two molten brown eyes smiled down at me.

"You okay?" Lukas questioned.

I nodded frantically because he was so close and my willpower was so low. All of my inhibitions had flown the coop, the alcohol only hurting my resolve in the long run. I wanted to lean in and kiss him right on those gorgeous lips. Damn him. "I'm great. Perfect! Wonderful!" Oh my God, why couldn't I shut up? "And why the hell didn't you tell Mason we knew each other?"

Using his pointer finger, he tapped his own chest. "Me? Why the hell didn't you?"

I threw my hands out in front of me. "Because it was awkward after you didn't!"

He grabbed my arm and dragged me down a small, dimly lit hallway near the bathrooms until we were alone. "Speaking of Mason. I don't think you should go out with him."

"What?" Of course I wasn't going out with Mason. I had no intention of dating Mason. I wasn't interested in him, but I didn't think that had anything to do with Lukas.

He ran a nervous hand through his hair and I almost softened. Until I saw his jaw tick and he ground out, "I don't want you going out with Mason."

My eyebrows landed at my hairline. "Excuse me?"

I couldn't be hearing him right. He did not get to tell me who I dated. "He's not the boss of you! Girl power!" Drunk me wanted to yell.

"Mason's not for you, Red." He had the audacity to look mad.

I scrunched up my face and crossed my arms. "Oh, please, tell me then, Luk. Who is for me?"

He stepped toward me and pushed in with his big body until he had me pinned between him and the wall behind me. He placed his hands on either side of my head and brought his head close to mine. I sucked in a breath at how close he was. His smell. God, it was addictive and intoxicating and if I hadn't been drinking beer all night I would've blamed that scent alone on how drunk I felt.

"I'm calling dibs, Scarlett."

I shook my head back and forth, trying to clear it. "Dibs?" I questioned. "Dibs?" I asked again because what the hell was he talking about? But the possessive look on his face said it all. And I didn't like it one bit. Oh, no, he wasn't. I wasn't a pork chop or a few Skittles. "You can't call dibs on a person, Lukas. What the hell is wrong with you?" Oh, the alcohol was out in full force now.

"I already did," he said from between clenched teeth, his face hard, unyielding. His nostrils flared as he took a few deep, calming breaths, but I was still hella fired up. "Come on, Red. I think you can feel this thing between us." He leaned even further into me and I caught that fresh pine wood scent that made my head spin and my knees weak. Like the girl from every romance movie I'd ever seen, I swayed in a bit, all the while loathing my poor choices.

This man. He made me angry. I was his sister's teacher. It was unethical as hell. He could break my heart. He had. It had only been a teenage crush, but nevertheless I'd felt destroyed. What would I feel like as an adult? An adult who wanted to be married and have children. And then I dared. I dared to dream about this sweet smelling man with his expressive eyes, plump pink lips, and square jaw covered in the most delicious scruff I'd ever seen in my whole life coming home from work all sweaty and dirty. I wouldn't make him dinner or greet him at the door with a highball of his favorite scotch. No. Oh, I'd give him a bath. I'd put him in the tub and soap him up with my bare hands, ditching the very idea of a washcloth and touch him in all the places I'd been dying to touch him since I was fourteen years old. Apparently drunk me loved baths and abs.

"I don't feel anything," I denied vehemently, lying through my teeth. I felt a lot, mostly right between my legs.

He smiled. The devil. "You do." His eyes bore into mine. "Right here." He tapped the spot right over my heart through my shirt with the tip of his pointer finger.

I brought my own hand there, rubbing the spot dramatically. "What? No! That's just heartburn. I had tacos for lunch."

"Fucking adorable." A low chuckle hit me straight in my girly parts and I pressed my thighs together and closed my eyes. He was winning. He was winning and he wasn't even trying. Because once that chuckle hit my ears, I was back in that bathtub and soaping up my hands for round two with the best pair of abs in the land. They'd be hard beneath my soft hands and I'd let my slippery palms travel up to the expanse of his wide, smooth chest with the most perfect nipples that ever existed in my imagination.

"What's it gonna be, sweetheart?" His breath across my lips snapped me back to reality like a bucket of ice-cold water over my head. Not my lips. Not a kiss. That would break me. I cleared my throat awkwardly even as my face burned. My fantasy vanished into thin air and once again I was pressed up against a six-foot-four tall muscled wall of total manliness and we weren't all wet and sudsy. And that was a damn shame because I was just getting to the juicy part of my bath time story and it just happened to be below his waist and under a mound of bubbles.

He moved in even closer if that was possible, totally invading my space and intruding on my barely hanging on sanity. And that's when I felt it. Long and thick and hard right up against my stomach, and heat rushed through me while my belly did so many somersaults you would have thought a gymnast was living in there.

But I had to get control. I was Ella's teacher, first and foremost. And this man was just another guardian I had to deal with. He wasn't the good-looking, carefree boy I'd tutored in grade school, and I wasn't the nerdy girl with braces and a pile of insecurities that could rival Mount Everest. I was confident. I was a badass. I was a woman. Not a silly girl anymore.

It was like he could read my thoughts because his tongue came out, darting across his full bottom lip, and my eyes nearly crossed. And I was suddenly back in high school and mooning over the star quarterback like a lovesick little girl. Run for your life, my mind screamed while my stomach brushed his erection and purred like a damn cat. My inner teenager was such a slut. And inebriated me wasn't much better.

Just no. Taking a deep breath, I summoned my innate redheadedness and got my shit together before saying, "There's only one thing I feel between us, Mr. Callihan." I somehow managed to sound sultry and sexy like every redhead I'd ever seen on TV instead of the hot mess I usually was. I pulled my bottom lip between my teeth and gave it a suck before releasing it with a smirk.

His eyes dashed to my lips, eating them up, and his pure look of desperation only spurred me on. "Fuck, but I really like it when you call me that."

I settled my hands on his broad shoulders and leaned over until my lips were right at his ear. Standing on tiptoe slowly, I made sure my stomach brushed low and hard against the bulge in his pants before whispering, "And your cock isn't *my* problem."

I pushed off him lightly before landing on the balls of my feet and pivoting on a heel. I wanted to run from that dark hallway like my behind was on fire, but instead I stepped forward slowly with an intentional swing to my hips I hadn't even premeditated. It just came natural, this teasing thing. Lukas wanted me! He wanted me! Like really wanted me because I'd felt it. I was awesome. A rebel. A renegade. A total badass.

For good measure, I threw a look over my shoulder that I hoped screamed sexy seductress that you'll never have and not pathetic girl who didn't know what she was doing. The small smile that played at his lips and the challenge in his eyes as I looked back told me all I needed to know. He definitely wanted me. Bad. Ohhhh, how the freaking tides had changed. And it felt good. Game on, Lukas "Last Minute Lucy" Callihan. Game freaking on.

As I was leaving, he said, "I'm not through with you yet, Scarlett Knox."

And a heady feeling washed over me. The absolute thrill of being in control. Of being the one he wanted. Being the wanted was so much better than being the wanter. Excitement buzzed in my drunk girl veins right along with a gallon of beer. And even though I knew him not being through with me yet was probably not a good thing, I couldn't help but absolutely bask in it.

I walked back to that table feeling like I was on top of the world. And that was the last thing I remembered.

God, something smelled so good. It smelled like I'd imagine heaven. But only if heaven were full of hot, musky, naked men. And maybe that was my heaven. Who was I to judge God's plan? But that smell, I was attracted to it like a moth to a flame. So, I moved toward it and buried my face in it.

My mouth watered as my nose hit soft skin and a hard body part. "Mmm. Heaven," I moaned, using my arms and legs to wrap myself around that smell. It was warm, too, and I couldn't get enough of that warmth and that pine scent. I was holding on for dear life and nuzzling and pretty much trying to bury myself.

Something warm enveloped me in its embrace and I sank further into that smell, wanting to stay there forever.

From the top of my head to the tips of my toes I was toasty and that smell was practically me now. We were one and I wasn't the least bit mad about it.

I ran my nose down a smooth expanse of skin and felt a low, rumbling sound from beneath me.

That sound made me stretch and curl around the warmth below me like a cat lying in the sun.

"You keep doing that, Red, and I'm really gonna show you heaven."

Instinctively, I froze. I knew that voice. But that couldn't be right. Because I was in my bed and I'd never ever let Lukas into my bed. Because that would be dumb and I wasn't an idiot. Was I?

I lifted my head that felt heavy and achy and popped one eye open slowly. I slammed it back closed because it was him. He was there and if the angle I'd seen him at was anything to go by, he was under me. For fuck's sake, no! I laid my head back on his chest and pretended I hadn't seen shit.

"That bad?" he asked, his voice an echo through my body, and I knew he was referring to my epic hangover, but when I said "yep," I was referring to the fact he was in my bed and his bare chest was under my ear, so yeah, it was bad. Like really bad.

But still I wrapped my arms tighter around him and he clenched around me as well. God, even in my sleep I knew I wanted him. In fact, I was directly on top of him. Clinging to him like a damn spider monkey. I was pathetic in high school and I was pathetic now, too.

I let out a long breath and breathed in his scent one more time before I made myself move.

But when I went to move off him, he pulled me tighter to him and ran his hands down the length of my back before they landed square on my ass and stayed there. "Stay," he ordered.

And who was I to argue? I was comfortable and he was sexy and still as sweet as I remembered and damn if I wasn't swooning. Even with an aching head and raging hangover, the man had me smitten.

He ran his hands over my ass and up my back before trailing back again, over and over, and I moaned softly because it felt so good. So sexy, but so good, too.

"We need to talk, Red," he said softly, continuing to stroke me.

"No," I mumbled right between his pecs where he smelled divine. "Less talking, more stroking." He had me now. I was in the enemy's clutches and I was staying there.

His chuckle vibrated in his chest and I smiled despite myself. This was a bad idea. An epically bad idea and yet I couldn't stop it. It was inevitable. Us. This thing. It was unstoppable and I felt completely powerless. How much longer could I keep up the fight? How much longer did I want to?

"While I appreciate how adorable you're being right now, there's something I want to say. Something I need to tell you."

And then I realized. He was rubbing my back and my behind. My behind that was only covered in my panties and I was pretty sure I was only wearing my sleeping cami. And he didn't have a shirt on. I hadn't checked for pants yet, but it didn't feel like he had any on, because the coarse hair of his legs against my smooth ones was wonderful.

I sat up again, this time with both eyes open, and it was a huge mistake because damn, Lukas looked marvelous in the morning. I wanted to rub my face all over his stubbly one. I wanted to run my hands through that thick mass of brown locks. I wanted to lick his full bottom lip.

Those lips gave me a closed mouth smile that said they knew exactly what I was thinking. And that snapped me right out of my lust filled fog.

"We didn't, ya know, do anything last night? Right?" I croaked out. Surely, I'd remember if I had got it on with my high school crush. But I didn't remember anything past my fifth beer. I wasn't much of a drinker and I probably should have paced myself, but I was in a state of duress.

His smile grew. "Like what?"

Oh, he was playing that game. I rolled my eyes. "You know what. It. That's what."

He palmed my ass hard and pressed down so I could feel him right there between my legs, hard and ready.

I squeaked and he laughed low. "It? Come on, Red. You can say it. Can't you?" He was teasing me, but with his hands palming my ass and his cock right there, it was too distracting for me to care.

He pushed up against me and it brushed right where I needed it and I couldn't help the small moan that passed my lips.

"Are you asking me if I brought you home, stripped you down"— he paused, clearing his throat for dramatic effect because he squeezed my ass while he did it—"with my teeth and then buried my face and then my cock in your pretty pussy?"

A shiver raced through me that I couldn't contain and he gave another soft laugh when he felt it as well.

I was flushed and hot all over at his dirty words. But more than anything at that moment, I wanted him to flip me over and have his dirty, wicked way with me. I was done. I had not one fuck left. I'd suffer the consequences later.

But first I had to know if I'd missed anything because that would have been a shame. I lifted my head and used my arms to brace myself against his chest so I could get a real good look at him when he answered me. "Well, did you?"

He rolled us until he was over me and I was gloriously under him.

He ran his nose down the length of mine and I was so tempted to lean up. To give him my lips, my mouth, my freaking everything.

"Baby, when I make love to you, you're gonna know it. You're gonna remember it. And you're sure as hell gonna feel it the next day."

I stared up at him, his eyes blazing down at mine enough to burn down the whole town of Summerville. So, we hadn't done anything. I breathed a sigh of relief.

And just like that he was gone, his heat and body only a memory. He settled in beside me and I got a marvelous view of his black boxer briefs. We may not have done anything, but he sure didn't have a problem stripping down and getting into bed with me. I threw my hands up over my head into the mattress. Why didn't he take me? He'd wanted me. I at least remembered that from last night right outside the bathroom. Hell, just minutes ago I'd felt how much he wanted me right between my legs. Why was he stopping when I was finally giving in?

"So what did happen last night?"

His eyes were full of laughter. "I brought your drunk ass home and tucked you into bed. I was going to leave you, but you kept saying you felt sick and I didn't want to leave you alone."

I looked down at my cami and panties. "But did you undress me?"

He grinned wickedly. "Oh, no, baby. You did that all on your own."

I groaned in embarrassment and then I sat up in realization. Oh, no. "But where is Ella?"

"She stayed the night with Allison."

Breathing a sigh of relief, I lay back down. "Oh, good. Thanks for staying." *And taking your shirt off*, I thought to myself.

"Don't thank me yet. You never know what I'll get home to. I may be calling you for a major cleanup."

I let out a small giggle when I thought of the last mess we'd cleaned up when Ella had hung out with Allison for too long.

"We need to talk."

Oh, no, not this again. This was bad news. We should have sex instead. I wanted to be spontaneous and crazy and let the man have me so tomorrow I could blame the whole thing on bad judgment and hormones. If we talked first, I couldn't do that.

"That's a terrible idea," I said to the ceiling.

"Why is it a terrible idea?"

I looked over at him and gave him my sexiest look. "Because we could be doing other things."

He threw his head back and laughed. Well, then. Clearly my sexiest look wasn't all that sexy.

"You're too fucking cute for your own good."

I batted my eyelashes. "Then why are you over there and I'm over here?"

"Because I can't focus enough to talk with you on me or under me."

I leaned up on one elbow so I could admire his broad chest, strong shoulders, and six pack. "Who cares about focus and talking? That was so last year, Luk."

He smiled big, all his teeth on display, and damn if he wasn't the most handsome man I'd ever seen. And he was in my bed. And he wanted to *talk*. I threw myself back dramatically against the mattress again.

He moved in closer to me. Until his torso was pressed to my side, his elbow to the bed, his face over mine. He looked devastatingly serious.

"The other night at my house. I lied."

I raised an eyebrow. "About what?"

"I don't want to be just friends. I've never wanted to be just friends with you, Red. Not a single day since I've known you."

I swallowed hard. My throat and eyes burned.

He looked away from me and let out a long sigh. "I shouldn't have kissed you."

I turned my head so I didn't have to look at him anymore. I couldn't listen to this. I couldn't hear him go on about how he shouldn't have kissed me. About how he regretted. It would gut me because that kiss had been special to me even if had hurt me down the road. I still thought about that kiss. My first kiss. From my first love.

His big hand cradled the side of my face sweetly, right at my jaw. "Look at me, Scarlett."

"I don't wanna," I mumbled, my throat feeling tight.

Using his hand, he gently urged my face back to his until our eyes met. "Hear me when I say this. I shouldn't have kissed you, but I couldn't help it. I'd been thinking about it for weeks. How you'd feel. How you'd taste. I was selfish. It wasn't fair to you."

I closed my eyes so I wouldn't have to look at him anymore. It was too much. "It doesn't matter, Luk. It was a long time ago," I said, my eyes closed, my embarrassment palatable.

"It does matter. Because I want you to know why I kissed you, but I also want you to know why I didn't ask you to wait on me. Why I didn't beg you to be my girlfriend. Because God knows I wanted to. I wanted it more than I wanted anything and that was a hell of a lot back then when all I wanted was to play football so I could make my dead father proud."

My eyes snapped open and his were liquid heat down on mine. They burned me up as they consumed me whole. Instantly, I was lost in those sweet baby browns that had stolen my heart all those years ago. It was glorious. It was awful.

My hand came up of its own accord, my palm meeting his square jaw and the rough stubble of his chin. "It's okay, Luk. I get it."

"Do you? Because I want you to understand. What I did that night on your front porch? I did for you." He let out a sardonic laugh. "Not the kiss. The kiss was for me. But when I told you goodbye? That was for you."

I shook my head slowly. I would've waited on him. I would've visited him. We could have made it work.

"No, baby. You deserved more. You were just a kid. I was already a man. You deserved first dates, proms, dances, and dates, and you wouldn't have had any of that with me being miles and miles away but belonging to me. I couldn't take that from you."

I stared at him, shocked. He meant it. He'd let me have my teen years and I had. Wow. I rubbed my thumb across his prickly face, hating and adoring him all at once. Because I wasn't so sure I wouldn't have traded prom and first dates for a night here or there with him. I probably would have and I probably wouldn't have regretted it a bit.

He leaned in and rested his forehead to mine. "But make no mistake. I'm home now. And fate would have it that you're here, too. And I'm done with this friend bullshit, Red. I'm done pretending I don't want you. I'm done making excuses to see you. And I sure don't give a shit that you're Ella's teacher. I want you and I'm done fucking around."

My hungover brain buzzed with awareness. He wanted me? Like for a booty call? Or for more? But before I could ask him, he pressed a long kiss to my forehead and got out of the bed.

I watched in a daze as he slipped on his jeans and T-shirt from last night. He turned to my mirror and ran his hands through his hair, pushing it into place. The man had no right looking so good right out of bed.

He stood at the foot of my bed and looked down at me and all I could do was lie there like an imbecile. He'd rocked my world. I was speechless. I had no clue what to say. What to do.

"I can see you need some time to take all of this in. And I'm going to give it to you. But know this, Scarlett. I want those lips. And I'll have them. If it's the last fucking thing I do."

He turned and marched out of the room like a man on a mission and I guess he was. Mission Lips according to him. He wanted my lips and I wanted his heart. Looked like we were at an impasse.

Chapter
SEVENTEEN

Lukas

It was Tuesday, my day off. And usually I would sleep a little late and make myself a big breakfast, but as soon as I got Ella on the bus to school, I came to the gym at the stadium to work out some of my frustration. And it had absolutely nothing to do with Scarlett. Scarlett, who hadn't bothered to call me back the countless times I'd texted and called. She was ghosting the hell out of me again. I didn't expect it this time. I'd laid it all out there. I'd put myself out there and now she was acting like I didn't exist. We had a past. Our present was rocky as hell at best. But I was keeping my head in the game and my eye on the prize—our future.

So I'd decided to get myself to the gym and work my ass off, so I didn't think about her or have the urge to call her again. It wasn't working.

I was headed back into the locker room after two long hours when I heard someone talking. I stepped up to my locker, telling myself it was none of my damn business.

I checked my phone to make sure I hadn't missed any calls and saw that good ole Aunt Merline was still stalking my ass hard. Jesus, she was getting on my damn nerves. I wasn't going to give her Ella. A person wasn't just something you could give away. Didn't she get that?

I was heading to the shower when I heard a voice again. "I know, baby. I'm sorry. I'm gonna try to get home soon."

I peeked around the corner and saw Trevon on the phone. Knowing this phone call was none of my business, I kept on to the showers and washed the grime of my workout away. I was drying off when I heard him again.

"What did they say?" He paused, listening. "What kind of testing? How can they test him if he's nonverbal?" He stopped again before continuing. "I know, honey. I know you're doing the best you can, but I'm worried about our baby. What are we going to do if something is wrong?"

I tried not to eavesdrop anymore than I already had, and by the time I'd finished drying off and wrapped my towel around my waist and headed back to my locker he was off the phone.

He looked over at me across the room and gave me a cold head nod. Hell, at least I was getting that now. The team and I were getting along a bit better and with our first game coming up, I was thankful they at least weren't kicking my ass that much on the field anymore. They weren't taking it easy on me by any means, but they'd at least stopped trying to kill me.

I'd just finished slipping on my clothes when I heard a loud bang and a "Fuck."

I looked over at Trevon, knowing the right thing to do, but worried I was overstepping. Still, I walked over to his side of the room. "You all right, man?"

His head darted my way and I realized I'd startled him. "I thought you were gone."

"Not yet."

He nodded. "Yeah, I'm good. Just missing home." I could tell he wanted the conversation to end there, but my momma never called me a quitter, so I kept going.

"Yeah, where you from?"

"Georgia," he said, stuffing shit into his locker distractedly.

"Not too far. Maybe you can take a trip home before the season really starts."

"Yeah," he clipped out, grabbing his bag and closing his locker. "Look, man, I gotta head—"

"I heard you on the phone," I interrupted because I didn't want to lose him. I felt like there was something he needed to hear.

He pulled at the braids on the top of his head and stared at the floor before finally saying. "It's my baby. He's three. He's not talking."

I nodded and sat on the bench nearby. "And what are the doctors saying?"

He dropped his bag to the floor and sat beside me. "It's not good. They are doing testing and throwing around words like autism and on the spectrum. I don't even know what that shit means, man."

"Yeah. It's a lot to take in. And I bet you're worried as shit and wanna go home."

He nodded. "Every fucking day, but I have a family to take care of and a team counting on me. I have to be here."

Leaning back, I reached into my pocket and grabbed my phone. "I get it, Childs. I really do." I opened my photos on my phone and scrolled until I found a picture of me and Ella. A selfie I'd taken of us on the couch at home, our faces squeezed together, her grin wide.

I pushed the phone out in front of Trevon. "This is my baby sister. She has Down syndrome. She's the whole reason I moved home."

He gave me a playful smile. "You mean you didn't come all the way home to play ball with my ass?"

I shook my head and laughed. "Not even a little bit. Playing ball with your cocky ass was just a bonus."

He laughed, too. "What about your parents?"

It still hurt to say it. "My dad passed away when I was a kid and my mom passed away a few months ago. So now, I have Ella."

"Ella. That's a cute name."

"Yep," I said, tucking my phone back in my jeans pocket. "She's a cute kid. She's smart and she's funny and she's loving and kind. I wouldn't change a hair on her head."

"No?" he asked, his face serious.

"No. You see, Ella's different, but that doesn't make her bad or weird. My mom just made sure she always had the resources she needed to get as far as she could and now she's pretty independent and awesome. I love her just the way she is."

I nudged my shoulder against his. "I guess what I'm trying to say is, if something is going on with your baby boy, you and your girl will handle it and you'll love him just the way he is, and he will love you, too. That won't change. Ever. And if he does have autism, it doesn't make him any less perfect or wonderful. You get me?"

His eyes full of emotion staring back at mine, he said quietly, "I get you, Lucy."

Lucy. He was coming around. The only person who'd called me that on the team was Mason. It felt good. I stood up, feeling like I'd accomplished what I wanted.

"Thanks for the talk, man." He pushed his hand out and we did some kind of bro handshake that I was totally winging because I didn't have too many friends.

"Anytime." I went back to my locker and grabbed my bag.

I was walking out of the room when I heard him yell, "You're getting good at standing up, Lucy. Now, we just gotta get you throwing the ball."

I grinned, but didn't turn around as I lifted my hand high in the air and threw up my middle finger. "What can I say? I'm a slow learner, but I'm getting there," I joked.

His laughter followed me out of the locker room.

My workout didn't do shit for my mood. So, I went to the grocery store and picked up something good to make Ella and me for dinner and by the time I got home, Ella was already there and had sent me the thumbs-up.

Imagine my surprise when I pulled up to the house and saw Mason's truck in the driveway. My guess he was there to mooch another meal off of me and my sister and still I smiled. I liked having Mason around. He was slowly becoming another member of the family.

139

I walked into the house to find Mason and Ella parked on the couch together, a bowl of popcorn in between them watching old reruns of *General Hospital*.

"Hey, Ellie Bellie!"

She didn't spare me a glance with Chase on the screen, but she did shout back, "Hey, Lulu!"

I juggled the groceries in my hands all the way to the counter. "Don't worry, I got it," I called out to them.

Mason looked at me as he shoved a fist of popcorn in his mouth and then went back to watching TV. Asshole.

"You don't have anything better to do than hang out with us?" Giving him shit was becoming my favorite pastime.

He shrugged. "Not really," he said, finally getting up off the couch and joining me in the kitchen. He muscled in and started looking through the bags. "What are we having?"

"Steak, potatoes, and asparagus."

"Mmm. Sounds good. I'll do the potatoes." He grabbed them out of the bag.

I quirked an eyebrow at him. "You cook?"

"Yeah, smartass. My mom taught me how."

"Where's your mom now?" I asked, putting away the groceries.

"Passed."

"Dad?"

He started to peel the potatoes. "Gone, too."

"Siblings?" Shit, this was getting sad. I was wishing I'd kept my mouth shut.

"One shitty ass drug addict brother I haven't seen in years."

Lord, I was just digging myself deeper, but now that I was there I might as well find out all the dirt. "Younger or older?"

He stopped and looked at me. "Twin."

"Fuck, man."

"Lulu, watch your mouth," Ella called from the living room.

"Sorry, Ells!" I called back, seasoning the steak.

"So, have you heard from Scarlett?" Mason changed the subject.

"Nope."

He shook his head. "See. No game. You shoulda let me try."

I threw a piece of garlic at his head and then picked up my phone, sending yet another text, this time asking if I could take her ballroom dancing again. What could I say, I was desperate. And desperate times called for desperate measures.

Chapter
EIGHTEEN

Lukas

ANOTHER MISSING TOILET PAPER ROLL, ANOTHER DAY. THAT WAS THE mantra of my life lately. It was the weekend and once again, I'd woken up to a missing toilet paper roll in my bathroom, no replacement. Curious, I checked the trash bin to see if the only other person in this house had thrown it away and it was nowhere to be found.

I'd had practice, so I hadn't had a chance to look around more, but now I was a man on a mission. This morning, I was feeling pretty good. Scarlett had let me go to ballroom dancing with her again this week. She'd even let me pick her up. She'd even signed us up for a Salsa class tonight. Turned out, she was pretty impressed by my dancing skills. I was tearing down walls and feeling damn good about it. I had a feeling I was pretty close to getting a kiss, too. I'd never been this excited for a simple kiss, but I guess that was what happened when the woman you were falling for all over again withheld something you really fucking wanted. And I wanted her kiss like I wanted my next breath.

But it was afternoon now and I was trying not to think about that as I scoured the house for the missing empty toilet paper rolls. I checked all the trash cans and walked past the porch where Ella was, doing her Zumba in some colorful leggings to the TV mounted on the wall out in the lanai.

I searched the kitchen drawers and the TV cabinet, curious.

Taking one more look out at Ella to make sure she was still out there, I headed to her room to do the most awful thing I'd ever done. I was invading her privacy. It made me feel like a damn sneaky ass parent spy, but I guess that wasn't too far from the truth.

I checked all of her dresser drawers and her closet before lying on the floor and looking under the bed.

I pulled out a long clothing container that was surprisingly light. I lifted the lid and then stared down at approximately five thousand billion empty toilet paper rolls, some paper towel ones, too, that I'd apparently not noticed going missing. What in the hell was happening? Why was she storing all these empty paper rolls in her room under her bed? Ella had done some odd shit before, but this took the fucking cake.

"Why you in my room?"

I looked up from the floor to find one pissed off Ella over me. I hadn't even heard her come in. I'd been too absorbed in the mountain of questions I had about all the rolls under her bed.

I leaned back until I was sitting on the floor because I wanted to appear as non-threatening as possible. If she got her hackles up now, we'd never have a rational conversation about this craziness.

"I was looking for something."

Her eyes narrowed behind her thick glasses. "Under my bed?"

"Well, yes. I was looking for the toilet paper roll from my bathroom." I motioned to the bin full of them. "And I think I found it." I was trying to crack a joke and keep it light, but she wasn't having it.

She marched over to me in her colorful leggings and put the lid back on the tub and shoved it back under the bed with her foot. "Out, Lulu!"

I stood up while she watched me like a hawk and then I sat down again, only this time on the side of her bed.

"I said out!"

"No, Ella. I'm staying because I think we need to talk. Want to sit here next to me on the bed?"

She looked at me like she wanted to say no, but she finally sat, as far away from me as she could, looking at the wall in front of her instead of me.

"Hey, Ells. Can you look at me?"

She turned her eyes to mine and my heart felt like it was in my throat. God, I loved her. She was really all I had left. I loved her surly moods and ridiculous need to watch old episodes of soap operas. I loved taking care of her. And even though doing it and having a career was the hardest thing I'd ever done in my life, I wouldn't trade it for the world. It may have been selfish keeping her instead of handing her off to another family member, but I didn't care. I needed her as much as she needed me.

"Why are there a million empty toilet paper rolls under your bed?"

She looked down at her hands as she twisted them around her lap. I waited for her to answer. Sometimes she just needed a little time. And she did.

"Momma and I take those to the community center. The kids use them for crafts."

I smiled because she and my momma were about the sweetest things ever. "Well, that's okay, Ells. We can drop them at the community center tomorrow." Problem solved and it turned out this wasn't that weird at all.

She shook her head. "No." She looked me in the eye. "Momma and I *always* drop them."

My heart left my throat and settled right in the pit of my stomach like lead. No. I wasn't ready to do this. I'd known it was coming. She hadn't really dealt with Mom's death. She'd been there, at the funeral, mostly emotionless. Merline had been convinced she didn't understand. But I knew my sister. She understood. She just didn't want to.

I kept my voice light. "Well, since Momma can't, I'll take you."

She shook her head. "No."

"Okay, then what do you plan to do with all the rolls under your bed, Ella? Are you keeping them forever?"

"No, Momma is going to take me."

I was going to be sick. I couldn't do this. I just couldn't. But I had to. It was time. She couldn't keep denying even if it did make her feel better at the moment.

I reached my hands out. I wanted to hold her while we talked. "Come here, Ellie Bellie."

She shook her head adamantly, almost angrily, and I swallowed hard.

"Okay. Cool. We can talk like this." I looked at her pale pink bedding covering her queen bed. Her elaborate white furniture that almost looked like a princess's. She even had a sparkly chandelier over her bed. I was about to break this princess's heart. It killed me.

My nose burned with emotion. "Momma's not coming back." There. I said it. I was sure it hurt me almost as much as it hurt her.

Her head snapped to me angrily, her words biting, her emotion wounding me. "She is coming home, Lulu. She told me."

I scooted closer to her on the bed, my heart bleeding for her and not understanding at all. I reached out a hand and cradled the side of her face. "What did she tell you?"

A tear slipped from behind her glasses and I wiped it with my thumb. "Come on, Ells. What did Mom tell you?"

Another tear from the other eye and trembling lip almost did me in. "She told me"—she stopped, sucking in air or courage or something—"she told me she would never leave me."

She fell forward onto herself, big hiccupping sobs echoing through the room, and I felt tears hit my own eyes as I pulled her into my lap.

I cradled her close to me and rocked her just like I had when she was a baby. One tear slipped down my cheek for every sob that left her mouth. Because I got it. I did. I missed Mom, too, but it was high time we dealt with it. We couldn't hide from it forever.

"Oh, baby. Momma didn't want to leave us. Especially you. She loved you so much."

"But she promised, Lulu. She promised she would never leave me," she cried into my T-shirt.

"But death isn't a choice, Ells. She would have stayed with you forever if she could have. Never doubt that."

"It's not fair."

Her broken voice splintered my heart. Still rocking her, I whispered, "I know. I know," over and over because what else could I do? Life wasn't fucking fair and I didn't dare tell her everything was going to be okay. Because I wasn't making anymore promises I couldn't keep. I wouldn't do that to her.

We rocked like that for what felt like endless minutes, just me and my baby sister wishing for our momma to come home, so we could be somewhat normal again.

And when Ella finally quieted, I prayed that now she understood. I kissed the top of her head.

"You know we're gonna be all right, right?" I whispered into her hair and rubbed her back. "As long as we have each other, everything is going to be fine."

She said nothing but it was enough for me that I knew she heard me.

I held her for a long while, until she finally fell asleep in my arms as I leaned back against her royal headboard. And when I was sure she was good and out, I slid out from under her and got to my feet, putting the pale pink blanket at the foot of her bed over her body.

I walked to the kitchen feeling like I'd been hit harder by grief than any fucking linebacker. I grabbed my cell off the table and as much as it pained me I canceled my ballroom dancing night out with Scarlett.

Ella needed me at home tonight and there wasn't a question in my mind on where I should be.

I got Scarlett's reply while I was loading the dishwasher.

Scarlett: Something wrong?

I fired one back immediately. I didn't want to worry her or for her to think I didn't want to see her. Because I did. All the damn time.

Me: Ella's having a hard day. I think she needs me at home. That's all.

I didn't hear back from her, so I started a pot of chili for dinner and did some laundry. I was kind of rocking this stand-in dad thing, if you asked me. It had been a hard day, but I'd powered through. And when Ella woke up from her nap, she seemed to be in better spirits.

We parked our asses on the couch the rest of the day and watched old reruns of *Charmed* on Netflix. I was only a little embarrassed at how much I liked it.

We were still on the couch and halfway through our bowls of chili with a side of cornbread when the doorbell rang.

Ella didn't even budge, so I set my bowl down on the coffee table and made my way to the door, grumbling about that bastard Mason interrupting my dinner yet again.

To say I was surprised when I opened the door to find Scarlett there in a pair of black leggings and a sweatshirt holding a baking dish would be an understatement.

"Hey," I said, dumbfounded, standing in front of the door and not even thinking to invite her in.

She raised her brows and gave me a close-lipped smile. "Hey," she said back, pushing the pan in my hand toward me. "I brought some brownies."

It finally registered that she was here to hang out with me. She'd brought us brownies. I moved out of the doorway and motioned with my hand for her to step inside. "Come on in."

We passed by the kitchen and she placed the pan on the counter and I inhaled the smell of brownies and my Red, already feeling better about my day.

"We're having chili and cornbread if you want to join us for dinner."

She looked around nervously. "Oh, I wasn't going to stay. I was just dropping off the brownies."

"You didn't have to bring me brownies to see me, baby," I joked.

"Oh, I didn't. Those are for Ella," she deadpanned and I threw my head back and laughed.

"Ms. Lettie," Ella called, racing into the room. "What are you doing here?" She went in for a hug that Scarlett was happy to give her.

"I brought you some brownies."

"Yay! Lulu made chili. Stay. It's good." And just like that she was done with us. She headed back into the living room and hit play on *Charmed*.

"That didn't seem like a request," she mumbled, looking around the room awkwardly. She rocked up on her toes and back. "Well, it looks like I'm staying."

"Have you had dinner?"

"Nope."

"Okay, well, get yourself settled in the living room and I'll bring you some food."

I finished whipping up some food for Scarlett and walked into the living room to find my girls parked on the couch together, totally engrossed in a very old episode of *Charmed*. My girls. Holy fuck. Realizing I wanted that to be true more than anything rocked my world.

I handed Scarlett her bowl and sat down so Ella was in the middle of us. We ate quietly until Ella excused herself for her nightly bath.

As soon as we could hear the bath water running, Scarlett set her bowl on the coffee table and asked, "What happened today?"

I sucked in a long breath before letting it go and leaned back on the couch. "I found a huge container of empty toilet paper rolls under her bed."

She stared at me for ten seconds straight. "I'm sorry. I'm not following."

"She said she and Mom always take them to the community center downtown."

She nodded. "Go on."

"She's been hoarding them, Red. I offered to help her take them and she said no. Said Mom was taking her."

Her face fell. "Oh, no, Lukas."

"Yeah, it fucking sucked. She cried. I cried. It was awful."

She scooted closer to me and laid her hand over mine that was resting on my knee. "I'm so sorry, Luk. That must have been terrible."

I turned my hand over and lined my fingers up with hers before lacing them together. I didn't give a shit if she wanted to hold my hand. I needed it. So I took it. "It was. But part of me is glad it happened. She was just pretending Momma was still here. It wasn't healthy, but it also tore me up to see her like that today."

Our hands still intertwined in my lap, she leaned in until her head was on my shoulder. "You're doing a great job. Your momma would be so proud of you."

I rested my head on the top of hers and breathed in her fruity scent. It calmed me and I wondered if Momma would be proud or if I was just fucking everything up. "I don't know, Red. Sometimes I feel like I'm doing more bad than good. Some days around here are a fucking doozy. Sometimes, I wonder if Ella would be better off with someone who could give her all the things she needs."

She leaned up, looking at me, our faces close. "What is it you think she needs?"

"I don't know."

She brought her hand up and cradled the side of my face, her thumb caressing the apple of my cheek. "She just needs you, Luk. That's it. Stop overcomplicating things, honey."

Honey. Fuck me. I wanted to kiss her more than anything in the world in that moment. I wanted to get lost in her lips and smell and warmth for just one night. Like Ella, I just wanted to pretend for a bit.

Scarlett's head crept toward me, but instead of pressing her lips to mine, she gave me a long, slow kiss to the cheek she wasn't holding. I closed my eyes and soaked up that kiss like I would the sun on a day at the beach.

She pulled back and let my face go. "Y'all are gonna be okay. I promise."

"But what happens if I fuck up?"

She laughed. "Oh, you're gonna fuck up."

I lay back and looked at the ceiling. "Great."

"We all fuck up. The important thing is to not give up. When you make a mistake on the field, you just try to do better next time. Right, Mister Quarterback? There's always next game, next season, even." She patted my thigh. "You got this."

The next season. I nodded. She was right. Fuck, but she was perfect. Every second. Every moment. Every hour I was falling for her more—harder. "When are you going to let me take you out?"

She grinned. "I don't know." She picked at a piece of imaginary lint on her leggings. "I haven't thought about it," she finished haughtily.

I grinned back. "Liar."

A banging on the door followed by the creak of the door interrupted us.

"Knock, knock, it's me!" Mason called out, coming on inside the house like he owned the place. "Something smells good!"

"Sure, come on in," I said sarcastically because the motherfucker was already in my house.

Scarlett was giggling as he entered the room. He looked at her, then gave me big eyes before looking back at her. "Well, hello there, Scar. What are you doing here?"

She nodded toward the kitchen. "I brought brownies over."

He patted his hard stomach through his T-shirt. "Well, shit, brownies and chili. It's my lucky day."

"Go on, help yourself. You know where everything is," I said.

Mason went to the kitchen as Ella came out of the bathroom and joined us in the living room again. She was decked out in fuzzy fleece pajamas and zebra slippers. She looked adorable and made sure to squish right between Scarlett and me, causing us to scoot over. Scarlett tried to hold in a giggle as she moved over and I smiled my face off.

Ella hit play on Netflix and Mason joined us.

"Sweet! *Charmed!*" he said, settling in next to me with his food. The sectional was pretty filled up.

"We're going to regret eating all this shit tomorrow at practice," I said to Mason as the girls watched TV next to us.

"Worth it," he mumbled back.

"Ms. Lettie?" Ella piped in quietly.

Scarlett's gaze met Ella's. "What's up, Ellie Bellie?"

"Will you take me to the community center tomorrow to drop off my paper rolls?"

My breath caught somewhere in my chest. And fuck if my eyes didn't sting. And damn it if my nose didn't burn. I swallowed down the huge lump of emotion in my throat. Because I was not crying in front of Mason's crazy ass. He would never let me live it down.

My Red lifted her arms and wrapped them around Ella. She brought Ella's head to her chest and squeezed her tight. Her wet eyes met mine over Ella's head and that look, that pure sweetness was like a shot right to my heart.

I was in love with her. There was no denying it. The girl with the Skittles. The sassy redhead who was terrible at ballroom dancing. The loving woman with her arms wrapped around my sister. She owned me. Heart. Body. And soul. She just didn't know it yet and I was done waiting on her to realize it.

We spent the next two hours eating brownies with ice cream on top and watching old reruns. But really, I spent those two hours learning that family wasn't always the one God gave you. It was also the one you chose.

Chapter
NINETEEN

Scarlett

Lukas: Are you seriously going to make me come up to that school?

It had been two days since I'd gotten that text from Luk. Four since our night on the couch with Ella. Three since I'd taken Ella to the community center to drop off her empty toilet paper rolls. And I was thanking my lucky stars he hadn't made an appearance at The Cottage House. I needed time to think. I knew he thought I was avoiding him, but in truth, I just hadn't decided what I should do about the Lukas situation. He'd said he wanted me, my lips. But he'd never said he wanted a relationship. A girlfriend. And if I was going to break all my rules, I needed more than I want your lips. I needed everything and deserved it, damn it.

I was cleaning up my classroom from a long day. My TA had called off sick and the kiddos had just been having one of those days. Where nothing went right. Where one meltdown turned into two and where I ended up putting on an educational show at the end of the day because I didn't think me or them could handle it anymore.

I was working on my lesson plan for the next day in my head while shuffling around the pile of papers on my desk when I heard the creak of my classroom door.

Looking up, I immediately froze. My lucky streak had run out. He was making good on his promise or threat. Whatever you wanted to call it.

He walked toward me like a predator stalking his prey and instinctively, I backed up.

His head shook back and forth slowly, as a wicked smile covered his face. "Imagine seeing you here," he said.

Rolling my eyes, I mumbled, "You didn't imagine shit."

He kept going until he had me pressed up against the far wall of the classroom. "Better watch your mouth, Ms. Knox. Have you forgotten where you are?"

Oh, I hadn't forgotten. I was all too aware.

He pressed in further like he had that night in the bar and he smelled so good. I'd forgotten. And that was my problem. Anytime the man was around, all my defenses melted away like a piece of ice in a glass of warm sweet tea. He made me forget what I knew. Forget what I needed. Forget what I wanted.

"I've missed you." Dipping his head close, he ran his cheek down the side of mine and whispered into my ear, "Why are you making this so hard on both of us?"

I whimpered and that seemed to be all the permission he needed. His arms wrapped around my hips and cradled me close. He nipped at the lobe of my ear and my eyes nearly crossed.

"We shouldn't be doing this," I whispered to no one. Because he sure as hell wasn't listening and I wasn't making a move to push him away. But then his mouth left my ear and hit the spot just behind it that I had no idea until this very moment that I loved. His tongue darted out, tasting the skin there before his teeth bit, and my knees got weak. But my mind, it prevailed. "I'm not even sure you really like me."

I mean, I knew he liked me. Or I knew his body liked mine. But I wasn't sure if he really liked me. Like more than a one-night stand liked me. Because I wasn't the one-night stand kind of girl.

He pushed me harder into the wall and I felt the evidence of his arousal against my hip and it did not disappoint. It didn't seem fair that the perfect boy of my childhood dreams was also packing that anaconda.

His hand creeped up under my skirt and coasted across my thigh, and my head flew back, exposing more of my throat to him, my body on auto pilot, and it was flying right into dangerous territory.

"I'm pretty sure you can feel how much I like you, Scarlett." His deep voice rolled over me, through me, setting me afire. The sheer amount of want in it was dizzying.

Scarlett. God, the man hardly ever called me that. He taunted me with Red when he was joking around. But Scarlett, him calling me that? Damn. It did things to me. More than goose bumps, more than weak knees. It caused an ache deep in me, past the sensitive tips of my breasts, beyond the apex of my thighs, straight to my core, and it scared the absolute bejesus out of me.

"Your cock likes me, Luk. Not you." Deny. Deny. Deny. This couldn't happen. We were in my classroom. I was his sister's teacher. He was my first kiss and he'd broken my teenage heart.

His head snapped back to mine in record time and his lips were there, back at my neck, eating it up. Licking, tasting, sampling every corner, every dip, every turn. He finished me off with a long bite to my chin. "Mmm. My mouth seems to like you, too."

"Your mouth is going to get me in trouble. We're at school."

He backed up just enough so he could look between us down at my form-fitting black pencil skirt and white blouse. "I know exactly where we are, Red. And it's the stuff that dreams are made of. Now how about you hop your ass up on that desk for me and make this more than a dream?"

I eyed the desk across the room, but I knew better. Whatever this was between Luk and me was just temporary. He wanted my body, not my heart, and I had to protect it at all costs. Because the fourteen-year-old girl inside me was still madly in love with him. Thank God, twenty-four-year-old Scarlett knew better.

I slid between him and the wall and took three steps away. Pulling down my skirt and straightening my blouse, I said, "This is not appropriate, Mr. Callihan. It's not the time nor the place." But then again, it never would be if I had my say. This whole thing had disaster written all over it. And poor Ella, what would she think of all this? I had to think of her and my heart. And less about the eight pack I knew Luk was sporting under his T-shirt. God, I remembered it from the other morning in my bed and it was magnificent.

His eyes were wild on me. Like he was going to pounce any moment, so I took another healthy step back.

He matched my step with one of his own. "Name the time and the place, then."

"What?" I said, backing up again. He wasn't supposed to say that. He was supposed to say, well, it was nice knowing you, but since you don't wanna give up the booty, I'm outta here.

"I said, name the time and the place." He took another step forward.

My mouth fell open, but nothing came out. So, I backed up again, my mouth opening and closing like a fish. Because I didn't know what to say. What in the heck was happening here? Was he asking me on a date? Were we arranging a booty call? Whatever the answer was, none of it was good.

Two more steps back up on my wobbly red heels and my behind was pressed right up against the front of my desk. And then like a predatory animal he prowled toward me. Slow enough I could escape, but there was no hope for me. He had me right where he wanted me. I was easy prey when he looked at me like he did right now.

His chest pressed into mine. His jeans brushed my knees and I shivered. I quivered at the mere brush of his clothing. I was so screwed. He was closer than close. He was on me like white on rice.

His hands came up and cradled each side of my jaw, and his forehead lowered to mine. His heavy breaths mingled with my own.

With eyes pinched closed like he was in pain, he said, "I'm going to kiss you."

My body locked tight. Oh, no, he couldn't do that. If he kissed me I'd think about it at least the next ten years and that would be awful. I still obsessed over the day he'd kissed me when he'd told me goodbye. I couldn't let him do that to me again.

"That's a terrible idea," I whispered, his lips a breath from mine.

Slowly his eyes opened and they were suddenly boring into mine. "Why, Scarlett?"

I couldn't tell him the truth. That his kiss had ruined my teenage heart. That I'd never moved on. That no other kiss had ever compared. That I still thought about that kiss and what I had meant to him. I couldn't tell him any of that because it sounded pathetic and desperate even to my own ears.

So I lied. I lied my face off. "It's just not appropriate. I'm Ella's teacher and you're her guardian."

His smile said it all, but it didn't have to because his mouth wasn't far behind. "That's bullshit. None of that has anything to do with me putting my lips on yours." He studied my face like he did when we were in school together. Like he was trying to figure me out. I prayed he wouldn't.

And while his eyes pillaged my very soul, his knee slowly wedged itself between my thighs, causing my skirt to rise. I turned my head to the classroom door, terrified someone would walk through even though I knew it was after hours and we were alone.

His hands left my jaw and traveled down my neck, past my shoulders and the outer swell of my breasts to settle on my hips where he squeezed.

"What are you so afraid of, baby?"

He called me baby and he was doing it again. That thing where he made me dizzy and stupid. He was making me forget why this was a bad idea. Why I shouldn't want this. Because he felt so, so good against me.

His warm palms left my hips and slid down over my ass and to the bottom of my skirt where he clutched the hem in his fists, slowly sliding it up more.

I should have said stop. Anything, but the farther he pushed up my skirt, the more his knee moved in and up until it sat right there against me. Right where I needed it.

A small squeak escaped my lips and one corner of his mouth lifted in a slow smile. "God, you're gorgeous." His nose brushed the side of mine and the harsh stubble on his jaw scraped my skin exquisitely. His massive hands moved under my skirt and right to the globes of my bottom, squeezing, before one moved up and snapped the top of my panties. "And you have a thong on. You're trying to kill me, Red."

He lowered his head more, zeroed in on my lips, and even though I was a mess of hormones and turned on more than I'd ever been in my life, I couldn't give it to him. I couldn't give him my kiss again.

I turned my head in the nick of time and his mouth landed on my jaw.

"You're not going to give me your mouth, huh?" he mumbled against my cheek before pressing open mouth kisses down my face to my neck.

"No," I whispered into the quiet room, my voice breathy.

"Mmm," he moaned right into the spot where my shoulder met my neck before giving me a bite there that simultaneously stung and lit my body on fire. "Then I'll just have to take what you give me. Now won't I?" he growled.

And then he was there. All over. All hands and teeth and skin. His lips moved down to my chest where he kissed me like he was worshiping me. His hands cupped my ass hard and using his teeth, he peeled back my blouse until the tops of my breasts were exposed.

He pressed his mouth there, biting them, nipping at the sensitive skin and sucking until I was a mindless, needy puddle of want merely held up by an edge of a desk and two hundred and ten pounds of muscle.

I tried to hold back. To not cry out, but I was weak when it came to Lukas Callihan and his magic. It had always been that way and before I knew it, I was sighing and then moaning and eventually begging for more. "Please," I cried, pressing my hot core against his knee as my hands gripped the edge of the desk so I didn't float away.

Leaning back, he demanded, "Unbutton your shirt. I want to see you."

It was a dare. It was a promise. And I was a fiery redhead. I'd never backed down from a dare.

I let go of the desk, my chest rising and falling like I'd run a marathon. I pushed one button through the hole, my eyes on his. Because I knew if I looked away for even one more second I'd lose my nerve and despite my better judgment, I wanted this. I loved that he wanted me. I'd dreamed about it for so long.

Two. Three. Four. Five. And my shirt was open and I was standing there, my cream lace bra visible to the one and only Mister Quarterback. If I hadn't been so worked up, I would have been shaking in my red pumps.

"Jesus, Red. I can't believe how beautiful you are."

I paused, feeling like a fool. Of course he couldn't believe it. I'd been too skinny and gangly then. I hadn't even gotten my breasts yet. And just like that all those old insecurities poured into me. I couldn't help but think of that day. The day he'd left. And kissed me. Virtually stealing my heart and taking it with him all the way to South Carolina. He'd never called. Never written. He'd taken my first kiss and disappeared. And God, how my heart still ached when I thought about it.

I lay back further on the desk clutching the open lapels of my shirt, realizing what a fucking terrible idea this was. I could get fired over this. Over a man who probably wanted to fuck me and toss me aside like yesterday's garbage. What in the hell was I thinking?

"Come back to me, Scarlett." He was over me, closer and pulling at my fisted hands, his eyes pleading. His eyes. They'd always made me weak. Even then. More so now.

I let go and his hands pushed each side of my shirt aside before heading south back down to my ass. "I can't kiss your lips, but I can kiss you here." He started at my chin. "And here." My neck. "And here."

And he was back at the swells of my breasts. He took the silky lace of my bra between his teeth and pulled each cup down under my breasts and my nipples beaded in the cool air and under his lustful gaze.

"And here," he said with finality before drawing one of my aching nipples into his mouth and laving it with his tongue. His wet mouth was hot against my aching nipple and with one hand, I clutched the back of his head, holding him to me.

"Oh my God," I moaned, knowing this was so wrong but felt so damn right.

"No, baby. It's just me, Luk. But I have to believe that God had something to do with this moment." He chuckled quietly against my breast and the vibration and his breath only made me hotter, wetter. God, I was soaking. It was embarrassing really, except for the fact I couldn't think long enough to even be embarrassed.

His mouth devoured my chest as his hands gripped my hips harder and pulled me toward his knee that was between my legs. And that was it. His knee was right there, creating a delicious friction right against my clit through the thin material of my panties.

My breath caught and I stilled. I hardly breathed. It felt like everything stopped in that moment. Or something snapped. Like I'd finally reached a breaking point. I felt my body lock up tight, ready for whatever came. Everything but my lower half, that is. Because I couldn't stop myself. He pushed me down on his knee and I went there willingly like the crazy, sex-deprived freak that I was.

I couldn't stop it. I didn't want to. It was the most amazing feeling I'd ever had in my life. Better than my hand. Greater than all the vibrators and dildos galore. A simple man's knee was doing me in. I was such a sexual novice.

His breath and lips and tongue pillaged my chest. His hands held my hips like they were a lifeline, like he was afraid if he let go, I'd fly right away and never come back.

While his mouth devoured the tops of my breasts and then farther down to the hard buds of my nipples, he used his hands to grip my ass and rock me against his knee in that same delicious spot that had me seeing stars behind my eyelids. Because my eyes were clenched closed. I couldn't bear to watch this man steal what little was left of my heart. I hadn't let him have my lips, but I realized in that moment it didn't matter. These feelings were something I'd never experienced with another man. He was just making more firsts for me to crave, want, need. Damn him.

I pulled at his hair, angry, needy, damn irate at the situation but unable to stop it. Because I was too caught up and he was too damn sexy for his own good.

He grunted from the spot right between my breasts and sucked hard like he wanted to punish me, too. Pulling me more tightly against his knee, he rocked me harder there in a rhythm that did more than just turn me on. No, it had me moving toward something I didn't think possible with my panties still on and his dick still in his pants.

My breathing picked up and my body curved inwardly until I was practically curled around him and begging him to keep going. "Yes," I panted right into the hollow of his ear.

"You're on fire, Red. And you're going to burn me up. Aren't you?" He looked down between us at the spot where I was pressed up against his knee. "Are you going to come right here on my leg leaned up against your desk like a good girl? Look at you making a wet spot right there on my knee."

My face flushed hot and my cheeks burned, but I didn't care. His voice was thick with anticipation and sex. It was deeper, more gravelly, more everything and I felt it right down to the tips of my toes. At this point, I was riding his leg and chasing the kind of orgasm I'd only ever dreamed about—one that wasn't self-induced.

"Fuck, you're pretty," he said, looking down at my face before leaning in. I tipped my head back and moaned as his lips missed mine and landed right on my chin. He worked his way down again, this time not even bothering with the tops of my breasts. He went straight to my nipples, sucking them hard enough to sting.

I cried out and pushed even harder against him, wet spot be damned. I needed to come. Now.

"That's it, Red. Ride me. Use me." He bit the tip of a nipple hard and held it between his teeth before finally releasing me and giving the nub long licks with his tongue, soothing the sting. "Come all over me, baby."

Those words and that deep voice washed over me like a tidal wave because in seconds both of my hands were in his hair and holding him to my chest while my bottom half was locked tight around his, my shorter legs so intertwined and tangled up with his that I didn't know where mine began and his ended.

I ground down and threw my head back, my orgasm shooting through me like lightning, so very unexpected in its intensity. "Yes, yes, yes," I cried as I rode it out, unabashedly unashamed. My legs and arms shook around him.

Luk's hand stayed at my ass, rocking me slowly against him while his mouth sucked gently at one nipple and the other hand played at the other, gently squeezing. A squeezing that caused me to contract at my core.

My body fell lax back against the desk and still Luk kissed every available surface of skin he could reach. Tender kisses that wound my body down, all the while wounding my heart.

Because I knew this couldn't go on anymore. Whatever this thing was, this attraction, it wasn't sustainable. Luk and I would never work. He was married to football and I was married to teaching. I was Ella's teacher. He was her guardian. He couldn't even make her a lunch she liked. He couldn't even commit to teacher conferences and I wanted to have a relationship with this man.

I stilled under him, my body locking up tight. Was that what I wanted? A relationship? No. no. no. That was a terrible idea. I thought of our time in high school. How I'd sit in class all day waiting until after school when I'd get to see him, pathetically counting down the hours, the minutes, and then the seconds.

I couldn't live my life like that again. Waiting on Lukas Callihan to notice me, like me, and hope that one day he could love me for it all to end up being a meaningless kiss followed by ten years of silence. No, there was no way I could let that happen again.

"I should get dressed," I said awkwardly, looking at the doorway to my classroom, not knowing the protocol for a moment like this at all. Was this where I did the walk of shame? Except without some of the shame since I didn't actually get laid? Although I did have an actual sex worthy orgasm. It had been epic, mind-blowing, and I knew I'd be thinking about it for the rest of my life, like I had that stupid kiss after school all those years ago.

He hadn't moved off me and I felt his heated stare, so I turned, my eyes meeting his dark, steely ones. They didn't look mad, but they didn't look pleased either. I diverted my eyes because I couldn't handle all the questions in his.

I blew a breath up and into my hair, ruffling the strands at the top of my head, trying to act all nonchalant but totally failing. "Okay, well, I should probably get back to work now." *Hint. Hint. Get the hell off me, Luk. This was awkward enough without you staring down at me like I had the answers to world hunger.* Or at least his hunger? Maybe he was thinking about how he could take this further. Ya know, and get me naked on this desk so we could actually do it. But hell would freeze over before I let that happen. The orgasm was fun and all, but he had to go. Now.

Just when I was about to sit up and demand he go, he leaned down, this time shocking me. It was the eyes. They were sweet. Emotional even and they completely threw me for a loop. Frozen, I watched as his face descended toward mine, his lips an inch from mine, and still I couldn't move. He was going to do it. He was going to kiss me. My eyes fell closed of their own accord. His sweet smelling breath ghosted past my lips and then he shocked the hell out of me by placing a small closed mouthed kiss right at the corner of my mouth. He was sure to not touch my lips.

"I'm not a patient man, Red. But I can wait for those lips. If I recall correctly they were definitely something worth waiting for." He said it softly right into the shell of my ear and I had to bite back a groan because I was ready to hop back on that leg like a dog in heat. What was Luk doing to me? This wasn't me. I was a good girl. And he made me want to be so damn bad.

He leaned back, pulling me up with him and finally letting go. I wobbled on my heels and he grabbed my elbow to steady me. "You okay there?" His mouth was smiling, but his eyes were smug as hell.

"I'm fine," I lied, buttoning my blouse and straitening my skirt with shaking hands and clumsy fingers.

He chuckled low and my eyes snapped to his and shot daggers. He thought this was funny? He could get me fired. He was laughing at my expense. I couldn't help I was so inexperienced. I just hadn't found the right partner yet and he was laughing at me.

I rolled my eyes and turned back to my desk, pretending to straighten papers that were already lined up perfectly.

I smelled his musky pine tree scent before I felt him against my bottom. And then his chest to my back. And lastly his mouth to my ear.

"Damn, baby. You liked that. Didn't you? And that was only my knee. Imagine what I can do with my tongue."

And oh, did I ever imagine. I was so busy imagining I didn't even feel him leave my body. I only noticed he wasn't there anymore when I heard the creak of my classroom door opening.

My head darted in that direction, my face on fire just like the rest of my body.

He looked back at me, his big body halfway through the door, his large hand on the knob, his smile and eyes smug this time. "Ella's birthday is Saturday. We are having a small party at the house at five in the afternoon. She'll expect you there."

And he was gone. He'd fled the coop. Elvis had left the building, people. Just like my damn sanity.

Chapter
TWENTY

Lukas

I'D NEVER SEEN A CHICKEN WITH ITS HEAD CUT OFF, BUT I WAS PRETTY SURE that's what I looked like right about now. That's what happened when a few family members and close friends were invited over for cake and the entire football team found out and invited themselves, too.

I had the grill going with burgers and hotdogs. Mason was manning that. Merline was in the kitchen finishing up a few sides and I was trying to avoid her by putting a few balloons on the mailbox and praying like hell I hadn't forgotten anything. Cake? Check. Food? Check. Gifts for Ella? Check. The entire fucking Alabama Cougars? Check. Scarlett? No check yet.

I knew she would come. If not for me, then most definitely for Ella.

She didn't disappoint. I was hanging the last balloon on the mailbox when her car pulled up. I watched, my breath stuck somewhere in my chest as she exited her car looking beautiful in a snug pair of jeans and a black T-shirt with "Purple Rain" across it in purple letters. Christ, she was cute.

"You made it," I joked.

"I did," she said, holding a small wrapped present in her hands.

"Where's the birthday girl?"

"Out back with Mason, I think." I walked up the sidewalk and onto the porch quietly. I didn't know what to say except that I was happy to see her and I thought that might scare her off. But I was. So damn happy.

Merline greeted us as we walked into the house. "Hi, I'm Lukas and Ella's aunt Merline." She put her hand out to Scarlett, who took it while she laid Ella's present on the counter with a million others.

"I'm Scarlett. But you can call me Lettie. All the kids do. I teach Ella at The Cottage House."

I wondered why Scarlett never told me to call her Lettie. I thought maybe it was because she actually liked the nickname I'd dubbed her of Red. I smiled like a smug bastard.

"Oh, how lovely." Aunt Merline beamed at Scarlett, clearly impressed. I rolled my eyes, because the old witch hadn't been nice to me since she'd been here. She hadn't been mean, but she wasn't throwing worshipping smiles my way, that was for sure.

"Come on." I grabbed Scarlett's hand and dragged her toward the back porch, where clearly a game of football was going on without me.

"Pass it to Ella," Mason ordered, running next to my baby sister. Rollins, our kicker, passed the ball to Ella and everyone crowded around pretending to catch her, but Mason picked her up in his arms.

"Don't let go of the ball, Ella!" He cradled her in his arms like he was carrying a baby instead of a teenager and ran like hell, the guys hot on his heels.

When he reached the tree covered shade of the yard, he raised Ella up over his head and said, "Touchdown!"

"Touchdown!" Ella yelled high above his head.

"Woohooo!" Scarlett yelled from beside me as I smiled my face off.

"Hey, Lucy. See how Ella did that? Ran that in for a touchdown? You should try that sometime!" Childs yelled over the hooting and hollering.

I smiled and flipped him the bird while Scarlett giggled next to me.

"You shouldn't let them toss her around like that. She could get hurt," Aunt Merline said from behind Scarlett and me.

"It's fine, Merline. Mason wouldn't hurt a hair on her head. He adores her."

She turned and went back into the house with a "hrrmph." She could suck the fun out of anything.

The guys played football with Ella a little more, then we all had burgers, hot dogs, and cake before Ella opened her presents.

My team did well and bought her cute, colorful workout leggings and bath bombs. They all knew her love for Zumba and long baths. I shared a lot with them now and what I didn't, Mason was happy to offer up.

Merline got her some coloring books and crayons, which she loved but already had a million of. I got her some new fuzzy socks and pajamas. Scarlett's gift was the last.

Ella unwrapped the present carefully like she knew it was extra special or maybe it was just because it was from her favorite teacher. We all watched quietly, until the last piece of paper was shredded and the small picture frame was revealed.

Ella held it in front of her, staring at it while the rest of us waited to see what the hell she was looking at.

I looked over at Scarlett, who was sitting right next to Ella on the couch. She watched Ella cautiously, nervous even, and I walked over and stood behind the sofa, so I could peer over Ella's shoulder.

My body locked tight as I looked down at the picture, my mom's smiling eyes shining back at me in the photo. She was standing next to Ella, outside somewhere and they had their arms around each other. They looked so happy it made me sad.

Feeling her eyes on me, I looked at Scarlett. Giving me a sad smile, she said, "I took it at the beginning of the school year. It was the school year kickoff picnic." She looked back at Ella and rubbed her hand along Ella's arm. "I thought you might like to have it."

Still staring at the photo, Ella said, "That's my momma."

"Yep," Scarlett agreed. "That's your momma and you."

"I miss her. Lulu says she's in heaven with Daddy." Her gaze finally landed on Scarlett's.

Scarlett smiled down at Ella. "She is. And I bet she and your daddy are having the biggest party ever for you today up there."

Ella seemed to be thinking about that as she nodded slowly and I felt relieved. Like maybe our talk had made a difference. It seemed like she was understanding and accepting. It was a good thing and Scarlett's gift had been so thoughtful.

"Thanks, Ms. Lettie." Ella leaned in and gave Scarlett a huge hug.

The doorbell rang just on time and Ella's face lit up. "I got it." She took off for the front door and I grinned at Scarlett shamelessly. It was Ella's favorite part of her birthday. Ella came back toting a dozen red roses and Scarlett's eyebrows rose.

"Are those for you, Ella?" she asked.

"Yep. Detective Chase sends me roses every year for my birthday."

Scarlett looked confused.

"Yeah, Detective Chase from *General Hospital*," I chimed in.

Ella grabbed her picture frame and carried it with her flowers. "I'm going to put this stuff on my dresser."

"That's a perfect spot for it."

Ella ran off to put her presents away and I couldn't take my eyes off Scarlett.

She couldn't take her eyes off me either. She seemed rather impressed that Detective Chase sent flowers to Ella every year. Shaking her head softly, she smiled at me and I grinned back.

And the rest of the evening played out to that same tune. I watched her play cards with Ella. I watched her laugh with the guys and when everyone was gone and only Merline and I and she were left. I watched her tell Aunt Merline off.

"Luk, you should really get a cleaner. This place is a pig sty. Luk, don't you think that Ella should eat more vegetables than she has on her plate?"

It went on and on. And I could tell Scarlett was getting really annoyed with her crap. And then the shit finally hit the fan.

I was telling Scarlett we should leave the decorations up. That Ella loved them.

"That's sweet, Luk. Make it a birthday week," she agreed.

"You can't leave these decorations up. Those balloons and streamers are a choking hazard," Merline butted in.

Scarlett turned and looked at her like she'd lost her damn mind. "Are you kidding me?"

Merline's hand came to her chest, all Southern innocence. "What?"

Scarlett walked forward until she was close enough to Merline that there was no mistaking she was talking to her. "Excuse my French, Ms. Merline, but you have no idea what the hell you're talking about. Ella is not a baby. And you mustn't treat her like one."

"I wasn't treating her like a ba—"

Scarlett cut off her lies. "You were. And all day you've belittled Luk and all his hard work. And not just his hard work for this party but his hard work all the damn time."

Merline got her hackles up and stepped up, toe-to-toe with Scarlett. "Our family is none of your business, missy," she spat.

"You sure wouldn't know they're your family from the way you treat them." And she turned and walked out of the room, just like that.

My mind was blown. I had to bite my lips to keep from smiling when Merline gave me a nasty look and grabbed her purse before heading to the door. Thank God. Not only had Scarlett told her off, she'd somehow managed to get her to leave as well.

We didn't mention the incident with Merline while Scarlett helped me put everything away and wash the dishes. I figured she was embarrassed about it when really I was impressed. I knew she had it in her. But she'd gone to bat for me.

When everything was done and Ella was tucked into bed after a busy day I asked, "Wanna watch a movie?"

She leaned against the kitchen counter and smiled. "I think I better head home. I'm beat and I have school tomorrow."

"Or you could just stay the night here?"

Her pink cheeks smiled. "Sweet baby Jesus, you are such a flirt."

"Thank you."

She grabbed her pocketbook off the counter, and my heart fell. Fuck, she was leaving and I couldn't make her stay. I had to give her time. It had to be her decision. I could be patient, I told myself.

I walked her out the front door and stood on the porch and noticed it had started to drizzle. "Do you need an umbrella?"

"No, it's only a little rain. I won't melt," she said from the top step. I wanted to beg her to stay. I wanted her to fucking kiss me. I'd never wanted to kiss a woman more than I did in this very moment.

She'd just hit the sidewalk from the bottom step when I called out, "Red!"

She turned around, a big smile on her face, the rain sprinkling on her. "Yeah?"

And then it struck me. Her standing at the bottom of the steps and me standing at the top. It was just like that evening all those years ago, except in reverse. Now I was the one standing on my momma's porch with worship in my eyes, begging for just one kiss.

And man, did I want to ever beg. "Kiss me!" I wanted to shout. But I promised myself I wouldn't. I promised myself I'd let her come to me. I promised myself that she would because I knew in my heart of hearts that she wanted us, too.

So instead of begging for a kiss, I said, "Thank you."

Her smile grew. "For what?" She pushed her wet hair off her forehead.

She didn't even get it. She didn't even know how amazing she was. And that made her all the more special. "For everything. For the picture. For having my back with Merline. For being you. Just thank you. You mean so much to us." And it was the truth. We wouldn't have made it through this without her. And I felt like we were finally coming out the other side. It wasn't what I wanted to say. Because I wanted to say I love you. But it didn't make what I did say any less true or meaningful.

Her smile fell from her face, as serious green eyes ate up mine. She looked like she wanted to say something, do something. Anything. And I stared back, willing her to walk up the steps to me. That's all she had to do. If only she would just take the first step, I'd be here waiting. I'd put in the rest of the work. I'd make us happen. I'd make us happy. She just had to meet me and I wasn't even asking for halfway.

"You're welcome," she said softly, giving me one more look over before turning slowly and walking to her car in the driveway.

My heart sank as defeat sat heavy in my chest. I swallowed down the huge lump of emotion in my throat as I watched her make that walk. Fuck. Just fuck.

But nevertheless, I still watched to make sure she made it into the car safely, but once she got to the vehicle she paused, her hand to the handle. I almost stepped off the front porch thinking she'd locked her keys in or something when she slammed the palm of her hand against the driver window and yelled, "Screw it!" She turned quickly and came running back up the driveway and then up the sidewalk and finally to the stairs before launching herself into my arms and wrapping her arms around my neck and her legs around my waist, her purse an afterthought, she'd dropped to the porch. She wasted no time pressing her cool, wet lips to mine, and my eyes fell closed.

She sucked my top lip into her mouth and then the bottom before finally sliding her tongue along mine. I groaned in shock and palmed her ass cheeks, damp jeans and all. Sucking and biting at my lips, she hummed lightly like she was enjoying a good snack and the sound drove me insane. I'd been waiting too long. I'd wanted this too much. She was going to make me come in my jeans on my mother's fucking front porch. I'd waited so long and it had been worth every second.

My shock wearing off, I finally kissed her back, tasting all corners and edges of her mouth, enjoying the flavor of her tongue. Lightning flashed in the sky behind her as I nibbled her jaw and kissed the corner of her mouth. I wanted to take her inside and put her in my bed and keep her there for at least a month, but I needed to know she was ready.

"What now?" I said, licking the pillowy softness of her bottom lip.

She ran her nose along the side of mine. "Take me to bed, Mister Quarterback."

Chapter
TWENTY-ONE

Scarlett

LORD HAVE MERCY. WHAT WAS I DOING? BUT HOW COULD I NOT? HE'D been standing there on that porch so sweetly, so patient. And there was no one in the world I wanted like this other than him. He'd scooped my pocketbook off the porch and thrown it in the entryway, carried me all the way to his room quietly and careful not to wake Ella, eating my lips like the starving man I knew he was. Because God, I was hungry for him, too. His kisses now were so different than that chaste sweet kiss on my porch all those years ago. No, they were fueled by need, passion, want. And I was on fire.

"God, I've thought about this for so long." His big hands palmed my ass and rocked me against him. Instinctively, my legs tightened and I groaned.

"Shh. We have to be quiet," he whispered into my mouth. I had a feeling his lips were going to be there a long while. He couldn't seem to get enough of them. He closed his bedroom door behind him quietly by backing up into it before moving us toward the bed.

Part of me was nervous, but the bigger part of me had been wanting this for so long. He pushed me down onto the bed and I made sure he came with me by pulling him down.

God, it felt good. The big, hard length of his body pressed to my small, soft one. His woodsy smell practically all over me. I would have basked in it a little more, but he pulled back out of our embrace.

"Fuck, I have to see you now. I want to see every inch of this creamy skin."

In record time, my wet Purple Rain shirt was in a pile across the room. My quarterback had a good arm. My bra and jeans followed until I lay there in nothing but my modest black panties.

He did a push up off me until he was kneeling right between my spread legs. "You're better than I imagined, Red. And I've been imagining you a fuck of a lot."

He looked down at me fiercely, while I blushed beneath him, not at all used to the kind of attention Lukas paid me but still loving it. The air kissed the tips of my nipples and I arched my back, pushing them out, begging for him to touch the aching buds.

But Lukas was a damn tease. He trailed one finger from my lips, my chin, and right through the middle of my breasts. He passed between my ribs and down the middle of the softness of my belly straight to my waistline.

I groaned low, my body and mind begging for him to do something more, but the man seemed determined to drive me crazy by taking his sweet ass time. His finger trailed down my silk panties to the cleft beneath them. It stayed there, rubbing up and down.

"Damn, baby, your panties are already soaked for me." His finger continued to torture, catching on my clit over and over until I was panting.

"Please," I whispered, trying to catch my breath.

"Mmmm," he rumbled as he hooked his fingers on either side of my panties and slowly brought them down my legs, like he was unwrapping a favorite gift instead of me. "Please what, baby? Want me to make you come?"

And then he was there, his knees to the floor, his hot hands at my thighs spreading them wide, his face inches from where I needed him. Desperately.

"Yes, please," I begged. I needed to come like I needed air.

His finger was back and this time he was watching. I felt so deliciously exposed.

Rubbing slow circles around my clit, he asked, "How do you want me to make you come? With my fingers?" He leaned in, until his soft hair tickled the tops of my thighs and his breath coasted across my core before he gave my clit a long, wet lick. "Or with my mouth?" He finished, burying his face there and giving me another long lick.

I'd never in my life had a man there, that close. It felt incredible, and I had little control over my mouth at the moment, so I blurted, "Your mouth," as my hands found purchase in his hair and pulled.

He didn't pass go. He didn't collect two hundred dollars, he just went for it. Licking and sucking and devouring me. I shamelessly rocked against his face, using his hair to control the pace in wicked ways I'd only read about in books I hid in my bedside table.

And then I felt it. It came on me quick like a flash of lightning hitting the earth and I shattered, broke wide-open. My eyes clenched close and my knees met the side of Luk's head while I trembled on his lips, shaking like a feather in the wind. Light flashed behind my eyes and I cried out, riding a delectable wave of ecstasy. And even when I let my legs fall wide and my eyes slowly drifted open, he licked and sucked me slowly down, drawing out the very last bit of my orgasm.

I lay there, depleted of every bit of energy, my mind blown and my body relaxed. I already wanted to have him do that to me again, but he was crawling up me, placing small kisses to my stomach, and then my chest and finally my lips, his tongue dipping into my mouth.

"Three," he whispered against them.

I opened one eye and looked at him with a smile. "Three what?"

"That's how many times you've let me have your lips."

Both of my eyes popped open. "I'm only counting two, Mister Quarterback. Outside your front door and just now," I smarted.

He smiled down at me. "Uh uh uh. You missed one."

My eyebrows scrunched together and he smoothed it with his thumb. "When?"

"Ten years ago. On your front porch," he said with soft eyes and I knew without a shadow of a doubt I was in love with this gorgeous, sweet man. He swept me off my feet over and over again. I loved every bit of him.

I pulled him down for our fourth time and kissed him hard and long before leaving his mouth for the lobe of his ear and giving it a tug with my teeth.

I was running my hands down his back when I realized something very important. "You still have all your clothes on!"

He chuckled low and it vibrated throughout my body before standing up and slipping his blue T-shirt off the way men only did in movies and books. My mouth watered at the sight of muscles on top of muscles covered by smooth, tan skin, with a speckling of hair. I watched on like a kinky voyeur as he slipped his wallet from the back pocket of his jeans and produced a small foil pack that he threw on the bed next to my head.

His hands met at the waistband of his pants and he stared down at me with a devilish grin.

Leaning up on my elbows to get a better view, I said, "Well, go on, Mister Quarterback. Let's see what you've got."

His cheeks were pink as he unbuttoned his dark denim and slid them down his legs, taking his black boxers with them. He kicked the pants off and walked the two steps toward me slowly. Slow enough I could get a good look at the gorgeous, long, thick cock that was swinging between his muscular thighs.

I lay back on the bed and looked at the ceiling, thanking God this man was my man, if even only for tonight. I wanted to throw my hand up and scream halleluiah but instead stared up into melty brown eyes. Reaching over, he grabbed the condom, ripping the package with his teeth and sliding his hand down between us, keeping us safe.

Laying his lips softly to mine, he breathed, "five," across them before kissing my jaw, then my neck and finally the tops of my breasts. "I have to be inside of you. Right this minute." He ran his hands down my thighs, pushing them open, and eased himself inside slowly, his face strained. Tears settled in my eyes like twin pools.

"God, baby, you're so tight," he ground out and my stomach flipped as he inched forward more, nervousness making my legs shake around him. More tears filled my eyes.

It was the third time he pushed that it finally registered. His mouth left my breasts and hot eyes landed on mine. "You can't be," he whispered reverently, his breath coming like he'd run a marathon. His forehead landed on the center of my chest. "I'm not that fucking lucky." He sounded choked up, full of emotion.

"But you are." The tears in my eyes overflowed and trekked down my cheeks and onto his bedding. He leaned up and tried to kiss them away. This was it. I was ready. I was scared, but I wanted it to be him.

"Are you sure?"

I nodded emphatically. "Yes, more than anything."

"Me?" he said like he couldn't believe it. That he somehow couldn't believe he was worthy of me giving my virginity to. Of course I wanted him to have it. I'd been saving myself for him. Not the him from high school. But for the first man I'd ever really loved. And Lukas was it.

I hit his chest lightly. "Yes, you! Do you want me to find someone else?"

With eyes full of emotion, he answered, "Never."

He brought his hands up and placed each one on either side of my jaw. "I'll be easy. I promise."

I gave him a tender smile. "I know. I trust you." And in that moment, I realized I really did. He'd earned it. The hard way. I hadn't trusted him when he'd come home, but he'd been nothing but open and honest and wonderful. And I trusted him more than I trusted myself in that moment.

One chaste kiss to my lips and he pushed hard into me, filling me up, piercing my virginity and only leaving a slight sting behind.

I smiled softly up at him as happy tears rolled down my cheeks.

"Okay?" he asked, my tears reflected back in his.

"I'm wonderful." And I was because he took care of me. He'd

taken his time. He'd done it right, just like he had all those years ago on the porch when he'd stolen my first kiss. He was perfect.

He moved over me, kissing away the stain of tears on my face, loving me with the slow rhythm of his body. And if I thought for one second that I wasn't completely in love and utterly devoted to Luk, I didn't now. He made love to me unhurriedly, savoring me, his eyes locked to mine, our souls so deeply intertwined, I didn't know if we would ever be able to separate them.

And when he finally froze over me, his muscles taut, his groan deep, I clenched around him and wrapped my arms and legs around his body, never wanting to let him go, never wanting this very moment to end.

I may have given Lukas my virginity, but he'd given me so much more—a night I'd never forget. A beautiful moment to cherish no matter what happened after tonight. I didn't care about the future. I didn't care what happened in the morning. I wanted to live in this very moment and so I did. With not a single regret.

"Did you sleep here?"

I cracked open a lid and found Ella standing right next to the bed and looking at me. I looked behind me for Luk and realized I heard the shower running. Uh oh. I was all on my own. I looked around for a clock but didn't see one, but what I did know it was dark thirty, so it was before I usually got up.

Sitting up in the bed, I grabbed the sheet and brought it to my naked breasts so Ella didn't get a show. "I did."

I looked around her, desperate for Luk to get out of the shower. I needed help navigating this. I was naked as a jaybird and Ella was standing in front of me in her workout clothes interrogating me. And I hadn't even had coffee yet.

"So are you and Lulu married now?"

My hand to my chest, I yelled, "What?"

"Momma said if you sleep with someone and have sex with them then you have to be married."

I heard the water turn off and prayed Luk was coming any moment because I had no fucking clue what to do. Because yes, her momma had told her the things you should tell a child, but no, that wasn't real life for most of us.

So I evaded as best I could. "What makes you think we had sex?"

She pointed to me. "You're naked."

Oh, for heaven's sake, but her mother had told her too much and I didn't know whether to be proud or jump from this bed like my ass was on fire.

Luk walked into the room with nothing but a towel wrapped around his waist, droplets of water running down his chest and shoulders, and my mouth dried up. My lady bits clenched and I felt a delicious soreness I'd never experienced between my legs. I couldn't decide whether to look at Ella or stare at his muscles. It was awkward as hell.

How was I supposed to do the walk of shame with her here? How was I supposed to lick his chest with her here? I was overwhelmed.

"What's up, Ells?" he asked, gathering some clothes out of the dresser and not freaking out at all like he should have been. I was naked. Ella was here. We'd had sex.

Ella pointed at me. "She slept here."

He nodded and slid on a pair of boxers under his towel. "She's going to be sleeping here a lot, Ellie Bellie. Better get used to it."

"Y'all had sex."

He nodded. "Again, Scarlett is going to be here a lot." He slid a T-shirt over his head and whipped the towel off before throwing some athletic shorts on. "I thought tonight you and I would take her on a date. How does Jasmine sound?" He looked at me. "Ella loves Greek food."

I watched on, my eyes big, my mouth hanging open because what the hell?

Ella shrugged. "Okay."

"Great, if you finished your workout, go get ready for school."

Ella walked from the room without so much as another word. I blinked, still in complete shock. Luk had been so mature, so in control, and I'd been a bumbling crazy person. I couldn't believe it, but it also made me so proud. He was so good at being her person. And he didn't even know it.

All dressed for the day, he came and sat next to me on the bed. "I have to get to practice. Allison will get Ella on the bus, so you can head out whenever you want. Take your time, but tonight I need you back here for a date with me and Ella. Okay?"

"Okay," I said because what the hell else could I say? I was uncaffeinated and he was ordering me about. I mean, I think he asked me on a date, but I couldn't be sure. I couldn't be sure about anything that had just happened, actually.

"Good," he said, kissing me on the head and then dipping down to hit my lips. "Six," he said against my lips. And then he grabbed a big bag from the corner and left the room.

I flopped back into the bed, exhausted, and my day hadn't even started yet. But I closed my eyes and smiled. I was going on a date with Luk and Ella tonight for Greek. It didn't get much better than that.

Scarlett

I WAS OUT IN LUK'S DRIVEWAY TAPPING MY FINGERS AGAINST THE STEERING wheel to a little Prince, feeling nervous as hell. I wasn't quite sure what Luk and I were doing. This morning he'd made it clear to Ella that I'd be around more often. He hadn't made it that clear to me why. Did he mean I'd be around more often as in his bed? Or did he mean I'd be around more often for dates like this?

He'd sent me a text today to make sure, yet again, that I was coming over for our date with Ella and of course I wouldn't say no. He'd told Ella I was coming. How could I possibly bail? But on top of that, I wanted to spend time with him. For heaven's sake, I'd given him my V card. But still, I didn't know what that meant for us. So you could say I was on pins and needles. I had, however, told him I was driving us tonight. I needed to have some modicum of control and this was it. Me driving. I shook my head at my crazy as Ella came out of the house first, a smile on her face. She climbed right into the front seat determined to ride shotgun and I pressed my lips together hard to keep from laughing.

Luk came out after checking his phone only to look up right when he got to the car to discover that Ella was in the front seat. He shot me a small smile and shook his head as he got into the back seat of my car. He climbed in not so gracefully, his legs almost clear up to his chest. A small giggle escaped my mouth that I couldn't contain any longer.

"Hey, Ells. Think you can move your seat up a little bit?"

Nothing. Not a nod. Not even a shake. She acted like she didn't hear him at all and my small giggle turned into a full on laugh.

Lukas rolled his eyes at me as I pulled out of the driveway and headed to Jasmine. I cranked up the radio and Ella looked over at me and smiled.

"Who you listening to?"

Apparently Ella was only ignoring Lukas. Seemed like she'd decided that it was just her and me on this date and it made me grin my face off. I looked in the rearview mirror at Luk and gave him a smile.

"Prince. Also known as The Love Symbol. Basically, the greatest musician of all time," I finished.

Ella stared blankly ahead.

"Don't worry. I'll teach you all about him."

Still, she ignored me and I checked the rearview again to see Luk grinning at me. He was clearly enjoying the fact that I, too, was being ignored now.

It wasn't a long ride to Jasmine, thank goodness, otherwise I was worried Luk was going to be perpetually stuck in my car. I pulled into the parking lot and unbuckled, but Ella was faster and before I'd even gotten all the way out of the car, she was already opening the door to the restaurant.

I practically had to pull Luk from the car he'd been so crammed back there and I wondered how we were going to broach the subject of the car ride home. "You riding back there on the way home?" I asked.

He laughed. "Hell no. I'm driving. You and Ella can duke it out for the front seat."

I giggled and started walking toward the restaurant only to be caught off guard at the feel of Luk's warm hand on the back of mine.

It didn't stop there. No. His fingers came around mine, intertwining, and I felt my breath catch in my chest as his rough fingers slid along the softness of mine and clasped. I walked slower, stunned. I looked down at my pale hand in his tan one.

"Are you holding my hand?" I asked, breathless.

He nodded, his face serious. "I am."

I stopped right outside the door and looked at him. "Why?"

One side of his mouth rose up in a barely there smile, before he brought our clasped hands to his mouth and kissed the back of mine sweetly. "Because this is a date, Red. And when I take a girl I like on a date, I hold her hand."

"Oh," I breathed, stunned, not knowing what the hell to say. So I said nothing at all as he opened the door for me but never let go of my hand. My heart was fluttering in my chest like it was full of butterflies. I was on a real date with Luk. He was holding my hand. This didn't seem like the recipe for a booty call.

We found Ella already seated in a booth and when we approached, Luk slid in across from Ella, making sure to scoot over and make room for me. But Ella wasn't having any of that.

"You sit here, Ms. Lettie." She tapped the spot next to her. I gave Luk big eyes but I wasn't arguing with Ella. I slipped in beside her, setting my purse between us.

"Ya know, Ella. This is a date so maybe Scarlett should sit with me."

Ella was looking at the menu, but I knew for a fact they came here often enough she already knew what she was getting. She was my routine girl. So, at first I thought she was ignoring Luk again.

I was surprised when she said, "But you said you and me were taking her on a date."

Luk full on smiled. "You got me there, kiddo."

"That's right," she sang back with sass and I tried not to laugh again. But completely failed.

We ordered drinks and food and made small talk about what Ella was working on at school and where I was taking the kids on their trip this month. Lukas talked about football and pain in the ass Mason, he called him. But it was said with so much affection I knew that he really liked the guy.

We were on dessert when the inquisition started. I was totally unprepared. Totally caught off guard. It was like I was back in the bed this morning buck ass naked while Luk was in the shower and Ella was standing over me in her workout clothes. It felt exactly the same and I shrunk into my seat when the first question flew from her mouth.

"Are ya'll having a baby?"

"What? No!" I answered quickly, ducking down like maybe I could disappear if I tried hard enough.

Luk followed me up with a patient, "Not right now. Right now, Scarlett and I are just dating, but one day if we decide to, we might."

I sucked in too fast and felt it. I was going to choke. He was trying to kill me. Did he say we might have a baby one day? I mean, the whole we were dating thing was shocking enough. Yes, he'd told me outside this was a date but did one singular date constitute "officially dating"? And babies? Why was this happening?

Luk pushed my water across the table at me like he knew I was going to die if I didn't have a sip. I slung it back, taking a big gulp, wishing I'd ordered an adult beverage instead. How had this happened? How had we gone from a front porch kiss the night before to dating and having babies?

Ella turned to face me. "Are you living with us?"

I shook my head ready to answer, but Luk cut me off. "Not yet. But I'd definitely like her to one day. Would that be okay with you, Ells?"

I wanted to shout what the fuck but I didn't want to scare the crap out of Ella, so I only smiled at her, but I was positive my face looked panic stricken. He wanted me to move in eventually? I felt like maybe we should have talked about this before, ya know, before talking about it with Ella.

Ella looked at me and then back at Luk and answered, "I don't mind. But she has to make brownies sometimes."

And even though I felt myself soften at her sweet words and her love of my brownies, I glared across the table at Luk who only winked back at me with a small smile. Damn him.

It was the final question that really did me in. That really reached into my heart and squeezed.

"Will you still be my teacher?" It was said so quietly, so softly and sweet. I lifted one arm instinctively and placed it around Ella's shoulders, hugging her to me.

"Of course, I'm going to be your teacher. I love teaching you. I wouldn't give it up for anything."

I looked over at Luk. "I have an appointment with Vice Principal Vega tomorrow to discuss my relationship with y'all."

I said y'all because in truth, it wasn't just Luk who was involved in this. It was Ella, too. I'd checked the teacher handbook for The Cottage House and there wasn't anything in particular there about dating a student's guardian or parent, but I still felt like running it past Vice Principal Vega would be for the best.

Luk seemed happy with my answer because he leaned across the table and took my hand that wasn't wrapped around Ella. "My girl," he said softly.

But not softly enough.

"I thought I was your girl?" Ella asked, looking upset and this was exactly what I hoped to avoid. I never wanted to upset Ella. I prayed that Luk and I didn't screw this whole thing up, for her more than anything. I didn't want her caught in the crossfires of a relationship gone bad. Because that seemed like what this was now. A relationship. We had a lot more at stake than just ourselves.

But I should have known Luk would have the whole thing under control. He slid his free palm across the table and grabbed for Ella's hand this time.

"You're my girl, too, Ellie Bellie." He gave her a soft smile. "Always. Is it alright if Scarlett is my girl, too, now?"

Ella looked between the two of us, clearly contemplating things. I held my breath along with Luk's hand. I hoped she knew how much

I loved her. How I'd never take Luk from her. How part of why I loved him was because he loved her so dearly.

Those flutters were back at full speed and I wanted to place my hand to my chest to keep them from flying right out but I didn't want to let go of Luk's hand. God, I loved him so.

"Okay," Ella said, breaking my train of thought like it wasn't a big deal. Like Luk and I weren't over here shaking in our boots waiting on her answer.

"Good, Ells," Luk breathed, letting our hands go and leaning back in the booth, his eyes darting from me to Ella. "My girls," he said again softly, his eyes thick and rich like melted chocolate.

"Lulu, Ella, and Lettie," Ella chimed in, obviously not wanting to leave Lukas out.

His smile widened. "Yep, Lulu, Ella, and Lettie. Sounds good, doesn't it?"

I couldn't help but smile, too. Because, God, it did. It sounded so, so good.

Chapter
TWENTY-THREE

Lukas

"**D**IBS." I KISSED THE SPOT UNDER HER EAR SHE LOVED. "DIBS." I kissed her cheek. "Dibs." And then her lips. "Dibs." Then her nose.

"You can't just call dibs on people's body parts, Lukas." She giggled beneath me.

I moved down her body until my face was right between her legs. "What were you saying?" I asked, my mouth an inch from her pussy.

"Nothing. Nothing at all," she sang back. "Who am I to argue? Have me."

I leaned in, giving her clit a slow lick that immediately set her thighs to trembling. Fuck, but I loved how responsive she was to me. It turned me on. It made me impossibly hard and I'd already had her this morning. It didn't seem like I'd ever tire of her. And we'd been doing this plenty over the last several weeks.

I slid one finger inside of her, fucking her with it, thinking how tight she still was. Yeah, I didn't have to call dibs on this pussy. It was all fucking mine. No other man had ever touched it and if I had anything to say about it, no other ever would. I licked and sucked and fucked her with my fingers and tongue until she came all in my mouth.

She lay there languid and worn out while I crawled up her body, stopping at her breasts to give both her nipples a suck before whispering, "Dibs," right between them with a smile.

"You're awful," Scarlett said, laughing.

I lay next to her in the bed. "And by awful you mean an amazing lover."

She swatted half-heartedly at my chest with her hand. "Yeah, yeah, yeah."

"I have to go to practice." I didn't want to leave her. It was the same every morning.

"Mmm, I'm still sleepy. I think I'm going back to sleep."

I noticed the dark circles under her eyes and worried maybe she was getting sick. "You feeling okay?"

"Yeah, just super tired lately." She gave me an evil grin. "I think you're wearing me out."

She was wearing me out, too, but the last almost two months had been the best of my life.

I faked right and tried to run the ball in. I was almost to the goal line when Mason's big ass head got me right in the gut.

"Jesus!" I yelled from the ground.

"Get up, Lucy, you big pussy."

I laughed. It was a hot afternoon at practice and I was getting my ass handed to me, but I was still in a fucking fabulous mood. I was going home to Ella and Scarlett soon.

Mason gave me his hand and I took it. He dragged me from the ground. "You must be getting laid. Scarlett finally give into your ugly ass?"

I raised an eyebrow. "If I'm ugly, then what the fuck are you?"

"A sexy, badass motherfucker," he answered too quickly and laughed. "So? What's going on with you and Scar?"

"I don't kiss and tell." It was cliché as fuck, but I wasn't telling. I wasn't telling him that I'd had her in my bed the past several weeks. I wasn't telling him I'd left her in bed all nice, warm, and sexed up this morning. That every night she was in bed waiting for me.

That I was living the damn dream. I was taking care of my sister. I had an amazing girlfriend. And I was the quarterback of the fucking Alabama Cougars. My momma would have been so proud.

Chapter
TWENTY-FOUR

Scarlett

MY HEART WAS HAMMERING IN MY CHEST LIKE AN ENTIRE BAND OF drums. My hands shook as I held the test below me and tried not to get pee on my hand because gross.

I hardly noticed the sounds of Ollie moving around our small apartment on the other side of my bedroom door. I had never been more thankful than right at this moment that my bathroom was an en suite.

I was supposed to be at Luk's tonight like I was most nights now. He was making pork chops on the grill, but I'd called and told him I wasn't feeling well. I wasn't feeling well was code for I need to take a pregnancy test. Or ten.

I shook off the test a bit and pulled it from between my legs. It said three minutes. That's how long it would take to get an answer positive or negative, but as I went to put the cap on it, it was there, the tiny plus sign that made my heart feel like it was somewhere in my throat. No. But it said three minutes. This couldn't be right. It had to be a defective test.

With my breath coming a mile a minute, I tore into the box of the pregnancy test like a savage. Lucky for me, I'd bought the bonus pack of three tests. I drank what felt like a gallon of water straight from the faucet, once again like a damn crazy person sat back on the toilet, and tore both tests open with my teeth.

Nope. The first test was wrong. That was too fast. It said three minutes. It had only been like two seconds.

I peed on the next two tests in record time, but as soon as I looked at them the little plus signs were there. With shaking hands, I grabbed the box I'd ripped and pieced it back together enough to read the directions, because surely the plus meant I wasn't pregnant at all but just a little bloated and maybe had a bit of a stomach bug. That was it. This test must give a plus for being sick.

Jesus. Now I was really reaching. The box only proved exactly what I knew already. I was pregnant. I was pregnant with Lukas's baby. A baby I was positive he wasn't ready for. Hell, he was still trying to cope with the loss of his mom and he had Ella to worry about. This wasn't going to be good news for him.

I sat on the bathroom floor in my panties and had a good old-fashion pity party but without the booze because I was pregnant. My ass was cold on the tile, but I didn't care. I deserved it, even. How did I go from virgin to pregnant in seven weeks flat? Only freaking me.

A tear ran down my cheek and I rubbed my hand over my stomach. Was I ready for a baby? I sure as hell wasn't married like I was supposed to be. My momma and daddy would definitely have something to say about that. True, things were going amazingly well between Luk and me, but that didn't mean either of us was ready for a baby.

I looked down at my flat stomach. Ready or not, though, it was happening.

And how it happened, well, who the hell knew. We'd been careful. I wasn't on birth control because prior to Luk, I wasn't having sexy times, but we did use condoms every time without fail.

Leaving the pregnancy test on the tiled floor, I left the bathroom and crawled to my bed and then creeped inside and tried not to cry. This was Luk's baby. And I loved him. This was a good thing, even if I wasn't ready for it. He was good to Ella. No matter if he loved me or not, Luk took care of his responsibilities. He was a good man. At least I could count on that.

I burrowed under the covers and reached my hand out to search for my phone on my nightstand. Once I found it, I called Hazel. She was the one who'd suspected it. I hadn't been feeling well for a week. I was convinced I'd had a stomach bug. She had mentioned I might need to go buy a pregnancy test. Now, I was realizing what a bad idea that was. Ignorance was bliss.

She answered practically before it even rang, "Well?"

"You were right."

She gasped. "What?"

"I said you were right." My voice was muffled by the bedding over and under me.

"Oh. My. God."

"Nope. Not God. Not immaculate conception. Just Lukas Callihan's super sperm."

The line was dramatically quiet and I felt a tear trek down my face.

"Wow," she whispered.

"Yep," I could barely get it out. I was going to lose it.

"Have you told him yet?"

"No."

"God, what are you going to do?"

I wiped the tears from my face on the sheets below me. "I don't have a fucking clue. I need to tell him."

"Yeah," she breathed, still sounding in awe and slightly terrified. "It's gonna be okay. You just have to tell him. Luk's a good guy."

Looked like we were all giving ourselves the same pep talk. A light knock at the door interrupted our conversation.

"Go away, Ollie!" I couldn't deal with him right now. I couldn't even deal with myself.

"Baby, it's me. Coming in!" Luk called back, followed quickly by the door creaking open.

"Shit, gotta go," I whispered into the phone to Hazel and hung up as fast as lightning. I lay there as still as possible, a lump under my thick covers, hoping he wouldn't see me there. Praying he left because he thought I wasn't in the room even though I'd just called him Ollie and told him to go away.

It was hot as hell under the covers all of a sudden and my breath sounded so very inconveniently loud.

I heard footsteps and then silence. And I wondered if maybe he looked around the room and realized I wasn't there and then checked the bathroom. Oh, God. Not the bathroom. And in the same day that I thanked God for the en suite in my room I was cursing it. I'd left the damn pregnancy tests on the floor. All five million of them.

I wasn't just hot anymore. I was sweating bullets. If he found those, the gig was up. He was too quiet. Why wasn't he saying anything? Where was he?

And still I lay there like a damn wuss.

I felt one side of the bed dip and my heart nearly jumped out of my chest. But he didn't make a move other than to just sit there.

"You're pregnant."

Two words that would change our lives forever. My breath caught. My eyelids snapped closed hard, but still tears leaked from them. I didn't say anything. What was there to say? It was the truth. Whether he liked it or not.

"Scarlett."

My breath was still caught somewhere in my throat as a torrential downpour of tears bombarded my face. I couldn't have said anything if I'd wanted to. And I damn sure didn't. I wasn't ready. I'd just found out. I wasn't ready to talk about it with him.

"Red, I know you're under there."

I finally breathed out and sucked another bit of air in before sobbing out, "No one's home."

He must have heard the distress and tears in my voice because the covers were ripped back and almost immediately I was in his warm, jean-clad lap and my face was buried in his white T-shirt that smelled like cotton and trees during the winter. I breathed and let out another deep sob while he rubbed small circles on my back and kissed the top of my head.

"Don't cry, baby. It's going to be okay."

I looked up at his face. "Are you mad?"

His face was full of confusion. "Why would I be mad?"

I just stared at him. I didn't know why I expected him to be mad. Maybe because it was too soon. Maybe because it wasn't planned.

"Because I'm pregnant with your baby!" I yelled.

Two seconds later, my bedroom door flew open and Ollie was there. "You're pregnant?" he thundered.

Picking up a pillow off my bed, I chucked it at his head. "Get out, Ollie. Now!" I screamed like a madwoman because I was. I was freaking crazy.

Ollie closed the door quietly because I think he could sense I was completely insane.

Luk grabbed my chin to hold my eyes steady to his. He used his other hand to wipe the tears from my eyes. "How could I possibly be mad that the love of my life is going to have my baby?" His eyes blazed down at me. Full of something more than passion. Love.

I blinked, stunned, my heart feeling like it stopped. My lungs felt like they'd seized up. "The love of your life?"

He rested his forehead to mine. "You have to know I'm head over heels in love with you, Red. How could you not?"

I brought my hands up and cradled each side of his face. "But you never said."

"I was giving you time. But in the meantime I was trying to show it. Every day. Scarlett, I could never be mad about you having my baby. It's what I dream of. You living with me and Ella. Us getting married and having a shit-ton of kids. This may be a little out of order and a little sooner than we expected, but we're gonna be fine. Because I love you and hopefully you love me?"

I pressed a soft closed mouth kiss to his lips. "I've loved you since I was fourteen years old, Mister Quarterback."

"Then I'd say it was high time you had my baby," he joked.

"But what if I suck at being a parent?"

He shook his head and rolled his eyes at me. "It's not possible."

"How do you know?" I cried.

"Because you've had lots of practice. Because children are your life. Because we're in this thing together."

More tears poured down my face as I realized there wasn't anyone in the world I'd rather be in this together with than Lukas. He was right. It was going to be okay. Even if we had done things all kinds of backward.

My hands fell from his face and I backed away so I could really see him when I said this. "Thank you, Luk."

"For what, baby?"

"For not letting me down. For being a damn rock. I freaked the hell out."

He looked at the array of pregnancy tests he had placed on the bed beside him. "I can't tell."

I laughed and laid my head back down on his chest. We were going to be okay. Because that was what Lukas did. He made things okay for the people he loved. And he loved me. I was eaten up with warmth.

"So, I'm guessing you're not sick."

"Nope, just knocked up."

"Well, good. Then I can take you to the house for dinner. Ella was missing you."

I leaned back in his lap. "Why'd you stop by, anyway?"

"To check on you. See if you needed anything." He pushed some hair behind my ear and kissed my forehead. At that moment, I would have married him five thousand times in a hundred different ways knocked up or not.

And that pretty much summed up my favorite quarterback. He'd come by to check on me and see if I needed anything and ended up saving the damn day. I was one lucky girl.

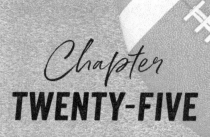

Chapter
TWENTY-FIVE

Lukas

I T WAS THE THIRD GAME OF THE SEASON. WE WERE AT HOME AND WE finally weren't playing like complete shit. Don't get me wrong. We didn't have a chance in hell at the playoffs, but the boys were coming around and so was I. We were finally starting to click. They didn't all hate the fucking sight of me. As a matter of fact, some of them even liked me. But better than any of that, we were playing well. Together. Which was a hell of a lot more than we were doing a few months ago.

It was halftime and I looked up into the stands. I'd somehow managed to get all the kids in Ella's class and their parents tickets. It had taken some begging and finagling on my part, but seeing all of them up there with Scarlett had been worth it.

I waved and Red gave me a big smile and nudged Ella to get her attention. I gave her a wave, too.

"Get your head in the game, asshole." Mason smacked my helmet.

"I don't know what game you're at, but we are killing it today."

He smacked the other side of my helmet. "Let's keep it that way."

I hadn't told him yet even though I'd wanted to, but Scarlett said that we shouldn't. We were having a baby. Me and Scarlett. A family with Ella. It was almost too damn good to be true. I wanted to propose to her right this moment, but I didn't want to overwhelm her and it seemed that she was plenty overwhelmed with just the shock of having a baby at the moment. The other stuff would come. I could be patient or at least I told myself that. I was happier than I'd been in a long damn time.

Halftime was almost over when I heard a commotion in the stands. I looked up to find a crowd huddled around where Scarlett and Ella were sitting, but I couldn't see them. I couldn't see anything but a huge mass of people.

Taking my helmet off, I tried to scour the stands again and noticed a medic running down the stairs nearby.

"I have to go," I said to no one and ran from the field, football be damned. My family was up there. My sister. My woman. My unborn baby.

I ran, pushing through people who yelled my name. I had to get there. By the time I made it to the entrance to where I knew they were sitting in the bleachers, two medics were pushing a stretcher out, Ella strapped to it, completely unconscious. Scarlett was right behind, white as a ghost, tears in her eyes.

"What happened?" I rushed to Ella, looking down at her body, so still. It scared the hell out of me.

"I don't know," Scarlett said. "We were standing there and then all of a sudden she fainted. She hit her head, I think."

"Excuse me, sir," one of the medics interrupted, but I could barely hear him. I couldn't focus. "She's breathing and vitals are good. We just haven't been able to wake her up yet. We're going to take her down-town to Baptist General to get her checked out. Might have just fainted from too much sun."

That didn't make me feel any better. This was my fault.

"I can ride to the hospital with her, Luk. You can go back. You have a game." Scarlett looked shaken enough without having to handle this all on her own. Ella was my responsibility and besides, I'd never be able to play a decent game knowing she was being rushed to the hospital.

"Ride with her. I need to get out of my pads and uniform and grab my wallet. I'll meet you guys there."

"Okay," she said, looking shaken. I kissed her quickly on the lips and told her the only thing I could. "I love you."

I never once thought about football or my team needing me. No, I thought about Ella and if I really was doing what was right for her. Maybe I wasn't. Maybe I didn't know what the hell I was doing. What if something was seriously wrong with her? How could I handle that? She was the only family I had left besides Aunt Merline. I couldn't lose Ella.

I dialed up Aunt Merline on the way and let her know Ella was at the hospital. It was the right thing to do. She loved her, even if she did drive me crazy. And maybe she was right. Maybe I didn't know what I was doing. Maybe Mom was wrong. Maybe I shouldn't be caring for Ella. I couldn't even make sure she got on and off the bus every day. I had to have help. Merline could do all of that.

By the time I made it to the hospital and back into a room with Ella and Scarlett, I'd worked myself up into a nervous wreck.

"Has the doctor been in yet?" I asked, rushing to Ella. She was still knocked out cold, but they had her hooked up to machines that were monitoring her.

"Not yet," Scarlett said, coming to stand at my side and wrapping her arms around me. "God, she scared me to death."

I rubbed the top of Ella's head. "Wake up, baby girl," I said. Seeing her like this was breaking my heart.

"Was she acting weird? Complaining about anything? Not feeling well?" Fuck, I felt like I was being accusatory, but I just needed to know what the fuck happened.

"No, nothing. She was fine and then all of a sudden she fell and hit her head on the concrete. One of the parents rushed to find a medic and that's it, Luk."

"Fuck," I breathed out, reaching out for Ella's hand, closing my eyes. And I prayed. I prayed that nothing major was wrong. And promised God all kinds of promises I didn't even know if I could keep if he made everything okay.

The doctor came in shortly after. He tried waking up Ella to no avail and panic ran rampant through my veins. He informed us they were going to run tests and take blood and left again. I was practically in hysterics. What would happen if she never woke up? What if I never heard her voice again? I couldn't breathe. I felt like I was being smothered.

"Luk." I barely heard Scarlett call. "Luk!" she said louder this time, placing her palms on my cheeks. "Are you okay, honey?"

Shaking my head, I pulled away. "I'm fine. I just need to know she's going to be okay."

I went from the highest of highs to the lowest of lows. I'd forgotten how you could lose everything in a split second. Maybe I'd been too happy. Maybe I couldn't have it all. The career and the family.

I looked over at Scarlett, who looked dead on her feet. She was pregnant with my baby. I had to keep Scarlett and that baby safe at all costs. "I can stay here, baby. Why don't you go home and rest?"

She gave me a look that said I'd lost my damn mind. "You're insane. I'm not leaving this hospital until I know Ella is okay."

"But the ba—" I tried to argue, but she cut me off.

"The baby is fine and agrees with me." Her face dared me to argue more, but the truth was I didn't have it in me. I felt wrung out and hung to dry.

I didn't have time to argue anyway because Merline came flying into the room like a bat out of hell.

The first thing she did was hug me and I felt the burn of tears in my nose. My aunt loved me and she loved Ella, even if she did rag on us.

"How is she?" she asked.

"Aunt Merline?" I heard from behind me and I swear my heart jumped right out of my chest. Ella was awake.

I raced to her. I'm not ashamed to admit that I jumped in front of Aunt Merline. She'd just have to wait her damn turn. "Hey, Ells," I said, rubbing her cheek. "How you feeling?"

"Okay," she answered, looking around. "Where are we?"

Scarlett jumped in. "The hospital. You fell and got a bump on your head at the game."

"Oh, no." Ella looked distressed.

"You're okay now, baby." I leaned over and kissed her cheek.

"I'm thirsty." Typical Ella.

We found a nurse to get some water and ice chips and waited on the doctor to come back with results. And the results weren't terrible. They weren't great, but they were at least something we could work with.

He informed us Ella had Sinoatrial Node Disease or SND. SND presented itself more in people with Down syndrome as they aged. And we all knew Ella was getting older. Hell, she'd just had a birthday. She'd passed out because the electrical signals of her sino-atrial, which is the area of specialized cells in Ella's heart that functioned as a natural pace-maker, wasn't functioning properly, causing her heartbeats to be irregular. Sometimes too slow, which could result in dizziness and fainting.

Lucky for us, he thought that a steady dose of antiarrhythmic meds would help. He said that one day, Ella may need a pacemaker, but for now we would just play it by ear. The doc got her started on meds and asked for medical history. He asked if she'd had any history of this in the past. I didn't think so, but I couldn't know for sure. I'd only been home months, but my mother told me everything. We were close. I would have known if something was wrong with Ella's heart, wouldn't I?

The doctor wanted to keep Ella overnight and monitor and get her meds started, so I agreed to take Scarlett home and grab the medical records as long as Merline stayed with her while I was gone and returned to sleep at the hospital with Ella for the night. I didn't care about football or the team. All I cared about was making sure Ella was safe, healthy, happy.

I was anxious to get to the house and back, but Merline asked to speak to me in the hall privately before I left.

I'd never noticed how old my aunt Merline looked. She was my mother's older sister by twenty years and lately she was really starting to age. Her hair that used to be mostly brown was almost white now. Her frame frail.

She started in on me right away. "I don't want you to misunderstand. I'm not blaming you for what happened today."

I sighed deeply right down to my damn soul because I couldn't do this right now. I was weary to my damn bones. I wanted to get home and get my shit and get back here to be with my sister.

She went on. "But, Luk. I just don't understand why you don't let me take care of Ella. It's not like you couldn't come and see her. I'd take good care of her. I love her. And you and I both know she had no business at that game today."

"Her being at the game had nothing to do with what happened today, Merline. You know as good as I do that it could have happened anywhere."

"You heard the doctor, Lukas. She could have gotten too winded climbing those stairs at the stadium. Any kind of exercise can trigger her heart problems."

"Come on, Merline. She does Zumba every damn morning. She's always active."

Her eyebrows rose. "She is and what are you going to do when you come home from a long day at the field and find your sister on the floor? You can't handle this. She needs more help now than ever. What are you going to do? Quit playing football and care for her? It doesn't make sense. I'm home all day. I can do it and you can keep playing ball. Your momma wouldn't want you to give up your dreams for Ella."

She was right. How was I going to care for Ella now? If I was worried about her being home alone before, it was even more so now. But maybe my dreams weren't football anymore. Maybe my dreams were just Ella. I didn't know how I'd support her without football. My momma hadn't been rolling in the dough and football was the only thing I knew.

"I can't do this right now. I have to go," I mumbled and walked back into the room to kiss my sister goodbye and tell her I'd be right back.

I collected Scarlett and we started a silent car ride home. I thought of all the things I needed to do, but didn't know where to start. I'd have to take Scarlett to get her car from the stadium at some point. I'd have to get Ella home. How many football practices would I miss? Would they let me go? My panic only escalated on the drive and by the time we got back to my place, I was growing angry at myself. I was failing. Just when I thought I had my shit together, everything was falling around me.

As soon as we walked in the door Scarlett set about collecting Ella some bathroom things and some pajamas while I opened the filing cabinet in my room.

Chapter
TWENTY-SIX

Lukas

MOM HAD TALKED ABOUT THIS PLENTY. HOW, IF ANYTHING SHOULD happen to her, there was a file labeled Ella with all of the information I would need to take care of her. I hadn't needed it until now. As I pulled out the manila folder, a small white envelope fell from it and onto the floor. Ignoring it at first, I looked through Ella's medical history, checking for any heart problems and coming up with none.

I grabbed the envelope to shove it back in the folder when I saw my name on the outside. Just a simple Lukas in my mother's handwriting. My breath caught and my heart kicked up a notch at the sight of it. It was sealed and waiting for me, all these months. I was both excited and scared to open it.

I slid my finger under the lip of the envelope, careful to not rip it. It was from my mother. It was important.

I unfolded the piece of paper on the inside, smelling the faint hint of my mother's perfume on it. I closed my eyes, missing her more than ever, needing her so very much.

It was clear to see it was a letter right away, her cursive handwriting so very distinctive to me. I pulled the letter close to my chest and held it there, thinking how odd, how amazing it was that today of all days was the day I should find this letter. Because I needed it so fucking much. I read the first line.

To Lukas, my son, but above all, Ella's Lulu

And instantaneously tears blurred my vision. But I kept right on, forging ahead because I needed to hear from my mother and I had a feeling she had something really important to say.

Hello, gorgeous boy. If you're reading this letter then I'm somewhere in the clouds, sitting on a beach and sipping margaritas with your dad. He says hi and that he's so proud of you.

I'm proud of you, too, you know. And not just because of all you have accomplished, which is amazing in itself. But you, Lukas, you are amazing. If I stripped you of your star quarterback status and your good looks, you'd still be the thing I'm most proud of in my entire life.

My children mean the world to me. I couldn't love you more if I tried. When I first realized I was pregnant with Ella, I was so excited for you to have a sibling. Someone you could love and play with. Family you would have long after your father and I were gone. Your father was gone, but he's left us with the greatest of gifts. A child. I was ecstatic. On cloud nine. Nothing could have prepared me for that twenty-week scan. The one that told us that most likely Ella would have Down syndrome. I left there devastated. I wouldn't be taking home a healthy baby girl. I didn't think I could be one of those moms. The moms who tirelessly supported and loved their children with special needs. That wasn't me. I couldn't do it. I was already a single mother. What the hell did God want from me? I wasn't that strong. I'd come home that day and crawled into bed, mourning what could never be. You came home from school and crawled into bed with me and we watched movies and ate popcorn. Do you remember that day? I didn't tell you about Ella then. Not yet. I just wanted one more day with my boy before our worlds were changed forever.

I thought of a lot that night. Mostly of you. Of how your life would change once the new baby was born. Of how I'd be trading in your football games for her occupational therapy. How instead of playing Uno in the evenings with you, I'd be struggling to get an infant with Down syndrome to sleep. I thought of all the things this baby would take from us. I thought of how one day when I was gone, she'd be your responsibility. And that brought me to a terrible low. You didn't ask for this anymore than I did. I'd been so silly, then. I worried the rest of the pregnancy. I feared the day she was born. Because how could I possibly know or understand how much she'd give us? How could I possibly know how much we'd love her?

But you did. From the very beginning. You may have been just barely a teenager, but your love for your family was bigger than the sky, even then. You're just so good in that way, Lukas.

The day Ella was born, I was a wreck. You sat in the waiting room with Merline, while I lay in that bed praying the doctors were wrong. Hoping against all hope for a healthy baby. I was terrified. And when it was all said and done and they put Ella on my chest, I looked down and all my fears were confirmed. My hands shook around her tiny body and tears slipped from my eyes. I didn't know what to do with her. How to care for her. I was one of those moms, now. But how? What did I do to deserve this? I was scared to death and a small part of me resented the tiny baby on my chest. She was going to change everything. Our tiny family would never be the same. I was heartbroken.

I had such guilt. Guilt over how your life would change now. Guilt over how I resented that sweet, innocent baby. I felt so desolate and alone. Until Merline brought you into the room and gave us a moment alone. Sweet Ella was lying in her bassinet. I was too scared to even touch her. But not you. You swooped into the room and went right over to her. You leaned your shaggy brown head over her and then looked back at me.

"Mom, she's so cute," you said, and fresh tears slipped down my cheeks. "Can I hold her?" you begged.

My words were lost in a heap of emotion, so I only nodded. You picked her up and cradled her to your chest like a football, took her little pink cap off and rubbed the fuzz on the top of her little head. You pressed your lips to one chubby cheek and walked over to the bed.

You sat on the edge of the bed next to me and I held my breath, scared out of my mind. How was I going to do it? How could I possibly raise you both on my own? Without your father?

And then you looked up at me with tears shining in the depth of your sweet eyes and said one word, "Dibs."

"What?" I asked, confused, too overwhelmed in the moment to even understand.

"I'm calling dibs, Mom. She's mine."

My breath caught and more wetness poured down my face like two rivers. But I knew in that moment, we were going to be okay. We were going to make it. You saved us, Lukas. You saved our family that day.

We both knew the day would come when you'd take Ella. We talked about it many times. Although, I know that probably did nothing to prepare you for how hard it would be. Lukas, you will have days with undeniable joy, where you wouldn't trade Ella for the world, and you'll have some days where she will make you want to pull every hair out of your head. But even those days, I wouldn't trade for anything. Those days are special and important, too. Those days help shape and mold us, build us and prepare us. Remember that.

There is no one in the world I trust more to care for my favorite girl than my favorite boy. And when there are days you feel like you just can't do it, know that you can. After all, you loved her first.

Your Momma

I gripped the letter in my hand as silent tears rolled down my cheeks. How had she known I'd need this? Because God, I had. I breathed out a soft chuckle. My momma. A damn know-it-all even in the afterlife, but I'd never been so thankful for that letter as I was right then. Thank goodness, I'd found it right when I had.

I was sitting on the floor of Mother's old room, which was now mine, holding her letter when Scarlett found me moments later.

Her lips turned down into a frown. "What are you doing down there? Are you okay?" She came over to me and sat down next to me on the floor. "What's going on?"

"Nothing," I said, already feeling lighter having read that letter.

"What's wrong?" I was sure she could see I'd been crying, but I honestly felt better in this moment than I had all day. Mom was right. I could do this. I loved Ella too much not to. I'd make it work.

"Nothing, Red. I'm good. I'm really fucking good." I pushed the letter out in front of her and she took if from my hands, giving me a nervous look.

"It's from my mom."

"Where'd you find it?"

"In Ella's file in the cabinet."

"Wow," she said, bringing it closer to her face. "May I?"

That was why I'd handed it to her. So she could read it. "Of course."

I grabbed her free hand and held it and I watched her read the letter, her heart in her eyes. My sweet Red. And when tears flowed down her face, I knew she understood. Just like she always had, even at fourteen.

"Oh, Lukas," she cried when she finished and wrapped me in a hug.

"I know." I squeezed her to me.

We held each other for a long while that day.

Eventually, Scarlett pulled back and palmed the side of my face sweetly. "She's right, Lukas. You and Ella belong together. I hope you know that. And it's not just you two. You have me and Mason and a whole damn team of players that I'm positive are up at that hospital by now."

"I know, baby." I leaned over and pressed my lips to hers softy. "We're gonna be okay. As long as we have each other."

EPILOGUE

I PULLED AT THE COLLAR OF MY TUX, NERVOUS AS HELL. I LOOKED AROUND the church as it started to fill up with people, and Mason nudged me with his shoulder.

"You look like you're gonna puke."

I shot him a shut the fuck up look. "I'm not going to puke."

He shrugged like it didn't matter to him anyway. "Then stop looking like it."

He was right. I did feel like I was going to puke. And not because I didn't want to be here. Because I wanted to be here more than any place in the world. I'd waited five months longer than I'd wanted to for this moment. But Scarlett had wanted to plan a big wedding and I'd pretty much do anything she wanted. Even wait for her.

But that didn't stop the nerves. It wasn't that I didn't want to make Scarlett my wife. I wasn't even a little nervous about that. I was more nervous about everyone watching us. Us being the center of attention. Turns out, I didn't like being center stage unless that stage was in the middle of a football field.

The room was quieting and everyone was taking their seats. Scarlett's parents had made the trip up from Florida and her mother gave me a finger wave. I grinned at her and tried to keep from losing my breakfast.

I loved that Scarlett's parents were here and we'd had so much fun visiting them in Florida a few months ago when I'd met them for the first time. We'd even squeezed in a trip to Disney for Ella. But I was sad my mother and father couldn't be here today to celebrate with us.

I looked on my side of the room where all of my people were. And my people consisted of my team. And not my Florida one. My real team. The boys I'd come to depend on—my chosen family. We weren't on our way to a Super Bowl anytime soon, but we were still fucking awesome.

In the front row, Scarlett had set up a picture of my mother and father when they were younger, before they'd had children. They were a handsome couple and I smiled knowing they'd be so proud and so very happy for me today. And I felt more than thankful that I had Mason's crazy ass as my best man.

The crowd quieted and music started up and everyone turned toward the double doors at the back of the room and I held my breath as I watched Ella walk in the room.

She was wearing a pink sparkly Cinderella type dress complete with a sparkly silver tiara on her head. Scarlett had let her pick it out and I hadn't been allowed to see it. She looked beautiful and happy. And for every flower petal she delicately tossed to the floor my heart skipped a beat. She came to stand next to me and Mason, and I didn't miss Mason lean over and kiss her cheek and whisper, "Good job, Ells." She blushed down to her toes almost the exact same shade as her dress.

Hazel was next down the aisle escorted by Ollie and I had to say they made quite the couple if that was what they were. We all weren't quite sure. Everything was very hush hush between the two, still. We were all just left to our assumptions. And assuming what was going on between those two was one of Scarlett's favorite things to do.

Speaking of my Red. The wedding march started to play and my hands were slick with sweat as my heart kicked up a notch. My throat felt tight, my mouth dry as I waited on her to come through those doors with bated breath.

And when she came around the corner, my nerves vanished into thin air. Because her? Here to marry me? It seemed almost unimaginable. This woman would be mine for the rest of my life. She'd be Ella's, too. She'd be ours. And that was all that mattered in that moment.

She was wearing a white dress that cinched in right at her waist, right over our baby, and then flared out in a tulle skirt. She looked like a ballet bride with her red hair up in an intricate knot and red lipstick on her lips. She was stunning and I will never forget how she looked walking down that aisle to me, pregnant with our child, for the rest of my life.

The ceremony was quick and easy, and I only cried a little. My boys were there and I couldn't have them giving me shit at practice next week.

Our reception was at the Cougars' stadium. We set up tents on the field and opted for a DJ instead of a live band. And when we danced our first dance, which wasn't really our first dance at all, to Prince's "The Most Beautiful Girl in the World," it was kiss number two thousand three hundred and sixty that was graced upon me by the blushing bride. Yes, I was definitely still counting. I didn't think I'd ever stop.

Since my mother was only at the reception in spirit, Ella and I danced together instead of a traditional mother/son dance. She lit up the room when I spun her to the sweet lyrics of "You are my Sunshine" through the DJ's speakers.

The night had grown late and the crowd had grown smaller, but Scarlett didn't want to leave. Instead, we were parked next to the candy bar that Scarlett had insisted on. She was popping Skittles into her mouth and I was standing behind her, my arms wrapped around her waist.

She didn't want the night to end and I couldn't wait to get her alone. I had plans on peeling back that dress slowly and savoring every inch of her delicious skin. She had plans on finishing all the Skittles at the candy bar.

"Ready to go yet, baby?" Please, dear God, I was about to pour the rest of the damn Skittles into my tux pockets, the rental fee be damned.

She turned toward me and wrapped her arms around my middle. "I just don't want today to end. It was so magical and wonderful, and I couldn't have asked for a better wedding day."

"I know," I said into the top of her hair. "But if we don't leave soon, I'm going to have to throw you down on this candy table and have my way with you here."

Tilting her head to mine, she pressed her lips to my cheeks. "Can't wait to get me alone, Mister Quarterback?"

"You have no idea the things I'm going to do to you next week."

Aunt Merline was moving in for seven days with Ella. I was betting in two, Merline would be ready to run for the hills. Ella was no picnic if you didn't know her schedule and respect the hell out of it. Mason was our backup plan for when Ella drove Merline crazy, since we'd be on a cruise to Alaska for the next week.

"Okay. Fine. Just let me fill this cup with Skittles and you can take me to the hotel and have your wicked way with me."

We'd booked a hotel for the night since we knew we'd want to be alone tonight. Scarlett had moved into Mom's place shortly after the night Ella had been hospitalized. I'd needed her help and I wasn't too afraid to ask for it anymore. It took a fucking village and lucky for me, I had one. And lucky for us, Ella's heart problems had been better since starting meds and we hadn't had anymore hospital stays.

"Let me grab my tux jacket and your purse, and I'll meet you by the front doors." I looked around conspiratorially. "We can make a break for it while no one is looking."

"Okay," she said, doubling her efforts at collecting candy quickly, and I dashed for the closet inside the stadium I knew our stuff was.

I threw the door open and stopped dead in my tracks. Because Oliver Knox was sitting in the bottom of that closet in his tux playing on his damn phone.

He squinted up at me, the light too much for his eyes. "Hey, Luk," he said, all casual, like he wasn't sitting in the bottom of a dark fucking closet.

"What the hell are you doing in here?"

He stuck his head out and looked around before popping it back in. "I'm hiding from Hazel."

"Why?" I was confused. Were they together or weren't they?

He just continued to stare at me.

"Spill it, Ollie. I don't have all damn day. My wife is waiting on me." Damn, my wife. That had a nice ring to it.

"Fine," he growled. "I'm hiding because imavirgin," he mumbled quickly.

"What?" I asked, thinking I'd heard him wrong.

"I said, Hazel wants to have sex and I'm terrified because I'm a fucking virgin. There! Are you happy? Now, close the fucking door!"

He couldn't be serious. I'd heard him time and time again talk about chicks. Was he for real?

"Luk!" Hazel called and I looked over my shoulder to see her walking toward me. I looked back at Ollie in the bottom of the closet, whose face was full of panic.

"Close the door," he whispered quickly.

So I grabbed my coat and Scarlett's purse as fast as possible and slammed the door shut and leaned against it. Just in the nick of time.

"Hey, Hazel." I leaned my elbow against the door like I was just hanging out. I was fucking terrible at lying.

She eyed me like I'd lost my mind. "Have you seen Ollie?"

"Who, me? No, I've been with Scarlett all night. Why? Do you need him?" Jesus Christ, I was shit at this.

"Yeah, there's something I've been wanting to give him."

I tried to stifle my smile. Because I bet there was something she wanted to give him. There seemed to be quite a story here and I, for one, couldn't wait to see how it would all play out. But for now, it would have to wait. My bride was waiting.

EPILOGUE

"**O**H MY GOD, LUK!" I SQUEEZED HIS HAND HARD AND NEVER IN my life did I think for one second that I could possibly possess enough strength in my tiny fingers to make Luk wince, but I was wrong. "I don't think I can do this."

"Of course you can, baby. You can do anything." He was playing the doting husband to a T and it was pissing me off.

"Don't you fucking patronize me, Lukas Callihan!" I shouted.

He looked around the room, terrified out of his mind. He looked like he was about to make a run for it. We were getting ready to have a baby and he was thinking about deserting me. I could see it all over his scaredy cat face.

"I'm not patronizing you, Red. I know you can do this. You are the toughest chick I know."

"What the hell is wrong with you? Don't call me a chick. I'm having your damn baby. And it's trying to kill me."

Poor guy looked pitiful. But there was pretty much nothing he could say or do at this point that wouldn't piss me the hell off. I wanted to kill him and I was definitely never having sex with him again. Ever.

Finally, the contraction passed and I loosened the death grip on his hand. His face visibly relaxed. "I'm so sorry, honey," I said for the twentieth time today. Any time I wasn't in excruciating pain, I was completely reasonable. Other than that, I was completely crazy town.

"It's time to push," the doctor said from between my legs. "Next contraction, it's go time."

I shook my head, my eyes bugging out. "No, I can't. Luk. Tell him I can't have the baby. It's too hard." Tears leaked out of the corners of my eyes. I'd been laboring for almost sixteen hours at this point. I was pretty sure I was past the point of exhaustion. Hell, Lukas looked like he'd been run over by a train and he hadn't done half the work I had.

I watched him take a deep breath and I was wondering if he was gonna grab my bag and get me out of this bed so we could hightail it out of here. There was no way I could push. I was too damn tired. Couple that with the sheer fact that having an actual child to care for scared the shit out of me, I made the snap decision that we just shouldn't. We should just go home and forget this whole labor thing ever happened. Even if we were ten months too late.

But Luk surprised me. He didn't reach for my bag. Instead, he reached for my hand again. He held it tight and he got that fierce look on his face like he did when he was playing ball. And that scared me. Because he looked like he was going to battle and I wasn't. I was going home.

"You listen to me, Scarlett Callihan." He made sure our eyes were connected. "We are having a baby today and when that doctor tells you to push, you are going to push."

My tears slipped down my face. "But I'm so tired. I don't know if I can."

"You can and you will. And do you know why?"

I shook my head.

"Because it's time for a new season. And that season is you, me, Ella, and our sweet baby boy cuddled up on our couch at home. She's out there in that waiting room right now, waiting on Nelson to get here. And I know you would never let Ella down. Ever."

He was right. I wouldn't, but I was feeling so worn out. But as it turned out, I didn't have much time to worry about it.

"Okay, let's do this. I want you to lean up and give me a push for ten seconds." The doctor looked over at Luk. "Count us down, Dad."

"Ten, nine, eight…" Luk counted down time and time again. I lost count of how many times I pushed, but I just kept Luk's words in my head. Ella, my sweet Ella, was waiting on Nelson. And it was time. It was a new season and I was ready to take my baby home with us.

I pushed hard one last time, and Nelson Lukas Callihan was born. He weighed a healthy nine pounds eight ounces, which totally explained why he almost killed me.

Ella and I had decided on Nelson and Luk didn't deny his girls much. It happened to be the late great Prince's last name and she had recently found a love for his music. I may have had something to do with that.

They laid him up on my chest and Lukas cried like a damn baby, my sweet, sensitive man. A healthy baby boy, no complications, thank goodness. We'd been told early on in our pregnancy that Down syndrome was definitely a possibility and that our risk for it would be high since it ran on Luk's side of the family. They wanted to do additional testing during the pregnancy to make sure the baby didn't have Downs. But we decided against it. Whether Nelson was born with the genetic disorder or not, he was still ours. And we would still love him. So knowing wouldn't have made a bit of difference, anyhow.

They wrapped Nelson's pink, hollering self in a blanket and handed him to me, and more tears fell down my cheeks. He was beautiful and perfect, and I couldn't believe that twenty minutes ago I was ready to call it quits and head home. I'd never ever loved someone so instantly in my life. How would I do this? How could I possibly love someone this much, raise them, and then set them free? Being a mom was scary as hell. I held him until he calmed.

"He looks just like you," I said softly.

Luk smiled down at both of us. "With your hair."

It was true. My boy had soft red fuzz all over his head.

"May I?" Luk asked before scooping Nelson from my arms and

pressing him to his chest. And I about died. It was the sexiest, sweetest thing in the world, seeing my big, strong man hold my teeny tiny baby. Maybe I'd have sex with him again, after all.

"Can we send for Ella?" he asked.

"Of course."

Luk asked the nurse to call for Ella out the waiting room and he settled into the chair next to me, Nelson snuggled into his chest.

"He's perfect," Luk muttered more to himself than to me, so I didn't bother responding as he played with Nelson's small fist and touched his cheek with his big finger. My boys. Oh. My. God. I had boys. My heart soared.

Ella peeked around the corner of the doorway and I smiled big at her. She looked nervous. I knew the feeling. I was, too. I was terribly worried about how Ella was going to take a crying baby in the house. How she would feel about the wrench in her routines. How she would handle Luk's attention being divided between her and Nelson. I loved her and above all wanted her to be happy.

"Hey, Ells!" I called and waved her into the room. I patted the spot right next to me on the bed and she walked over and sat down gently.

She bit her nails and stared at the floor instead of greeting me with a hug like she usually did.

"You okay, baby?" I asked and shot Luk a glance in the chair next to me. He was still cuddled up with Nelson, but he gave me a look that said I should handle it. We'd gotten really good at this over the past several months. In fact, I'd say we were pretty awesome at co-parenting.

"Yeah, I'm okay." She finally looked at me.

I leaned up and rubbed my hand down her arm. "What's going on? You sad?"

Her head moved back and forth slowly. "No."

"Are you upset?"

"No. Just worried."

Ah. Now, we were getting somewhere. "What are you worried about?"

Her brown eyes shined back at me with tears in their depths from behind her glasses. "You. I was worried because you said having a baby hurts."

Aww, my precious girl. I pulled her to me and held her close in a long hug. "Oh, my Ellie Bellie. I am fine. It did hurt a little, but you can see for yourself that I'm fine."

"I'm so glad," she choked out.

I held her a minute more and then pulled out of our embrace. "Are you going to let Lulu hog Nelson all day or do you want to meet him?"

She looked over at the baby and Luk.

"You can't have him! He's mine," Luk joked.

I scooted over in the lumpy bed and motioned for Ella to sit next to me against the pillows. She scooted around until we were sitting in the bed side by side.

I threw my arms out at Luk. "Bring us our baby!" I demanded.

He grinned at me as he walked Nelson over to us and placed him gently in my arms.

I held the baby near Ella. "What do you think, Aunt Ella? Is your nephew the cutest baby ever?"

Nelson let out a small squeak and Ella laughed. "Yes, he is!" she exclaimed.

"Would you like to hold him?"

She looked nervously up at Luk and he gave her an encouraging nod. "Go on. He's dying to meet you."

I used one arm to bring the baby over to Ella and my other to wrap around her to support Nelson on the other side. She brought her hands up the middle until we were both holding him securely.

"Look how happy he is there with my girls," Luk said, his voice watery enough to cause me to look up. His eyes were full of unshed tears as he gazed down at us.

It was hard to believe there was ever a time that I didn't think he worshipped the ground I walked on. The man was the most amazing husband in the world. And he wasn't at all bad at this parenting thing either.

He was living the dream. Football and family. And he was balancing it all with the kind of grace I greatly admired.

I'd been dealing with my own juggling act lately and decided to take the rest of the school year off to be with the baby and Ella, but I'd be back next year. I loved teaching too much to give it up.

"Well, what do you think, Ells? Should we keep him?" Luk joked, waiting on his sister to say anything at all. I had a feeling he was just as worried about her adjusting to life with a baby in the house as I was.

She looked over Nelson's face for a minute, really taking him in, and Luk and I watched on, nervous as hell and dying to know what she thought.

But then she kissed the top of his head and uttered one small but significant word that set all our fears to rest and let us know that everything was going to be more than okay.

"Dibs."

ACKNOWLEDGEMENTS

This book was incredibly fun to write. And I know that the reason is mostly Ms. Ella, who was inspired by my sweet, wonderful cousin Dee. A lot of the sweet and funny moments that you read between Ella and Luk were all conjured up by her. So, thank you, Dee, for being amazing you. We love you so completely.

Thanks to my husband, Tony and my kiddos, Jackson and Violet. You guys make writing books and being your wife and mom super easy!

Thanks to my momma for reading every book I write and for always calling the latest my best one yet.

Kelly, Megan, Miranda, Aly, Ashley, Danielle P., Jamie, Kate and Leigh. Thanks for being my book buddies. But really, thank you for being my real life friends.

Maria Luis and Jennifer Van Wyk, I should give y'all the credit for this book. After all, it never would have been written if not for all of our sprinting. I love y'all! #sprint4yourlife

To the most awesome, amazing, sweet, wonderful beta readers ever! Thanks for making The Red Zone something I can be proud of. Thanks for all your hard work, Danielle R., Megan, Danielle P., Dani, Kelly, Leigh, Miranda, and Renee.

Hang Le, thank you for never letting me down. Your talent amazes me. Amber Goodwyn, you are incredible. Never leave me! Thank you! Amor Caro, I can't believe how long we've been together. I feel so fortunate to call you friend! Stacey Blake, you make my books beautiful. And you don't get annoyed when I change dates on you. I love you! You're amazing. Julie Deaton, I wish you knew how beloved you are in this community. I can't have a release without you. <3 Emily Lawrence, thank you so much for all your hard work. Sarah Ferguson at Social Butterfly, thank you for being patient with me and for all of your hard work on this book. I'm so glad to be able to call you friend.

Renee McCleary, you're priceless to me. I am so lucky you found me and stalked me. Best PA ever.

And, finally, to all the authors, bloggers, and readers who support me and share and love my books, thank you, thank you, thank you!

ABOUT THE AUTHOR

Amie Knight has been a reader for as long as she could remember and a romance lover since she could get her hands on her momma's books. A dedicated wife and mother with a love of music and makeup, she won't ever be seen leaving the house without her eyebrows and eyelashes done just right. When she isn't reading and writing, you can catch her jamming out in the car with her two kids to '90s R&B, country, and showtunes. Amie draws inspiration from her childhood in Columbia, South Carolina, and can't imagine living anywhere other than the South.

FACEBOOK: www.facebook.com/authoramieknight

TWITTER: www.twitter.com/AuthorAmieKnigh

GOODREADS: www.goodreads.com/AmieKnight

INSTAGRAM: www.instagram.com/amie_knight

WEBSITE: www.authoramieknight.com

GROUP: www.facebook.com/groups/amieknightssocialites

NEWSLETTER: http://eepurl.com/cPHIuT

OTHER BOOKS

Made in the USA
Monee, IL
09 November 2019